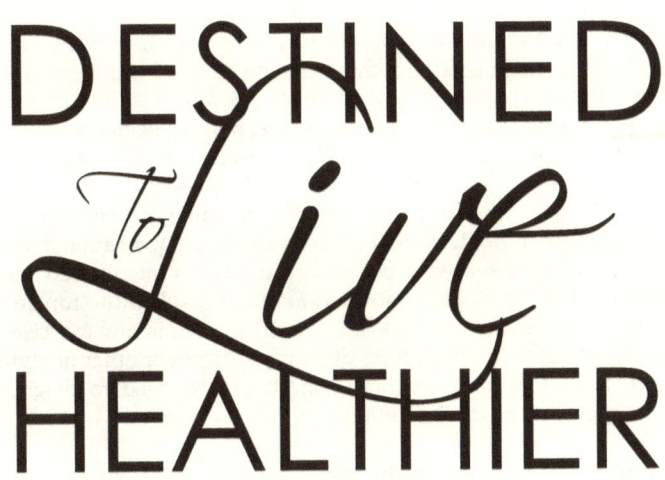

DESTINED *To Live* HEALTHIER

Mind | Body | Soul

BRIDGETTE L. COLLINS

Destined to Live Healthier: Mind, Body, and Soul

Published by Origins Publishing Company
P.O. Box 542671, Grand Prairie, Texas 75054-2671
Copyright © 2008 by Bridgette L. Collins

Publisher's Note

This is a work of fiction. It is not meant to depict, portray, or represent any particular real persons. The author has encountered many people through the years as a fitness consultant, and these stories were inspired by some of the things that she has experienced. The characters, places, incidents, and dialogues are based on the author's imagination, or if real, used fictitiously. Any resemblance to actual persons, living or dead, business establishments, events, or locales is entirely coincidental. The health information presented is intended to facilitate the author's account of the characters' lifestyle choices. Information in this book is intended for general reference purposes only and is not intended to address any specific medical condition. This information is not a substitute for professional medical advice or a medical exam. Prior to participating in any exercise program or activity, you should seek the advice of your physician or other qualified health professional. No information in this book should be used to diagnose, treat, restore, or prevent any medical condition.

The author and publisher of this book specifically disclaim all responsibility for any liability, loss, or risk, personal or otherwise, which is incurred as a consequence, directly or indirectly, of the use and application of any of the contents of this book.

Readers should be aware that Internet Web sites offered as sources for further information may have changed or disappeared between the time this book was written and when it is read.

Printed in the United States
Cover design by www.MarionDesigns.com
Interior design by www.Cover2CoverBookDesign.com
Photography by Kevin Brown (www.digitalproshots.com)

ISBN 13: 978-0-9790932-2-7
ISBN 10: 0-9790932-2-8

To My Parents,
Mr. Earnest L. Collins and Mrs. Doris J. Collins.

This book is dedicated to you.
I thank God for allowing us to continue to share a vision
that has blessed people all over the world. I thank you
for your unfailing love, support, guidance, advice, and
encouragement. And above all, I thank you for your
sacrifices and continuous prayers throughout my life.
I love you – you are the best.

CONTENTS

PART III
The Heel and Forefoot of the Golden Years

INTRODUCTION

The faith to understand and follow your destiny to live healthier in the midst of unprecedented challenges requires determination, courage, and good judgment. Too often, people give up, throw in the towel, and settle for the status quo rather than for change. They lock themselves into a routine and go through the motions, placing one foot in front of the other, trying to maintain stability among unforeseen trials and discomforts. A closer look into the lives of those seeking to overcome the burdens of unexpected financial problems, relief from the pressures of myriad relationships, and resolution of issues from a troubled past will shed invaluable insight on the difficulties of implementing healthier lifestyle habits.

In the pages that follow, Trevor MacElroy, a renowned fitness consultant from Dallas, Texas, spotlights three of his most inspiring clients. In doing so, he strives to help others relate to and understand the common struggles shared by those wanting to live healthier, while simultaneously facing concerns related to their careers, family, health, finances, and relationships. He encourages and empowers his clients to rethink their priorities and exposes them to constructive ways to transform their unhealthy habits. A change of perspective leaves them refreshed, renewed, rededicated, and ready to balance daily demands, obligations, and pursuits in healthier living.

As this story begins, you'll meet Laura and Leslie, two sisters forced to sever their unique bond after Leslie becomes pregnant at the age of seventeen and has to move away. Thirty years later, Leslie moves back to town, filled with anger and resentment toward her parents. A swift trace of their lives illustrates how the events of their collective past linger on in their future. Strained by Leslie's arrival, the sisters move to embrace a clean break from the past in order to receive the new things God has orchestrated for their lives. In the midst of internal chaos and family crisis, they learn to search and find the antidote for conquering a life built on blame, deception, insecurities, worry, and bitterness.

Next, you'll meet Brenda, a devoted wife and mother of three who seems to have it all; however, after fourteen years, Brenda's marriage is teetering on the edge of divorce. Inundated with marital conflict and mounting financial troubles, Brenda learns she has a medical condition that has the potential to evolve into a series of lifelong health problems. She relies on her faith and believes that God will deliver her from the problems associated with a verbally abusive husband, unhealthy spending habits, and poor lifestyle choices.

Finally, there is Maurine, a retiring occupational therapist whose life has been consumed with family, work, and pursuing the American dream. The moment of truth regarding her family's years of misplaced priorities and unhealthy habits surfaces during the funeral service of a co-worker who dies from breast cancer. Maurine's concerns become a reality when her husband suffers a heart attack. Recognizing that God has a purpose for her husband's survival, Maurine accepts, confronts, and tackles the culprit behind her husband's health scare: unchecked family traditions.

Laura, Leslie, Brenda, and Maurine begin to put into practice what health experts and medical professionals tell them will be necessary to live a longer, healthier life: taking responsibility for their actions and learning that sacrifice, determination, and perseverance are necessary for rearranging their priorities and embracing healthier lifestyle habits. With an understanding that a continuum of poor lifestyle choices will eventually evolve into health concerns like diabetes, heart disease, and cancer, they realize the one thing they have to their advantage is the power of choice.

Trevor's clients are placed strategically throughout the book to motivate you in the hopes that you will discover solutions that are meaningful to your personal situation. Reading about how others resolve issues involving depression, worry, betrayal, anger, forgiveness, marital conflict, emotional

& verbal abuse, caring for a sick parent, an overweight child, genetic predispositions, and financial distress will hopefully serve to inspire and empower you to change your priorities. As long as your lifestyle habits teeter between good and bad choices, a clear and present danger of disease and illness looms.

PART I

A Tale of Two Sisters

CHAPTER 1

The Homecoming

As the sun pierced through her bathroom window, Laura's face glowed with excitement. She thought about her older sister, Leslie, moving back home to Houston, Texas. The memories of the two of them playing with their dolls and the traditional childhood games — Mary Mack, dodge ball, hopscotch, and hide and seek — reminded her of their fun and happy childhood, a childhood shared by two young girls, one thin, tall, graceful, delicate, and kind-hearted, yet hard to discipline; and the other, round and pudgy, awkward and tom-boyish, yet intelligent and independent.

No two sisters were closer than Laura and Leslie. Even though they argued over who would use the restroom first, who would perform which chores, or whose turn it was to use the telephone or watch their favorite TV show, they enjoyed each other's company and companionship. Their interests, attitudes, personalities, and goals were different, but the two of them were compatible in every way and loved each other beyond measure.

Toweling down her body, Laura thought to herself, *I'm so glad my sister is finally coming back where she belongs. I hope her return doesn't stir up painful memories. I pray the events of the past haven't damaged our lives beyond repair.* Her thoughts were interrupted as she turned around to look at a large antique sterling silver picture frame hanging on her bathroom wall. Inside was a black and white photograph of Leslie and her sitting at their piano. Leslie would play the piano while they sang the theme songs from their favorite '70s sitcom shows: *The Jeffersons, Good Times, Love Boat, Gilligan's Island, and The Brady Bunch.*

Laura and Leslie were raised by strict disciplinarian parents, Richard and Lucille Olson, in their inner city, wood-framed, two-bedroom, one-bath home in Houston. Guided by their convictions on education, work, and economic stability, Laura and Leslie's futures had been meticulously mapped out by the time Laura was only four years old and Leslie was eight. Their parents involved them in various educational, social, community, and religious activities to facilitate their development into independent, responsible, and successful Christian adults.

Leslie's failure to conform to her parents' plans, though, led to monumental consequences. When she was of fourteen, she took an interest in boys, and, as life would have it, she was pregnant by the age of seventeen — five months before her high graduation. The family was engulfed in chaos, crisis, and confusion when Leslie was forced by her parents to make plans to marry the baby's father, Hunter, who was twenty-two and studying law at the University of Houston. A handsome, well-built, and popular young man, Hunter exemplified strength, prestige, and power, and he was given two options by Leslie's parents: either marry Leslie or face their attempts to ruin his noteworthy name. Following his graduation from law school and Leslie's graduation from high school, and prior to the birth of their baby, Hunter and Leslie married and moved away from Houston. Hunter's parents were adamant about his continuing on to law school and had agreed to assist Leslie and him financially — but only if they moved to Baltimore.

Through the years, communication between Laura and Leslie consisted only of quick telephone calls, infrequent letters, overdue holiday & birthday cards, and out-of-date photos. Laura hoped Leslie's return would be the antidote to remove feelings of hurt and abandonment and initiate thoughts of love and peace.

A unique bond between sisters, which they both cherished beyond comprehension, was severed very early for Laura and Leslie. For thirty years, they attempted to stay involved in each other's lives, but their parents and Hunter kept them separated. At present, Leslie, age forty-eight, has lived in Baltimore for thirty years with Hunter, and three children. Laura, age forty-four, lives with her husband, Marti, and their one-year-old daughter, Jessica, in Alvin, Texas.

Removing the stopper from the bathtub drain, Laura, on her knees, began to focus her thoughts on the reunion. Startled by the sound of the doorbell, she stood to look out the bathroom window: there was a black Lexus RX parked in the driveway. Her sister had arrived. Frozen by uncertainty, Laura stood still, thinking about the visual encounter.

It's been thirty years since I've seen her. What should I do first — say 'Hi,' hug her, or offer her something to drink? It's been thirty years!

As Laura pondered her thoughts, Marti entered their bedroom and announced that her sister was downstairs.

"Hey, baby, your sister is here!" Marti yelled out as he looked around for his wallet and keys. He knew Laura was in their bathroom, but she didn't respond. Opening the door, he noticed that Laura had a faraway look in her eyes. "Are you alright?" he asked.

"Yes, I am," Laura replied, securing her bathrobe. "She's early. I haven't curled my hair, put on my makeup, or figured out what I'm going to wear."

"Baby, it's okay. Calm down," Marti said, seeing that Laura was anxious.

"I just don't know if I'm ready to see her."

"What! All you've talked about is your sister coming back home — the two of you catching up on your lives, you introducing her to Jessica, and how you hated not having the chance to see her children grow up."

"I know, I know, but—" Laura said, moving hastily across their bedroom toward her closet.

Following close behind, Marti responded, "But nothing!"

"You don't understand, Marti. All the things I've been thinking and feeling for so many years — I remember the day like it was yesterday."

"What day?" Marti asked.

Laura's voice began to quiver and tears began to well in her eyes as she responded, "The day she said 'Goodbye' — the day I lost my sister — the day my heart was shattered."

"Baby, I love you, but now is not the time for crocodile tears. Put the past where it belongs: behind you," Marti said, hugging her and wiping the tears from her face with his hand. "Your sister is here, and you can't keep her waiting. You've got so much to catch up on."

"You're right," Laura said, pulling away from Marti. "Go and let her know I'll be right down. It'll just take me a few minutes to do something with my hair and makeup. Let me figure out what I'm going to wear."

"Okay, but fifteen minutes. You should have been ready by now. You knew she was going to be here at one o'clock," he said, leaving out of the closet. After a brief moment, he returned with a damp washcloth and said, "Wipe your face."

"Thank you," Laura said, taking the towel.

"Do you want me to take Jessica downstairs to meet your sister, or do you want to bring her?"

"I'll bring her down. Go," Laura sighed, pushing Marti out the closet door.

"Are you okay now?" Marti asked.

"I'm okay. Thank you."

Minutes later, Laura appeared downstairs in their family room with baby Jessica in her arms, and the sight of her sister brought on a flood of tears. Laura motioned for Marti to take Jessica so she could embrace her sister. Entangled in each other's arms, they held each other tightly.

"Hi, li'l sis," Leslie said, tears flowing down her cheeks.

"Hi," Laura said, fighting back the same flow. "This is my husband, Marti. I guess the two of you have already met." Laura looked to Marti for a quick intervention.

"I think I need to go get some Kleenex," Marti laughed. "This is our precious baby girl, Jessica Leslie," he said, raising their baby high.

Leslie stood, admiring Jessica as Marti raised her up and down. "Wow, my sister with a little girl."

"Leslie, I've heard a lot about you," Marti continued. "It's great to finally meet you. Laura always talks about the two of you and your childhood escapades. Sounds like the two of you were quite a pair."

"That we were. It's a pleasure to meet you, baby Jessica. You named her after me?" Leslie asked, reaching for Jessica.

"Yes, we did," Laura replied as Marti positioned the baby in Leslie's arms.

"She's a beautiful baby. Look at her curly black hair," Leslie said, feeling the top of the Jessica's head. "She has a pretty strong grip. Look at her squeezing my fingers."

"I'll take credit for the beauty," Marti said proudly.

"Wow, she's a big baby."

"That she is," Marti responded.

"You're a beautiful baby. I look forward to getting to know you," Leslie said, handing Jessica back to Marti.

"Ladies, I know you all want to play catch-up, so Jessica and I will give you some time alone. Laura, I'll see you later. I'm going to get the boys."

"Thanks, baby. I'll see you later."

"Leslie, I look forward to getting to know you better."

"Same here," Leslie said while waving goodbye to baby Jessica.

Other than an email announcing Leslie's return, it had been over six months since the two had communicated; they didn't know where to begin. Laura knew she needed to update Leslie on their parents but decided to wait for the right moment.

"This is a cute and cozy home you have with Marti. Looks like it's a great neighborhood for raising a family, with an elementary school conveniently nearby. I love your granite kitchen counters, and there's something about this room that draws you in. Maybe it's the lovely brick fireplace..." Leslie paused, staring at Laura, who was looking stylish in a long-sleeved, scoop-neck dress. Uncertain about what to say next, and clearly trying to move beyond an awkward moment for both, she said joyfully, "I've missed you so much."

"I'm glad you're back home," Laura said, giving Leslie another tight hug.

"I don't know if I'm glad to be back, but I know I've missed you, Laura."

"I was so upset when you left. My best friend was gone. I didn't have anyone to talk to late at night, no one to share my secrets with, and no one to give me advice. No one to sing 'Movin' On Up' with — I missed you so much."

"I felt the same way, but I had no choice," Leslie said, holding Laura's hands.

"Can I get you something to drink?" Laura asked.

"Marti gave me a glass of water in the kitchen," Leslie responded. "Whose boys is he going to see?"

Laura motioned for Leslie to have a seat on their sofa.

"Marti has three other children from his previous marriage: Drew, Marti Jr., and Tisha, ages eight, thirteen, and eighteen. He's going to pick up Drew and Jr. and take them to get some new tennis shoes. At their ages, they grow like weeds."

"You never mentioned his kids in your emails or letters."

"I know," Laura admitted. "Some conversations you simply hold off on until you're face-to-face."

"So, tell me about you, your life, your career, the hubby, and life with a baby at forty-something," Leslie inquired. "I was surprised when you married. From the tone of the emails and letters, your career always seemed to be first and foremost."

Laura had followed the path that her parents had orchestrated. She attended the University of Texas at Austin and majored in chemistry, eventually becoming a chemist for a major pharmaceutical company. She then worked for over seven years as a chemist for Western Forensic Laboratory, and she had recently been promoted to Vice President of Business Development.

"Still tagged as a newlywed and new mom at age forty-four, I'm experiencing elevated dimensions of multi-tasking like I never imagined. Managing a family, cooking dinner for three — and sometimes six — rather than one, washing clothes for three rather than one, managing household expenses that have tripled, and managing a ten-state territory, which includes over one hundred employees — it can all be challenging at times."

Leslie emerged from her seat and scanned the pictures of Laura's new and extended family, as well as those of their parents. Laura had pictures everywhere: the coffee table, console table, end table, and the entertainment center.

"You are a very busy lady. It looks like Marti is very helpful and involved with Jessica."

"He's wonderful. I never thought I'd get married. At age forty, I was pretty sure I wouldn't. After years of hearing 'Oh it'll happen when you're least looking for it,' I was surprised when he came into my life. I'm glad God blessed me with the right person. We connect on so many levels, and I'm head over heels in love," Laura confirmed.

"So, tell me. How did you guys meet?"

"Tim, a mutual friend, introduced us during the church picnic a few years ago." Laura talked about how they'd already heard a lot about each other through Tim. "I was so nervous that I dripped barbecue sauce on my cute white linen shirt imported of Italian material from Neiman Marcus. I was so embarrassed and felt sure I wouldn't ever communicate with him again. Nevertheless, the next day Marti asked Tim for my telephone number. A few days later, we met for lunch at a Thai fusion restaurant located in Bellaire. From that point forward, we were never apart. To my surprise, his kids accepted me and were there when he proposed to me on New Year's Eve six months later."

"Doesn't sound like you knew each other very long before you got married," Leslie commented while continuing to view the pictures.

"Neither one of us wanted a long engagement or a big wedding, so the next summer, in front of forty friends and relatives, we got married at our church."

"And what about the honeymoon?" Leslie laughed, showing a silly sense of humor.

Sitting cross-legged on the sofa, Laura replied, "We didn't get to go on a honeymoon right away due to some financial obligations. A few months after we were married, we took a vacation to Clearwater, Florida. The CEO of Marti's company owns a vacation home there. For nearly a week, we enjoyed his luxurious two-bedroom vacation home, completely furnished, with a pool and jacuzzi. It was two blocks from Clearwater Beach, close to a lot of shopping and restaurants. The trip was our delayed honeymoon. Aside from the traditional honeymoon activity, the second most memorable activity during our trip was our dining experience at Bahama Breeze, a restaurant that features the best tasting Caribbean food. Every time I think about that place, I get excited about the Creole Baked Goat Cheese, Jerk Chicken Pasta, and their famous Fresh Fruit Mojito made with ripe tropical mango."

"I love Mojitos. I've never had a fruity one before," Leslie added. "What in the world is Creole Baked Goat Cheese?"

"It's goat cheese served in roasted red bell peppers served with vine-ripened tomato salsa. It was great. I can't forget the grouper burger we tried at one of the local restaurants. The entire vacation was perfect."

"So, where is Marti from? Does his parents live in this area? What about brothers and sisters? You've never mentioned anything, other than the fact that you were married."

"He's from Houston, the northside. Graduated from Kashmere High School. Both his parents are living. He has a brother, Jeremy, who lives in Seattle with his wife and two kids, and another brother, Ted, who is single and lives in New Mexico. Jeremy and his wife both work for the federal government and travel a lot, so Marti's parents spend quite a bit of time in Seattle taking care of their home and two kids."

"What kind of work does he do?" Leslie asked.

"Actually, he's an aircraft mechanic for one of the airlines at Hobby Airport," Laura responded.

A surprised look came over Leslie's face. "Um, a mechanic? How did Mom and Dad take you marrying a blue-collar worker who's divorced and has three kids? I bet that was a heartbreaker. They would have expected Leslie, the rebel daughter, to marry a mechanic — not the well-to-do attorney."

"You know Mom and Dad. They expressed some concerns, but I wasn't going to let their prejudices deter me from marrying the man I love. For a while, I had to endure Dad's negative comments, like, 'You really settled for the bottom of the barrel this time. If you'd spruce up your look, you could get a professional man.' "

"Wow! That was harsh, even for Dad."

"I just ignored him. It wouldn't have mattered to me if Marti were a ditch digger. He's a loving, honest, hardworking, strong, and Christ-centered man. He's an amazing dad who reads to his little girl every night. He's a supportive, hands-on dad who takes care of his children and tries to be involved in every aspect of their lives."

"He sounds like a wonderful man. You go, girl, for standing up to the folks. Sure hate I wasn't around!" Leslie exclaimed.

Branded as the new middle-aged mom, Laura was glad she had waited to marry and have a child. Life experiences surrounding her career and personal goals had made her more seasoned, tolerant, and patient; however, in the midst of getting an education, developing a career, building a nest egg, and working in the community, she had not considered the other factors that came along with waiting and marrying someone with children. She was at a point in her life where she not only had to balance her current life and new role as a wife and mother, but also the role of caring for her elderly parents, befriending her stepchildren, and preparing for retirement.

"Enough about me. What about you?" Laura asked. "Hunter's been in Houston for about three months, right? What happened? How did you end up back in Texas?"

"Because of his new position, he moved down in December. A couple months ago, he purchased a 5200 square foot two-story home with five bedrooms and four bathrooms in The Woodlands," Leslie said. "By the way, you've got to come out soon and see it. The house is fabulous. It has an Italian Tuscany style kitchen and a media room with a wet bar, concession bar, and adjoining arcade room. Our bedroom has a gas log fireplace, not to mention the bay window with a view of our wooded back yard and custom designed pool and spa."

"Wow! It sounds like a home for the rich and famous," Laura said, sounding skeptical. "What's his new position?"

"He's the top legal advisor to Houston's newly appointed district attorney," Leslie responded as she sat down.

"He's really done well for you all."

Leslie briefly summarized Hunter's career. "After college, Hunter continued his legal studies while I raised our three children. Occasionally, I would work a part-time job. Attending and finishing a prestigious law school, Hunter has emerged as a well-respected and well-accomplished attorney."

"That's pretty impressive. How did you all afford law school?" Laura asked.

"After Casey was born, Hunter's parents were adamant about him going to law school. For years, they helped us out financially, and that allowed Hunter to focus on getting his law degree. Once he passed the bar exam, his career soared in county government. For the past ten years, he's worked as a director over various divisions, such as child abuse and sexual offenses, family violence, and violent crimes."

"What kind of part-time work did you do?" Laura inquired.

"I haven't worked very much in my life, but my last job was at the local police station performing administrative work. While the kids were in school and involved in extra curricular activities, Hunter never wanted me to work, but he allowed me to on occasion. I'm hoping he'll agree to let me work here. I like having my own money to spend as I please."

"Since the kids are grown and gone, Hunter should be okay with you working."

"He likes for me to be at home and available whenever he needs me. He says there's no need for me to work because he makes enough money to take care of me and the kids."

Concerned about Leslie's comments about Hunter, Laura slowly nodded her head up and down. "What about the kids? How are they doing?"

Leslie paused to look at a picture of their parents on the fireplace mantel, then added, "The kids are fine. Both Courtney and Charlene are doing great! Courtney received her bachelor's in marketing last year, and Charlene is working on her master's in public administration. Casey is thinking about moving down here. His job as a sales representative with Prime Time Communications in D.C. ended, so he's looking. His little girl, Donna Gale, was born two months ago."

"A little girl!" Laura shouted. "Why didn't you call and tell me about my great-niece?"

"Life's been stressful lately," Leslie admitted. "That's probably why I'm eighty pounds overweight. Plus, I found out I have a thyroid condition."

"What? A thyroid condition?"

"I don't mean to burden you."

"We're sisters, and I love you, Leslie."

"Laura, we haven't been sisters for a long time."

"Well, not by my choice, Leslie. You're the one who's allowed Hunter to isolate you from your family. If it hadn't been for my attempts to maintain some sort of contact with you—"

"Laura, let's not go down that road, please," Leslie pleaded. "After everything that happened, he thought it best to accept his parents' offer to help us, so we left Houston and everybody associated with it behind. But, I don't think he should be totally blamed. Mom and Dad were contributing factors, also. When I left home, you were fourteen, and they forbid you to have anything to do with me. Even when you went off to college, I never heard from you. With over fifteen years of no communication between us, it was inevitable that we'd drift away from one another. But, I thank you for the last fifteen years of letters, cards, and emails."

"I'm just glad we found our way back to one another," Laura said peacefully. "But, I'm still hurt. He took my sister away."

"Me, too. I'm glad you took the first step and wrote me. I still have that letter from 1993. As a matter of fact, I have all of your letters, emails, and cards..." Leslie paused, staring at Laura. "Tell me one thing."

"What's that?" Laura asked.

"How have you maintained a perfect body all these years, and after having a baby at forty-something? You are *wearing* that dress, girl — looking like one of the *Sex in the City* women. You definitely have that sexy look. You look nothing like my little round, pudgy sister. What brand is it — Dolce & Gabbana, Prada, or Armani Collezioni?" Leslie questioned as she tugged on Laura's dress.

"Thank you, Leslie, for the compliment. I definitely can't afford dresses by those top designers anymore. Actually, I found this dress at a thrift store," Laura smiled. She stood up and went into the kitchen to get a bottle of water sitting on the counter. Returning to the family room, she continued, "I've never considered my body perfect, nor myself as sexy.

Once I hit my mid-thirties, trying to maintain a shape became somewhat of a challenge. Although I exercised and ate fairly regularly, from time to time I'd fall victim to the food industry's attack on my weaknesses. For years, I allowed myself to become comfortable with being sixty pounds overweight. So, after Jessica was born, I decided to make some changes, and I started eating healthier and working out on a regular basis," Laura responded.

"I always wondered why I stopped getting pictures of you," Leslie said. "Well, you look great. Life is funny. I was always the thin and tall one, now look at me."

"I'm not gonna say it's been easy. Through a health problem of my own, I've learned that good health habits are necessary for longevity, as well as for reducing my chances of developing diseases and illnesses that come with age," Laura responded. "Plus, having a baby in my forties has motivated me to do the right things so I can be around for all of the family milestone occasions."

"What health problem are you talking about? You never mentioned anything to me about a health problem in your letters or emails," Leslie said.

"For a period of time, I had a bout with depression," Laura shared.

"Depression!" Leslie exclaimed. "What were you depressed about? You've always had everything: the great career, the affluent lifestyle, the joys of the single life. Of course, you were the favorite daughter."

"From the outside looking in, it probably appeared as though I had everything, but my life was filled with all the wrong things."

"What wrong things?" Leslie asked.

"It was very difficult having Mom and Dad's world centered on setting their own goals and standards for my life. I'm the one who had the pressure of trying to live up to their expectations," Laura said, her eyes beginning to tear up. "In high school and college, I had to be an honor roll student or suffer the wrath of Dad. As long as he was supporting me, nothing less was acceptable. Once I entered the workforce, the series of promotions on my jobs was never good enough; my pay was never high enough; they believed I wasn't moving up to an executive level because I was plain, unappealing, and overweight. Then, of course, at the time, I wasn't married and didn't have a kid. I felt like a useless barren woman."

"I can't believe they were so demanding of you and — you're beautiful, Laura," Leslie said, mildly annoyed.

"So, now that I'm married with a child, Dad's questions have gone to when will I become president of my company and when are we going to move out of this small two-story house?"

"I can only imagine how hard it's been for you," Leslie said.

"From the time you left up until a few years ago, I led a life of desperation and uncertainty. Dad's constant reminders of how he and Mom positioned me to succeed made me feel indebted to them for life," Laura said, wiping away the tears. "My whole life was about pleasing them. Trying to keep up with their demands had me spiraling out of control. Although I managed to be functional at work and advance in my career, other aspects of my life were on the decline."

"How can that be? Reading about all the highlights of your life in your letters, I just knew you were destined for greatness. And honestly, I was somewhat envious of you," Leslie said, amazed by what she was hearing. "How did you know you were suffering from depression?"

"When I'd get home from work, something would come over me, and I'd just start crying for no reason. My friends stopped hanging around me and inviting me to happy hour because I was always sad and miserable," Laura said.

"Did they try to help you?" Leslie asked.

"Yes, but I was too caught up in self-critical mode," Laura said. "They encouraged me to go to counseling, but I didn't want to go. I *wanted* to wallow in self-pity. I *wanted* to keep the covers pulled over my head and not deal with reality. The only thing that helped me get through the day was food and alcohol."

"Food and alcohol. Not you?"

"Yes, food and alcohol. For breakfast, by ten o'clock, I would have eaten a southern-style chicken biscuit, banana nut muffin, cinnamon raisin bagel with cream cheese, and drunk a caramel macchiato. Then, for lunch, a 12-inch sub, a package of chips, and a super-sized drink. An assortment of packaged donuts, popcorn, and sodas would follow throughout the remainder of the day, and I closed out the night with a box of Twinkies and a glass of Cognac."

"Wow! Even now, I don't eat that bad. How did you eat all of those breakfast items by ten o'clock?"

"Easy. On my way to work, I would pick up the chicken biscuit and eat it while driving. There was a coffee shop in my office building, so around nine o'clock I would go get the muffin, bagel, and macchiato," Laura responded.

"I'm sure Mom and Dad's criticism had a lot to do with the way you felt about yourself," Leslie interrupted. "Dad's comments must have been emotionally debilitating for you. Sounds like you've been subjected to a lifetime of unforgiving remarks."

"It's been a journey. I made many bad choices over the years. My finances got out of control because I felt I had to portray an image of success. I bought a big home in an affluent neighborhood, drove an expensive car, shopped at upscale clothing stores, and ate at the finest restaurants — all of which caused me to get deep in debt. After having just enough money to pay my mortgage, car, and utilities, I charged everything else. And truthfully, I lost my house," Laura said, her voice trembling. "The only way I could afford my home was to seek special financing. As a result, I was lured into one of those adjustable rate mortgages — and the balloon payments that come with them. Before long, I couldn't afford them anymore."

"I am so sorry to hear that," Leslie said, giving Laura a big hug.

"Now, it's funny listening to government officials talk about programs to help people stay in their homes and escape foreclosure."

"You've dealt with a lot. Did you take pills or something for your depression?" Leslie asked.

"Yes, I took antidepressants for a while, but, after joining my church, attending bible study, praying everyday, reading my bible, and getting involved in a women's ministry group, I let them go, along with happy hour, clubbing, and my compulsion to spend."

"How do you just let that sort of medication go?" Laura questioned.

"Let me rephrase that. I didn't just let them go. My psychiatrist weaned me off the medication. I must say that the withdrawal process was pretty tough," Laura said, clarifying that professional help assisted her with getting off the medication. "Once I developed a relationship with Christ and came into an understanding of God's purpose for me, my life changed. I realized that I had to live my life for God and not for others. More importantly, I realized that all the stuff I allowed Mom and Dad to deem important for me wasn't consistent with what I myself had come to believe," Laura said, sounding relieved.

"You are definitely together now, my sister," Leslie exclaimed.

"Every day is a journey. If I stay in the Word and remain consistent with my beliefs, then I'm able to stay on track with fulfilling my purpose," Laura said, reaching for the box of Kleenex. "No more crying, sadness, restless nights, feeling like a failure, living for others, or suicidal thoughts."

"Suicidal thoughts?" Leslie shouted, placing her hands on her cheeks.

"Yes, for a moment I let my thoughts wander to that point. The thought of being out from under the pressure and stress of pleasing our parents was more comforting than living. Being afraid that others would find out about my financial problems was more comforting than living. I thought that once the extent of my financial and emotional states was revealed, I'd be ten feet under — and it wouldn't matter to me."

"Wow, that's deep," Leslie said.

"I came to the realization that nothing is worth killing yourself over. I couldn't give up the hope that something better was waiting on me. I came to the understanding that I needed Christ in my life. If I wanted God to handle the problems I was having in coping with the pressures and distractions of life — all I can say now is that God was with me when I wasn't with him. Life for me is good now. Don't get me wrong, though: there are still times when I get burdened down, but now I have something inside that empowers me to recognize and respond differently," Laura said, assuring Leslie that she was okay. "I am truly happy and living in peace, which is something I never thought was possible for me."

"So what happened to the big house and the fancy car?" Leslie asked.

"I had to get rid of the house before it went into foreclosure. I moved into a one-bedroom apartment so I could focus on reducing my credit card debt and saving money."

"That's huge!" Leslie shouted. "A lot of folks would have tried to stay in the home until…"

"Yes, it was a big deal to go from a 2500-square-foot home to a 650-square-foot apartment. I sold and gave away a lot of expensive furniture. Plus, I traded in my Land Rover for a used Honda Civic," Laura admitted. "I loved my Land Rover, but I know it wasn't in God's plan me — especially considering how high gas prices are now."

"Now, you're married with a child — or I guess I should say children — and have an executive-level job," Leslie said proudly. "What about the folks? How did they handle everything you went through?"

"They expressed their disappointment and shame. Dad said my irresponsible behavior caused me to lose my home and car, that I was like all the other people in America who couldn't manage their money. I remember him saying in his deep tone, 'Your monthly income is three times what I earned when I was working, and you can't own nothing, not a single thing.'"

"Wow — that was hurtful," Leslie commented.

"You know what, though, Leslie? It was okay. I was at a different place in my life. I had gotten hooked up with Jesus Christ, which connected me to God's power and strength. I now understand that God uses situations to bring us into His purpose for our lives. I firmly believe that all I've been through prepared me to do the things I'm involved in at my church," Laura affirmed, "and because of my faithfulness, I was blessed with Marti, Jessica, and three wonderful stepchildren."

"That's awesome."

"Even with all the good stuff, there was still an area of my life that needed attention, and that was my lifestyle."

Looking at her body, Leslie shared, "I've tried for years to lose weight. My addiction to sugar and caffeine — my favorite sweets and lattés — is probably going to be my downfall. Every time I eat a pint of banana pudding ice cream late at night, I hate myself the next morning for doing so."

"When I got serious about eating healthier, I discovered that the combination of my favorite breakfast items tallied over 1,470 calories; super large caramel macchiato made with whole milk, 340 calories, blueberry muffin, 430 calories, cinnamon raisin bagel without the cream cheese, 280 calories, and the southern style chicken biscuit, 420 calories. I was too afraid to add up the grams and milligrams of fat, sodium, cholesterol, and everything else bad. And I dare not think about the number of calories, fat, sodium, and cholesterol in the other foods I consumed in the same day."

"Please don't share any more with me," Leslie said, laughing with amazement.

Laura continued, "My fitness consultant, Trevor, told me the other day that a large majority of people suffer from nutrition deficiency. He says the reason a lot of people crave sugars and caffeine is that their bodies aren't getting the vitamins and minerals they need. Unfortunately, most of us are overfed and undernourished."

"Fitness consultant? You go, girl! Since you have a fitness consultant, I know you can help me get on track," Leslie said, laughing. "I don't know if I have a nutrition deficiency, but I know I eat when I'm stressed, unhappy, or lonely."

"Those emotional situations cause a lot of people to make poor choices."

"Oh, I forgot to mention that I have high blood pressure and high cholesterol along with the thyroid condition. I've tried every diet on the market and can't lose weight. Last year, to get the weight off quickly, I started taking fat dissolving injections."

"What are fat dissolving injections?" Laura asked, her eyebrows raised.

"Actually, I was undergoing treatments that consisted of injections in various parts of my body — the arms, belly, and thighs — that would break down the solid form of body fat and convert it to liquid form. In the liquid form, the body fat would eventually leave my body as waste," Leslie shared.

"Whew! It sounds scary to me," Laura admitted.

"Actually, it was okay. But, after three injections the company went bankrupt."

"How much did something like that cost?"

"The average cost per treatment area ranged anywhere from $500 to $1200," Leslie said. "After I was forced to stop the treatments, I decided to try the exercise route earlier this year. I joined a 60-day, gut-buster boot camp to help me get rid of this stomach. But, as the title suggests, the program was too strenuous for me. So, I stopped. Before moving here, I made up my mind to do the lap-band surgery, but, after listening to a lady at my old job about it, I got scared and decided to wait."

"What did she say to change your mind?"

"First, she said that if you don't chew your food very well it can get stuck. If you eat too many bites, you may experience tightness in your chest. You can't drink with your meal. Then, there are the fills you need to get that help guide the rate of weight loss. She talked about the various foods she was unable to eat, like bread, broccoli, oranges, and rice. She said it may take a while to find the right combination of foods for your situation."

"I'm sure everyone's experience is different," Laura said.

"I know. Mentally, I wasn't ready, so I decided to wait."

"I want you to visit with Trevor. He conducts all kinds of fitness sessions. If you're truly ready to make some lifestyle changes, I believe he can get you on track. His method of coaching causes you to broaden your horizons, but you must be willing to step out of your box and explore your options for replacing old habits with new ones," Laura said. "What's going on with your thyroid?"

"I have an underactive thyroid," Leslie responded.

"A lady at my church has that, too," Laura said.

"It appears to be fairly common; however, it took forever for my doctor to make a diagnosis. I wasn't eating a whole lot, but I'd gained a significant amount of weight. I was tired all the time, and I had difficulty concentrating," Leslie admitted. "Even if I wanted to exercise, I couldn't because I was too tired and sluggish."

"I remember reviewing an article the lady had from the American Association of Clinical Endocrinologists about an underactive thyroid. According to that info, the lack of thyroid hormones decreases the body's metabolism, which affects the process of converting your food into energy," Laura said. "It was a lot of other information included in the article, but that's all I can remember."

"I'm so glad my doctor has me on medication. I'm hoping it'll straighten everything out."

"If you'd like, I can make an appointment for you to visit with Trevor. His main office is in Dallas, but I believe he's in town for the next couple weeks."

"Let me think about it — I'm not sure I want to be involved in another fitness program," Leslie said, politely. "My new home has a mirrored exercise room off the master suite, but I can't fathom having to look at my body while trying to exercise."

"Do you have any equipment in it?" Laura asked.

"Yes, Hunter has a treadmill, stair master, exercise bike, rowing machine, and a home gym system in it," Leslie responded.

"You don't have to commit to anything with Trevor; I just want you to talk with him. He can provide you with some options for eating healthier and implementing various exercise activities. Since you have all of that equipment, he could show you how to use it. Don't limit your thinking; considering the current state of your health, it's an important time in your life. You have to understand that God has greatness in mind for all of us. However, you'll never experience His greatness if you don't place Him first and your overall well-being second. In order to experience His greatness, some things will have to change in your life."

"Okay, sister. Don't start getting preachy on me," Leslie said, avoiding eye contact. "By the way, how do you keep your belly so flat?"

"This past Fall I tried some different activities."

"Like what?" Leslie asked.

"Belly-dancing and salsa-dancing classes."

"Okay, salsa I can see... but belly dancing?"

"Yes, belly dancing," Laura laughed. "Experiencing firsthand the battle with the bulge in my mid-thirties, I definitely wasn't happy with my body image, and not necessarily because of what I believed others thought, but because of how I felt. I hated not being able to cross my legs at the knee or being unable to touch my toes or feeling self-conscious every time my arms jiggled when I'd wave at someone or raise my arm at work, not to mention being unable to climb a flight of stairs without my heart pounding. Like you, I didn't like looking in the mirror at my fat thighs, stomach, hips, upper arms, and butt. I'd cringe every time, thinking 'How did I allow myself to get to this size?' Although I probably wouldn't have admitted it at the time, I was depressed about how I looked; Dad's hurtful comments about my weight probably just made matters worse. And, frankly, standing five feet and six inches and weighing one hundred and ninety pounds, I was afraid of the potential health risks associated with being obese, as well as the risks associated with belly fat."

"I wish I could switch bodies with one of those beautiful, tall, slender actresses on television. I would love to be a size six, or even a size eight."

"The main thing you should focus on is being a size healthier," Laura stressed. "Everyone is not designed to be a size six or eight. If, through implementing healthier eating habits and a consistent exercise program, you end up being a size twelve or fourteen, it's important to understand that you're still healthier. Changing your lifestyle to incorporate those two key factors will help you prevent, eliminate, and manage any current or unforeseen health concerns."

"I've read that belly fat can be dangerous because it's associated with increased risk for heart disease, diabetes, and some forms of cancer."

"Exactly. My doctor says it also interferes with liver function because it hampers the processing of cholesterol and insulin," Laura added.

"Sis, I don't mean to cut you off, but I'm a little hungry. I haven't eaten anything all day," Leslie stated. "We've been talking for over an hour."

"I'm so sorry. We've been chatting so much, I forgot about the food. Marti set up the grill for me so I could grill us some burgers. Let's go in the kitchen."

Leslie got up, trailing behind Laura. "Burgers? Not you!"

"Burgers made with ground white chicken; they have less fat," Laura said, turning on the oven.

"Right now, I don't care what they have less of. I'm hungry. Let me help you."

"Actually, I've already shaped the patties, but you can place the sweet potato wedges on the baking sheet in the oven," Laura suggested, pointing to the refrigerator.

"Sweet potato wedges!" Leslie said, surprised.

"Instead of regular potatoes, we make our fries with sweet potatoes. With the right seasonings like ground cumin, ground red pepper, paprika, thyme, garlic powder, or dry mustard, they taste great," Laura said, "and they're very nutritious."

"Interesting. Sounds really healthy."

"People tend to make eating healthier restrictive. For me, it's about discovering ways to make my favorite foods healthier," Laura said.

"I see," Leslie replied, while getting the tray of sweet potato wedges out of the refrigerator. "Moving back to the Houston area is going to be great. With you guiding me, maybe I can get rid of this fat the right way."

"Trevor has really helped me, so I know he can get you moving in the right direction, too," Laura said. "I definitely want you to try belly dancing. It's a lot of fun. Plus, it's a great workout. There are some whole-wheat buns in the refrigerator, and some mixed greens and sliced tomatoes. Can you get them out?"

"Sure. I'll heat the buns," Leslie said. "You don't use lettuce."

"I prefer mixed greens or fresh spinach because they provide more nutritional value, like vitamins A and C, calcium, fiber, etc."

"I guess I should consider that a good thing," Leslie smirked.

"Yes, that is a good thing. Eating foods with an abundance of nutrients like vitamins, minerals, and antioxidants helps us all stay healthy; they protect our cells from disease and illness."

"I see. So tell me about Mom and Dad. How are they?"

For thirty years, there had been intense animosity between Leslie and her parents. Laura had always hoped that they would be able to communicate someday, as well as come to respect and listen to one another. However, harboring the pain of past events prevented Leslie and her parents from doing so.

"I didn't know where your head was about them, but they're fair. I told them you were moving back."

"What was their response?" Leslie inquired.

"They want to see you."

"That's a surprise," Leslie responded quickly. "Wish I could say the same. It's going to take me some time to get to the point where I can see them."

" 'Some time to'?... It's been thirty years," Laura said, hesitating. "Come, let's have a seat for a moment."

"Some time to come to terms with how they treated me. For years, I've struggled internally with guilt, abandonment, emptiness, shame, and loneliness," Leslie shared, sitting down at the dinette table. "You were the good daughter. I, on the other hand, was a major disappointment. I brought shame on the family by getting pregnant at the age of seventeen, which resulted in me being banished from the family tree. It'll be a little much for me to sit and visit with them and talk about the good ol' times."

"Parents make mistakes, Leslie. You've got to let it go."

"It's more than them banishing me from the family. What do you think drove me to find solace in boys?"

"What?" Laura asked.

"Our father's verbal abuse toward our mother — the way he would belittle her in front of others," Leslie said, her anger rising. "The way he controlled her every thought and movement. The way he made her ask for permission to talk on the phone to her mother, to buy Coke instead of Pepsi, to go to Wednesday night prayer meeting. I figured if there were a God, he wouldn't let a man treat his wife that way."

"Leslie, let's not bring up old stuff," Laura begged.

Ignoring Laura's plea, Leslie continued. "I know it didn't change when I left, did it? I bet she really got it when I got pregnant. So what was the story? How was my absence explained?"

"Leslie, all that stuff's in the past. Let it go. It's time you focus on the here and now."

"Have you let it go? I bet his actions had a lot to do with your depression. That's probably why it took you so long to get married: afraid you'd end up with a man like Dad. I'm glad they tossed me out. At least I was able to get away from the dysfunction."

"Dad had a difficult childhood. His mother abandoned him when he was only six months old. He was raised by his Aunt Betsy, who was sixty-four at the time, and his father never claimed him," Laura said. "As a child, love for Dad was nonexistent. A man with his background showed love the best way he knew how, and that was by providing for his family."

"Listen to you making up excuses for his cruel behavior toward our mother. To me, his behavior is unforgivable," Leslie said. "I bet she told you those things to justify his behavior. The poor little disadvantaged boy didn't have anyone to love him, so he had every right to act out his hostility on her and others. Women excuse too much. When their man is going through something, they allow him to abuse, misuse, and take their frustration out on them. Something is wrong with that picture. What about women? We have a heavy burden placed on us daily."

"All I am saying, Leslie, is that it helps you to understand the foundation that created Dad's demeanor. I'm not condoning his behavior, but I do understand it."

"I'm sure their church members would be surprised to find out what kind of person their Deacon Olson really is, which is not the loving, devoted husband and father he portrays himself to be. The Olson Family has done well hiding dysfunction. The family that looks like the symbol of strength, stability, and spirituality to the outsiders is, in actuality—"

"Leslie, where is all of this coming from?"

"While working at the police department in Baltimore, I met a lady who was the founder of a domestic violence organization. I did some volunteer work for her. While doing so, I learned about the different forms of abuse. I had always thought it was only physical, but I learned that it's also emotional and verbal. As I became more familiar with the traits, I recognized the actions of an emotional and verbal abuser while reminiscing about our childhood. I guess we thought it was normal for Dad to talk to Mom any kind of way — talking about her childhood and how poor her family was, how she was lucky to have him — that she wouldn't have anything without him. Ridiculing her — calling her stupid and dumb when he became jealous of her. He was always jealous of others' admiration of her love for God and her good deeds. He may not have beaten her black and blue, but his verbal abuse was just as bad."

"Leslie, all of those things might be true, but God is a forgiving God. You can't allow yourself to stay trapped in your childhood, holding onto unhealthy thoughts and feelings."

"Laura, I'm not trapped. Unfortunately, I don't have selective memory like you. I'm just reflecting on the fact that we didn't have a good role model of a husband or father. Then, I was forced to marry someone just like him."

" 'Just like him'?" Laura paused. "What do you mean, 'just like him'?"

"Just forget it," Leslie responded. "I'm just rattling off."

"Is everything okay between you and Hunter?" Laura inquired.

"Everything is fine. Do you have something I can snack on until the food is ready?"

"There are some oranges and apples on the counter," Laura said, getting up from the table.

"Any cookies or candy?"

"No. We try not to bring sweets into the house. It helps not to have tempting foods available."

"I guess I'll eat an orange. Let me guess: it's loaded with something nutritious, right?"

"Oranges are great sources of vitamins C and potassium, as well as fiber," Laura responded.

"For now, I just want something to eat; I'll let you get into the nutritional specifics another time," Leslie said, getting up.

"Okay, and we'll also get more into the hazards of going all day without eating. Letting yourself get hungry will lead to poor choices. If you establish regular intervals for eating, you'll be less likely to make unhealthy choices out of desperation. Let's go outside and get these chicken burgers on the grill."

Laura's home had a covered patio in the back with a huge backyard with plenty of room for kids and outdoor activities. Laura and Leslie spent the remainder of the day there catching up on their lives, laughing about the silly things they did as kids, and talking about old classmates. They laughed about the evolution of musical devices — record players, eight track players, and cassette players, and their collection of LP's and 45's from the seventies and eighties. Laura reminded Leslie of how much she loved to dance.

CHAPTER 2

Disruptive Family Matters

*I*t was the beginning of another workweek. Laura was exhausted from spending the entire weekend helping Leslie shop for furniture and new pieces to decorate and furnish her new home. They visited some of the finest furniture stores in Houston, including Ethan Allen, Zealie, and Noel, in the hopes of finding the right blend of contemporary and traditional furnishing.

Walking through their bedroom door, Marti paused a moment to watch Laura, who was buried in thought. Interrupting her, he jumped into their bed, wrapped his arms around her back, and greeted her with a hug. "Good morning, baby. What's on your mind? You have that faraway look again."

Lying in bed, she turned around and kissed him. Displaying her usual sign of affection, she began poking him. "What time is it?"

Looking at the clock on their nightstand, Marti responded, "It's 5:36 on a fabulous Monday morning. Again, what's on your mind?"

"I was just thinking about stuff — Leslie is still angry with our parents."

"Sounds like they treated her pretty badly when she got pregnant," Marti said.

"That's just the way parents were back then. If a girl got pregnant, she had to move out and get married."

"You're right about that," Marti responded.

"Anyway, I enjoyed our visit. I just hope I can help her work through the hostility and anguish. I've got to figure out how to stop her from living her life in reverse."

"Did you tell her about your father?"

"No, not yet."

"When are you going to?"

"I need to tell her this week. Dad will be going back to the doctor, and I want her to be involved in the medical decisions."

Laura and Leslie's father, Richard Olson, had recently been diagnosed with Stage IV prostate cancer at the age of seventy-seven. Overlooking the seriousness of prostate cancer, Mr. Olson often joked about being poked and prodded by doctors during his prostate exams, and for nearly twenty years he refused to get annual check-ups. For months, he had ignored the signs and symptoms of someone experiencing prostate problems: difficulty urinating, pain during urination, lower back pain, and pain achieving and maintaining an erection. Eventually, ongoing excruciating pain isolated in his bones forced him to seek medical attention from his physician, leading to the cancer's discovery.

"If you want her involved, you should go ahead and tell her quickly."

"I will," Laura confirmed. "I just hope she's ready to go to Mom and Dad's home for the reunion. Even though the home has gone through numerous renovations in fifty years, the remnants of the emotional fallout still linger. I want her to put the past behind her. Even though my parents have never talked about it, I know they regret how things turned out. A few years ago, they invited Leslie and her family down for a holiday, but because Hunter had Leslie and the kids under his control they didn't come."

"What do you mean 'under his control'?" Marti inquired.

"That's another story that would require a lot of time to recount; nevertheless, I believe seeing our old blue and white, single-speed, pedal-braked Huffy bikes will probably remind her of the fun we had as kids."

"That is too funny! I had a Huffy, also. It was my primary mode of transportation from the second through the sixth grade. I rode that bike at least twenty miles every day, going back and forth from my house to the neighborhood store and my grandmother's house. Around the fifth grade, I'd outgrown that bike and wanted a ten-speed, but we couldn't afford it. One Christmas, I asked Santa for a new bike, but it never came. That's probably when I stopped believing in Santa Claus."

"Sorry, honey. I didn't mean for you to relive any childhood horrors," Laura responded, rubbing his head.

"It's okay. God has blessed me to be able to buy any bike I want," Marti said, assuring Laura that he was okay. "I'm looking forward to teaching Jessica how to ride her first bike."

"I'm looking forward to her dressing up and playing with dolls and her Easy-Bake Oven," Laura said.

"The other day, I found myself thinking about this past year of adjusting to life with a new baby — the lack of sleep, that is. It's been pretty amazing watching our baby grow over the past twelve months — from the point when the nurses gave her to us in the hospital room to her taking her first steps to her saying 'Ma-Ma and Da-Da'."

"It's unbelievable how babies grow and learn so quickly within the first year. The first three months, they learn something new every week. It's like they go from just lying down to looking at you to making noises to reaching for you to eventually walking. I'm so glad God blessed me to experience it firsthand. It's amazing!"

"Truly amazing — especially trying to dance to her music!" Marti interjected.

"This year has started out pretty interesting. My promotion at work has me on the fast track. Now, I have to figure out how to balance home, work, church, and getting back into my outdoors exercise routine — and, above all, my parents—" Laura stopped mid sentence.

"What were you getting ready to say, Laura?"

"Nothing," Laura said, as she hesitated before continuing. "I'm really excited about the baby jogger and trailer you got for me and the baby for Christmas."

"Oh, yeah, I guess I need to get to work on the assembly, right?"

"You're absolutely right, Mr. Marti Tyler Mason."

"I'll get to it this weekend," Marti said.

"It's almost six. I'd better start getting ready for work. I have a busy day ahead of me; a lot of meetings. What's the baby doing?"

"She's playing with the toys in her playpen. I finished bathing her. She's dry and clean. Listen to the monitor."

"I love it when you're off during the week," Laura said, enjoying the moment. "You bathe, feed, and dress the baby, leaving me more time to fit in some exercising. By the way, you've been promising to do Pilates with me."

"And, if I must say, your Pilates has you looking lean. You look great! But I'm not interested in doing it — Thanks, though."

"Thanks for the compliment, honey," Laura said, giving Marti a quick kiss. "Listen! Jessica is crying."

Looking at and listening to the baby monitor, Marti responded, "I'd better go get her fed."

"Are you following the nutritional guide for the baby?" Laura asked. "I want to make sure our daughter gets started on the right track with eating healthy."

"Yes, honey, I'm following the guide — approximately two ounces of whole grain per day, one cup of fresh fruit per day, three-fourths cup of vegetables per day, and so on."

"Great! I don't want her becoming comfortable with drinking sugar-laden drinks and foods and consuming high calorie foods that don't offer any nutritional value. I don't want my child to be a pudgy little preschooler like me."

"I know, sweetie. You're probably still thinking about all those kids at the church harvest fair last Fall who had a can of soda in one hand and a slice of cake in the other," Marti responded while walking out of the room. "Let me go take care of the baby so I can get to work. By the way, did you see that she has another tooth?"

Marti was still adjusting to Jessica's ongoing feeding. Laura's new job had her traveling occasionally, so Marti had taken on more of the caretaker role.

Laura entered the kitchen as Marti was finishing Jessica's feeding.

"There's a children's festival in South Houston this weekend, and I'm thinking about taking Jessica on Saturday after I check on my parents," Laura announced, taking Jessica out of her highchair. "Are the kids coming over this weekend? I know Drew would enjoy the storytellers, puppet shows, games, jugglers, and other activities."

Marti started to wash some dishes in the sink. "I really don't know," he said, sounding irritated. "Sydney is acting like some scorned woman again. Ever since she and Luke broke up, she's been hard to get along with. I was hoping things would work out with him. I truly want her to be happy. It's like the bitterness she feels for me is destroying her. For fifteen years, I never figured out how to love her the way she wanted to be loved. I was devoted, respectful, and faithful. I worked hard every day so I could move up on my job and increase my income. I worked my fingers to the bone to provide her and our children with nice things, but it was never enough for her. Our entire marriage was filled with her continuously comparing me to her sister's husband who earns six figures as an engineer. It was clear to me that I would never be able to make her happy. Our constant fighting and hurting was destroying our children. I was hoping she could find the same magic with someone that I've found with you. I was just hoping the hurt feelings would go away. Her actions are blatant manipulation."

"Why haven't you said something about Sydney before now?"

"I didn't want to worry you. Between work, having to travel, Jessica, and your parents, you have enough to worry about, especially since your brother and sister aren't helping you. Sometimes I feel like our marriage has been consumed with all these outside forces rather than our new life with Jessica," Marti said, embracing Laura and Jessica.

"What about spring break? Are the kids going to stay that week with us?"

Jessica was starting to get fidgety, so Laura grabbed a stuffed animal off the counter top to distract her.

"I really don't know. They're supposed to," Marti responded with frustration, as he a placed a dish in the dish rack. "What are you eating this morning? I'm having yogurt, toast, and some of the fresh fruit you mixed together the other day."

"I'll have the same." Laura sat Jessica back into her high chair with her toy. She opened the refrigerator to get a carton of yogurt. "Marti, you are my husband, and our life is a partnership. Please don't exclude me, and don't worry; our marital bond is solid. I love Jr., Drew, and Tisha as though they were my own, and whatever friction is going on between you and Sydney, I want to know about it."

"I'm sorry for excluding you," Marti said, placing her toast and fruit on a plate. "She's probably going to say she's taking the kids out of town again this weekend. She's trying so hard to limit my contact with them."

"Don't worry, everything will work out. What about Trevor's kids camp at church this summer? It might be a good idea for you to register Jr. and Drew. I'm worried about Jr.'s size. He's thirteen, five feet, three inches tall, weighs 166 pounds, and is still growing," Laura voiced, looking concerned. "And worse: his best friends are the television, music videos, and video games."

"You're right," Marti replied, sitting down next to Laura.

"And it doesn't help that you spend the majority of your time playing video games with him and Drew the few times you all are together. Since you love video games so much, you should look into buying the *Nintendo Wii Fit*. One of my employees bought it, and he loves it. He says he's doing activities he was reluctant to do like jogging, step exercises, and yoga. It's helped him improve his balance and posture, as well as his strength. He says there are over forty different activities, like pushups, lunges, and leg extensions. He also talked about a virtual personal trainer. You should do some research on the Internet to find out more specifics."

"I think I'll check it out," Marti said, putting a smear of honey on his toast. "You're right to be concerned, and I do take responsibility for my contribution to his lack of physical activity. Jr.'s weight and lack of exercising are sore subjects with Sydney. I told her about the summer camp a few months ago, and I know there's a deadline for us to register to get the discount."

"As someone who works as a pharmaceutical sales rep, you'd think Sydney would be promoting wellness and fitness. It's disturbing to think about how conditions like diabetes and heart disease keep increasing among kids because parents won't foster good habits in them," Leslie said, irritated. She looked across at Jessica, who was playing with her toy. "How much is the summer camp going to be this year?" Laura asked.

"For the two, it's around $130 per week for ten weeks. This year, they've added Spanish classes and field trips to some different museums. Plus, they'll have Trevor's standard physical fitness classes and basketball. Also, I thought it would be a good idea for Trevor to help Sydney develop healthier lifestyle habits for her and the kids."

"What did she say?"

" 'Not interested'."

"Did you tell her that he's been in the fitness business for over fifteen years? That he's the owner of Faith-Based Fitness Solutions, a fitness-consulting agency in Dallas? That he conducts fitness workshops throughout the Houston/Dallas/ Fort Worth areas at recreation centers, hospitals, nursing homes, churches — everywhere? *And* that he has special programs for kids?"

"Yes, I told her all of that and more," Marti said.

"Did you tell her he runs in marathon races all over the country?"

"Yes, I did. I even told her I would pay for the consultation and a few sessions. That's one reason I was working the overtime," Marti confessed. "She seems to think Jr.'s excess weight is baby fat."

"Looks like the only time they eat healthy meals is when they come to visit us," Laura said.

"You're right. I wish she'd take time out to cook sometimes," Marti said. "Still, I'll try to find out something about spring break."

"We've been saving for months to take the kids to Corpus Christi's beautiful beaches for spring break," Laura said.

"I know. I was looking forward to my time with them, strolling along the shore, watching them laughing, playing, and splashing in the ocean water. There's nothing more invigorating than fresh, crisp ocean air. Not to mention watching the seagulls floating through the air and the boats scattered throughout the harbors," Marti said, his excitement growing. "I'll call her this evening."

"Great! Plus, you also need to talk about our contributions toward Tisha's prom, graduation, and college. She's a high school senior, and no one is talking about the expected college contributions. Over twenty-seven percent of your payroll check goes toward child support, and the court order states that you'll continue to pay while your children are in college," Laura said with frustration. "And then there's the summer camp for the boys."

"Laura, please don't start with the child support again," Marti said. "On a different note, what about your parents? That's another bill we're looking at having to pay."

"I'll call Leslie when I get a free moment. I would like to have someone come and care for my parents during the week and on weekends, which can only happen if Leslie and I contribute additional funds," Laura said.

"How much are you talking?" Marti asked.

"I've checked with some assisted care providers. After reviewing their income from retirement and social security, our portion for a care provider would be around $1,800 a month," Laura said.

"That's a lot of money, Laura," Marti said. "We're already paying $500 a month in daycare, plus my child support. We're pretty strapped for money. Now that the price of gas has soared, the cost to fill your tank has tripled with you working at the corporate office near downtown."

"And our food bill — milk has really increased," Laura interrupted.

"We haven't even considered what my portion will be for Tisha's college."

"I really don't have too many options as far as my parents are concerned," Laura said. "Depending on the medical care my dad will need for his prostate cancer, the care provider can take him for his treatments or whatever is necessary."

"The way I figure, since your sister isn't working she could help care for your father. That saves us from having to pay another bill."

"Let me talk with her this week, but I really don't think that's going to happen."

"Also, what's our strategy for getting a sitter for Jessica on Saturday mornings when you're coming in from out-of-town trips or wanting to exercise? I've got to work on Saturdays."

"I thought you were going to change your hours back to Monday through Friday," Laura said, getting up from the table.

"One moment you're glad I'm off during the week so you can exercise, then the next you want me off on Saturdays," Marti said, sounding irritated. "Either I can work Tuesday through Saturday or Monday through Friday."

"There's no need to get testy," Laura said, clearing off the table.

"I'd better finish eating my breakfast. Jessica and I need to get out of here before the traffic gets too bad."

"Okay. We'll talk about it later," Laura said, picking Jessica up to kiss her.

"I love you. We'll see you later," Marti said. "We're having Men's Forum at the church tonight, so you'll need to pick Jessica up."

"Okay," Laura said, waving goodbye to Jessica.

The following day, while sitting at her desk reviewing some paperwork, Laura received a telephone call from Leslie.

"Hi, Laura. Just thought I would check in with you. I wanted to see how your day is going."

"Hi, Leslie. It's good to hear from you. The job is going okay. Supervising is a challenge, but I'm adjusting. It gets tiresome having to contend with people calling in sick, dealing with low performers, and the like. Today, I received a complaint about one of my managers. Apparently, he's taken an interest in one of the workers, sending her instant messages about getting together with her. Now, she's filed a complaint against him for harassment."

"Sounds like fun," Leslie responded.

"Not that part of the job. The best part of my job is developing strategies for promoting Westerns' criminalistics and forensic services to criminal justice facilities, medical examiners, and government crime laboratories. Like other women in an executive position, the other challenge is striking a balance between being authoritative, tough-minded, and empathetic. I have to make tough decisions everyday — decisions that leave my employees having to step up their game and move beyond their comfort zone. I'm often referred to as the 'B' word—" Laura said, stopping in mid sentence.

"By the way, I need to talk with you about something. Can you meet me after work for dinner?"

"Sure. What about one of my old favorites: Kelly's Country Kitchen, over on McGowan, near downtown," Leslie suggested.

Laura frowned in disapproval. She knew the food selections at Kelly's were high in calories, fat, sodium, and cholesterol — all the bad stuff — so she responded, "I was thinking about something a little healthier."

"I know you're into the healthy stuff, but ever since I moved back I've been longing for their country-fried steak, mashed potatoes and gravy, and those big country biscuits. Can't you find something healthy there to eat?"

Later that evening, Laura and Leslie met at Kelly's Country Kitchen. Walking into the restaurant, Laura saw Leslie sitting at the bar with a drink and a plate of Buffalo wings in front of her.

"Hi, Leslie. I'm sorry I'm a little late, but I had to get some last minute information to my boss."

"It's okay. I decided to order an Amaretto Sour and a plate of Kelly's finger-lickin' good Buffalo wings while I waited for you," Leslie said. "I guess I shouldn't be drinking this, right? It has a lot of calories, I suppose. Did you schedule my appointment with Trevor?"

"The day after tomorrow, Thursday, and you're right: those are the sorts of foods and drinks you want to eliminate from your diet," Laura suggested. "Trevor is also facilitating a living healthier class on Friday. I think you should attend."

Leslie motioned for the hostess to direct them to a table. "I'll see. By the way, Ethan Allen delivered my furniture yesterday."

"That was quick."

"Sister, money talks," Leslie boasted. "I hired a lady to help me get things in order. Earlier today, she helped me put up the wall pictures and decorative accessories we picked out."

The hostess escorted Laura and Leslie to a nearby table. With her purse on her shoulder, Leslie lagged behind, carrying her drink and plate of wings.

Laura motioned to assist Leslie as they began to sit down. "Did Hunter like the bedroom set you bought for your room?"

"Girl, he doesn't care about that kind of stuff. He's mainly concerned with the outside looking good. He hired a company to professionally design and install landscape — crape myrtles, magnolia trees, and flowering shrubs. He had a pond installed, as well as special lighting and a landscape wall. He added the works. All I know is that I've been working myself to the bone trying to get our house in order. I want it to be a showplace for all to drool over."

Laura hesitated. Listening to Leslie talk about her home made her have a flashback of how she allowed material things to consume her. Regaining her focus, she was unsure about how to start the discussion about their father. Grabbing the menu on the table, she continued, "Wow! That's a lot."

"That's nothing for Hunter. My husband is a big spender."

"Leslie, I wanted to talk with you about Dad."

"What about him?"

"He's sick, Leslie."

"Sick how?" Leslie asked.

"He's recently been diagnosed with Stage IV prostate cancer, and the cancer has spread to his bones."

Laura went on to share how they were faced with having to help their parents determine his treatment options. Laura explained that she wanted Leslie to be involved in examining the benefits of each treatment option against the possible outcomes, side effects, and risks.

"I'm so sorry to hear about his situation. Life has been hectic with Hunter settling into his new job as top legal aide to the new district attorney. He needs me right now. I'm sure you'll help our parents make the best decision."

"Excuse me, but how does Hunter's new job impact you? Am I missing something? Let's see: he goes to work everyday and works long hours, then he comes home to a dinner waiting for him. Besides all of that, he was placed in that position back in January, and it's now March. As for you, your dad is terribly ill, Leslie."

"Excuse *me*, but I just found out about his illness."

"Still, you haven't managed to squeeze five minutes out of your busy days since you've been back in town to call and check on him or Mother — But you know what? I'm not gonna dwell on it. I'm hoping your conscience is going to kick in at some point. I would like for us to come to some consensus on long-term care for him and Mother."

"Okay, let me act concerned. What do you mean 'prostate cancer'? What is 'Stage IV'? Why does Dad think he has it?" Leslie said, rattling out questions. "And please give me the abbreviated version."

"Apparently, Dad has been having problems urinating for a long time, and Mom couldn't get him to go to the doctor," Laura said. "Now he's been diagnosed with Stage IV prostate cancer."

"Millions of people have some sort of cancer. That's why there's chemo, radiation, surgery, and all the other stuff available to them," Leslie said sarcastically.

Growing irritated with Leslie's insensitive comments, Laura said, "Leslie, I'm trying real hard to be patient with you. I know the hurt and anger has you responding this way. And probably the alcohol—"

"Whatever." Leslie said as she took a sip of her drink.

"Dad went to see his doctor. His doctor performed some exams and tests. After the exams and tests, he referred him to an oncologist."

Interrupting Laura, Leslie said, "Men know they should go to the doctor to have their prostate checked annually. Dad is seventy-seven. He should have been getting regular screenings, such as the digital rectal exam or the blood test called the prostate specific antigen, commonly referred to as the PSA."

"Sounds like you're not as ignorant as you're pretending to be about cancer. In fact, it sounds like you're quite familiar with prostate cancer and its associated tests," Laura stated.

"A friend of mine in Maryland worked in a lab. She would always talk about tests people should be getting regularly at various ages, like the colon test around forty-nine or fifty," Leslie added.

"Anyway, the tests Dad took two weeks ago revealed some abnormalities, which led the specialist to conduct further tests. The results of the additional tests showed advanced prostate cancer."

"So what does that really mean? Is he going to die?"

"Leslie, it's a little premature to start thinking about death. The results prompted his doctors to explore the extent of the cancer within his body. They wanted to find out if the cancer had spread from the original site to other parts of his system," Laura said.

"So what now?" Leslie asked.

"Now that we know what stage cancer he has, we need to work with the doctors to come up with the best treatment plan."

"Have you tried to contact Walter? He needs to know about Dad," Leslie said.

"No, I haven't. I'm so tired of the neglected childhood syndrome."

"I spoke with him a few weeks ago. Our brother is dealing with the physical trauma his son, our nephew Pete, suffered in Iraq," Leslie shared. Disturbed by Laura's unforgiving attitude toward Walter, Leslie became frustrated. "At least Walter is worthy of forgiveness. Pete's arm was ripped off during a roadside bombing five months ago, and Walter's been helping his son maneuver around the poor medical treatment of soldiers injured while fighting for our country. Pete is just twenty-two years old — not some old hateful man like Dad!"

Laura ignored Leslie's comment. "Where is Pete?"

"He's at Fort Sam Houston in San Antonio," Leslie responded. "You really should call down there to check on your nephew."

"I'll check on him," Laura replied.

"Whatever you decide as far as Dad is concerned is fine with me," Leslie said.

"Leslie, I need you to meet us at the doctor's office next Monday. The address is 8610 Covert Lane in North Houston."

"Okay, let me check with Hunter. I'll see about coming."

"Check with Hunter?" Laura asked. "I've scheduled your appointment with Trevor on Thursday. Is that okay with Hunter?"

"Let's just order. I'm ready for my country-fried steak, gravy with mashed potatoes, and biscuits. Where's that waitress? I need another Amaretto Sour."

CHAPTER 3

A Balancing Act to Live Healthier

*T*he growing demands of a new position and family life began requiring Laura to look for innovative ways to find the right balance for living healthy.

"Hi, Baby. I'm sorry I'm late; we had some executives from the corporate office in town today, so, Mr. Mitchell and I had to take them out for dinner," Laura said. "I hate I missed your dinner. Afterwards, I needed to run by and check on Mom and Dad. How long has Jessica been asleep?"

Marti was sitting on the sofa watching his favorite show, *Wife Swap*. "About an hour. Laura, it would have been nice of you to let me know you would be this late," he responded.

"I'm so sorry," Laura said, hugging and kissing Marti. "The battery in my cell phone went out, and my car charger is in your truck. Looks like your show is keeping you company. How was your day?"

"It was fine."

"Anything new happen?"

"Management is interested in sending me to school to get a Federal Aviation Administration Airframe and Power Plant Mechanic's license."

"Wow, what a tongue twister — but that sounds great, Marti!"

"They're developing some lead aircraft mechanic positions at Bush International Airport. Getting the license would mean going back to school for twelve to twenty-four months."

"That's not bad," Laura responded. "You had talked about opening your own shop."

"We have too many financial obligations facing us right now for me to be thinking about opening a shop or even going back to school. Sydney called, and Tisha's been accepted to Texas Women's University in Denton. She gave me the rundown of what we're looking at for Tisha's college: $4300 per semester for tuition, another $650 in books, about $3000–$4000 per month for housing, and money for food. Then, we have our portion of the costs for graduation and the prom."

"Has Tisha applied for any scholarships?"

"Her grades aren't good enough for her to get scholarships."

"Had we hired tutors for the math and science classes like I suggested, she probably could have brought her grade point average up," Laura said, opening up her laptop.

"Laura—"

"Nevertheless, we'll manage our portion, Marti. My promotion has given us an extra $40,000 annually. I think you should go to school. Will your company pay for any part of the cost? How much more money would you make after completing school?"

"At least another $25,000 a year. My company will help some with the classes. The only thing is, you're traveling now — What about child care arrangements?"

"Honey, I forgot to mention it, but my traveling will be diminishing. Initially, I needed to travel to develop a rapport with my managers. Now, we have a new teleconferencing system that serves as our means of conducting meetings," Laura confirmed. "What about the kids? Are they coming for spring break?"

"No, Sydney is taking them out of town," Marti said. "We'll definitely have them for the summer. We can go somewhere then."

"Don't worry, things will get better. If you don't mind, I'm taking Leslie to meet Trevor tomorrow after work. I'm going to take off a little early. I'll be home by six o'clock, though, so Jessica and I can have some quality time together."

"Okay," Marti said.

"I'm going to check on Jessica and then get ready for a presentation at work tomorrow," Laura said, as she took her laptop and proceeded down the hallway.

Leslie and Laura met as scheduled in front of The Memorial Park Fitness Center where Trevor conducted fitness classes. While waiting for Trevor to arrive, Leslie shared with Laura the excitement she felt driving through the park, including how she admired the beautiful scenery and the variety of outdoor recreation opportunities — tennis, soccer and softball fields, and jogging trails. Moments later, a tall, dark, athletic-looking handsome male walked up behind them holding a gym bag in one hand and a notebook in the other.

"Hi, Trevor. How's everything going?" Laura asked.

"All is well. I can't complain," Trevor replied.

"Thank you so much for scheduling an appointment on such short notice. I just wanted my sister, Leslie, to meet you. I believe she's ready to get serious about implementing some healthier habits."

Trevor positioned his notebook and gym bag and shook Leslie's hand. "I know it's March, but Happy New Year's to you, Leslie. Let's go over to the picnic table and have a seat."

"It's great meeting you, Trevor. Laura has said some wonderful things about you," Leslie said, with a sad expression. "She's right, though. I'm ready to get this weight off and get healthy."

"I'm proud of you. It's easy to settle into an array of excuses, but I'm glad you've made a decision to discover ways to balance the things going on in your life and get fit," Trevor replied.

"Trevor, I told Leslie about your strategic plan for living healthier," Laura said. "I had never considered the words 'getting fit' and 'strategic planning' in the same sentence."

"I like to use the concept of strategic planning with fitness because it's important for my clients to understand that there must be a roadmap for accomplishing their health and fitness goals. In business, strategic planning identifies where the organization wants to be at some point in the future and how it's going to get there. The same concept applies to implementing healthier lifestyle habits," Trevor said. "My role is to help you figure out where you want to be at some point in the future and how you're going to get there. As your fitness consultant, my job is to help you adjust your plan when the roadblocks and detours of life affect your progression."

"The only place I want to be is eighty pounds lighter," Leslie confirmed.

"I know you want to lose the excess weight, but it's important to assess the internal and external factors that have led to your unhealthy habits. Once you identify the root causes of your condition, the direction for change will be clear. You can't plan for the future if you don't review, reveal, and resolve the reasons for past behaviors."

"For years, I've flipped myself inside out to balance the priorities and stresses in my life. My whole life has been consumed with my husband and my kids. Well, my kids are grown now, and my husband is consumed with his career," Leslie said, her eyes beginning to water. "The root of my problems is the hurt, pain, and resentment I've held onto for so long. It's time to address that component of my life, which

I've neglected for so long. My sister says I need to stop living in the past and start living in the here and now. So, here I am ready to make some changes."

"Well, I'm glad you're here today. One of my favorite scriptures in the Bible talks about our bodies being a temple of the Holy Spirit. This Scripture helps us to understand more fully that our body is the temple of the Holy Spirit and that God has a vested interest in how we maintain it. The body is a gift from God."

"Hallelujah!" Laura exclaimed.

Trevor opened up his notebook. "Do you have medical clearance from your doctor to start an exercise program?" Trevor asked.

"Yes, I do."

"Great. I need you to complete some forms for me. Basically, they will provide me with information to evaluate and design a lifestyle program to meet your health and fitness needs."

Trevor and Laura chatted while Leslie completed a series of assessment forms. Afterwards, he conducted a comprehensive physical evaluation to assess Leslie's aerobic fitness, body composition, muscular strength and endurance, and flexibility. He explained to Leslie that both the evaluation forms and physical assessment would more clearly identify any specific health concerns, facilitate setting personal goals, and establish benchmarks to measure her progress. He retrieved various items from his gym bag. He took her weight, blood pressure, and percentages of body fat and lean muscle mass.

"Let's prepare to walk," Trevor said. "Let me put my bag and notebook in my car, first."

"Laura, you're coming, too, right?" Leslie asked.

"I'll be right behind you."

Trevor returned. "I do want you to be clear about my strategy for helping you achieve your goal. Oftentimes, when people make a decision to start exercising, they go in with a preconceived notion to lose a lot of weight in a short period of time. However, the real goal should be to discover ways to implement long-term healthier lifestyle habits, which include eating healthier, eating less, drinking plenty of water, getting enough sleep, and exercising. I'll develop a structured program to help you with all of those things."

"I want her to attend my belly-dancing class," Laura said, with enthusiasm.

"That would be great. For now, let's focus on building your strength and endurance with consistency and intensity. Progression is the key," said Trevor. "Your training program will include a mixture of walking and running. Each week you'll receive a training schedule that outlines your activities for the week. You'll start off doing more walking than running, and then, as the weeks progress, you'll be doing more running than walking. Following the training schedule will be critical to your progress. We'll also merge some resistance training into our sessions to build muscular strength and endurance. Lean muscle tissue helps increase your metabolism and burns fat throughout the day."

"Sounds like a plan."

"Let's get started. Here's a bottle of water for the two of you. Never exercise without having your water with you or near you. We're going to start walking west toward the tennis courts. The walk route will be around two miles."

"Two miles!" Leslie shouted. "Isn't that a little aggressive for a beginner?"

"You'll be okay," Trevor assured her. "It's important to warm up five to ten minutes before your main aerobic activity. Then, you'll start to increase your pace. Okay, it's time to speed up our pace," Trevor said. "What have you eaten so far today?"

"Okay," Leslie said, picking up her pace. "Well, for breakfast I ate a sausage and egg biscuit sandwich and my favorite caramel macchiato. Sometimes, it's a blueberry muffin and café mocha."

Laura flinched listening to Leslie talk about her breakfast items. She thought to herself, *I told her the other day about the number of calories in a blueberry muffin and caramel macchiato.*

"Okay, what about lunch?"

"I was hoping you wouldn't ask. It wasn't a good day for lunch."

"What did you eat?"

"Well, I treated myself to one of my favorite restaurants, and I had the cheesy bacon cheeseburger," Leslie admitted, hesitating to continue.

"A cheesy bacon cheeseburger!" Trevor said, raising his voice. "That has to be one of the unhealthiest burgers. I'm talking about an artery-clogging menu of beef, pork, and cheese. That kind of food leads to obesity, diabetes, and heart disease."

"I guess adding the fries and chocolate shake were a really poor choice," Leslie said, avoiding Trevor's eyes.

"Leslie, if you're serious about living healthier, you've got to be committed to making better eating choices. Whenever you eat out, you're going to be faced with good and bad choices. The key is to avoid the selections high in calories, fat, cholesterol, and sodium — like the cheesy bacon cheeseburger and fries."

"Trevor, today was really stressful. I have a lot of stuff going on at home, and I needed one of my favorite meals to help me deal."

"The other day, she had two Amaretto Sours, a plate of Buffalo wings, a country-fried steak, gravy with mashed potatoes, and biscuits," Laura recited. "That was dinner."

"My sister, the tattletale. Some things never change," Leslie said with irritation.

Trevor ignored the back and forth comments. "Most people traditionally eat more and make poor food choices in response to their feelings — feelings of depression, loneliness, anger, stress, problems at work and/or home, and issues with kids."

Trevor paused to look at the sports watch on his wrist. "It's been fifteen minutes; time to take a drink."

Trevor retrieved his water bottle and instructed Leslie on how often and how much to drink.

He continued, "You can't allow food to be your reaction to life's trials and discomforts. There will always be things you don't have control over, like the actions of a boss, husband, or kid. But, your health is a different story. You do have control over the choices you make every day."

"You're right," Leslie agreed. "My doctor told me I need to lose weight, follow a healthier diet, and exercise. He says doing those things will increase my chances of getting off my high blood pressure and cholesterol medications," Leslie said, looking for confirmation. "He gave me a handout listing low-sodium, low-fat, and low-calorie foods, but it all looks boring."

"You've got to discover creative ways of making your favorite foods healthier, which involves preparing the majority of your meals at home. For instance, the primary goal is to eat more fruits and vegetables. In order to boost your veggie intake, add vegetables every chance you get. Start with breakfast: you can prepare a Frittata using superior eggs, fresh spinach, tomatoes, mushrooms, and a low-fat cheese. When making your favorite pasta dish, like spaghetti, add vegetables like broccoli, zucchini, and squash to the meat sauce. Use half as much pasta and twice as many vegetables. When ordering out, instead of fries, get the restaurant's veggie ensemble; most will have steamed vegetables. Or, you can substitute with a fruit medley."

"Those are some good suggestions. I've never thought about making my own Frittata."

"Let's alternate walking and running for twenty minutes," Trevor said.

They walked for three minutes and ran for two minutes, and Trevor explained that Leslie should continue the same routine when exercising on her own.

"I've never done an exercise program like this before," Leslie said, motioning for a break.

"How much water did you drink today?" Trevor asked.

"I generally drink one of the 16-ounce bottles," Leslie answered. "And you just gave it to me." She smiled.

"You should drink at least the recommended standard of eight to ten glasses of water a day; a rule of thumb typically used for the average adult. Keep in mind that if you're physically active that number increases. If you apply a more recent rule of thumb, you can drink half your body weight in water. However, someone with a medical condition should seek guidance from their physician as their water intake may be considerably less."

"Half my body weight? I weigh 230 pounds!"

"So, for you, that is approximately 115 ounces," Trevor stated. "It's important to understand that your body is comprised mostly of water, and, as a consequence, if you're not getting what your body needs to function properly, you could be placing your health in jeopardy."

"That's entirely too much water."

"It's well documented that drinking sufficient amounts of water can help lessen the chance of kidney stones, keep joints lubricated, prevent and lessen the severity of colds and flu, and help prevent constipation. It helps the body to digest and absorb vitamins and nutrients. It also detoxifies the liver and kidneys, and carries waste away from the body. The consequences of not drinking enough water every day can be tremendous. You can become dehydrated, you can incur a build up of toxins and waste in your body, you can develop bladder infections, kidney stones, and a series of other health problems. With all of that said, water is critical to our health."

"How do you know if you have enough water in your body?" Leslie asked.

"Look at your urine. If it's clear or pale yellow, you're doing a good job of staying hydrated. But if it's intense yellow or gold, you probably need to drink more water," Trevor stated.

"Trevor, she drinks a lot of alcoholic beverages," Laura announced.

"Laura, you saw me with two drinks. How in the world does that constitute 'a lot of alcoholic beverages?' Does Trevor know about your Fresh Fruit Mojito in Florida?" Leslie questioned.

"Nearly three years ago. I haven't had one since," Laura smirked at her. "Now what?"

Trevor began to laugh at the fiery exchange.

"Can we stop running?" Leslie asked.

"We're almost near our starting point. We've exercised for nearly forty minutes. That's the goal for today. Let's cool down the last five to ten minutes. I'll show you some stretching exercises. Stretching helps to improve your flexibility, your range of motion, and to reduce your risk of injury," Trevor said.

"Trevor, I read an article recently that said that many foods are also good sources of water," Laura said.

"Water in juicy fruits like oranges, grapefruit, grapes, watermelon, and apples can help keep you healthy and hydrated. Carrots, tomatoes, and cucumbers also contain plenty of water," Trevor said. "Leslie, there's the fitness center."

"Great!" Leslie said, sounding relieved. "What about drinking soft drinks, fruit juices, sports drinks, and coffee? They contain water."

"Don't slow down. We still need to keep walking, but slower for our cool down phase," Trevor said, monitoring her pace. "Be careful about drinking soft drinks, fruit juices, coffee, and other drinks. All these drinks can help quench your body's thirst for fluids, but they typically contain a lot of calories. They may quench your thirst, but their true effects are deceiving; because you're not dehydrated, you think everything's okay. The typical 12-ounce soda contains about 39 grams of sugar, not to mention the bargain saver sizes, such as 20, 24, and 32 ounces. An 8-ounce glass of cranberry juice contains about 33 grams of sugar. Take note of how much sugar is in your beverages of choice. Sugar decreases the rate at which fluid is absorbed into the body.

Plus, caffeinated drinks like coffee, tea, and sodas will prompt the body to lose water."

"Not to mention alcohol," Laura chimed in.

"There's a lot to living healthier. Still, though, I'm thankful I have time to get on the right track."

"Thanks again, Trevor, for scheduling Leslie on such short notice," Laura said. "I'm glad you were in town."

"Me, too. I'm excited about the possibilities," Leslie shared.

"You're absolutely welcome. I'll work on your training program this week," Trevor said. "For now, just do the same routine we did today."

"Although I'm excited, I'm also a little scared," Leslie admitted. "Eating healthier and exercising — it's a little overwhelming thinking about all the things I need to change. I've gotten so comfortable with being this size that I've accepted things as they are."

"Coach has educated me on how to set realistic goals. Sweets were a real weakness for me. Now, I keep nutritious and satisfying snacks, like fruits or nuts, available at home and work." Laura hesitated before continuing her comments. "Trevor, tell her about the importance of exercising more to lose weight. I read an article the other day that said that thirty minutes of exercise is the minimum. It also said we need to do more if we want to lose weight."

"You're absolutely right. When the medical professionals and health experts talk about thirty minutes of mildly intense exercise beyond the usual activity, they suggest that amount of time in order to lower the risk of chronic diseases; however, if your goal is to manage your current body weight and prevent unhealthy weight gain, you need to strive for about sixty minutes of moderate to vigorous exercise most days of the week. And that's without any additional caloric intake. If your goal is to lose weight, you need to strive for at least sixty to ninety minutes of daily moderate to intense exercise, while not going beyond the recommended caloric intake requirements."

"I know I need to lose weight, but sixty to ninety minutes of exercise is out of the question. I'm not interested in devoting that kind of time to exercise," Leslie said, her hands on her hips.

Trevor jumped in with, "Earlier in our conversation, you said you were ready 'to address that component of your life you'd neglected for so long'. The road to optimal health includes the right attitude about exercise. First, I want to encourage you to focus your attention on learning to redefine exercise in a way where your mind and body are connected. During your redefining process, any unfavorable thoughts are removed, and exercise becomes something pleasurable that you want to do from your heart. Once you reach that point, exercise will become a part of your life for life. For now, I'm introducing you to walking and running, but there are many other activities. Once I get your endurance and strength to a certain level, I'll encourage you to find other activities that'll motivate you to get moving a minimum of thirty minutes each day. Some other options include cycling, swimming, hiking, stair climbing, rowing, elliptical cross-training equipment at your local gym, or group exercise classes, like yoga, Pilates, and jazzercise."

"And there's always my belly-dancing class!" Laura shouted out.

"Right," Trevor responded.

"Trevor, you've given me a lot to think about," Leslie said. "I know I'm tired of feeling disappointed and disgusted because I lack self-control. I'm tired of wearing big sweaters and loose clothing to hide my layers of fat. I'm tired of wearing out my jeans between the legs because my fat rubbed the legs together. I hate feeling that my husband doesn't want to be intimate with me because I'm fat; I'm just tired . . ."

"Leslie, a lot of people share those same sentiments — But you know what? You can do something about it. Although it's March, we're still at the top of the new year. Time for a new beginning — time for you to take responsibility for your actions," Trevor emphasized. "Always remember that a continuum of excessive caloric intake, without sufficient calorie burning, will result in unwanted body fat. The storage of excessive body fat will eventually evolve into health concerns like heart disease and diabetes. One thing you have to your advantage is the power of choice. You choose whether you will exercise for thirty minutes, three times a week. You choose whether you will eat vegetables for breakfast. You choose whether you will eat an orange or a slice of pie. The power of choice is yours."

Laura chimed in, "Trevor, tell Leslie about your basketball analogy. He's a true sports fanatic."

"I'm often reminded of how at the end of a game the losing team fouls the winning team. By doing so, they hope the winning team will miss their free throws, giving the losing team more opportunities to get the ball and add points. This common tactic makes the game longer and helps the losing team improve their chances of winning, only if the other team misses their free throws and doesn't score any additional points. Unfortunately, the game of life doesn't work that way. The only stall tactics you can initiate to improve your numbers related to blood pressure, blood cholesterol, and blood sugar, and increase your chances of adding healthier years to your life is to make better choices."

"Thanks, Trevor," Laura said, glancing at her wristwatch to check the time.

"Also, I work with a registered dietician, Vanessa Daniels, at Barley's Wellness Center over on West Stephens in North Houston. I like working with the staff at the centers in Dallas and Houston because they offer practical solutions for balancing daily demands with healthy habits. Modifying your daily food consumption is probably the most challenging habit to transform. Despite the disclosure of potential health risks, most people continue to eat foods that are high in calories, fat, cholesterol, sodium, and sugar — like fast food, candy, cookies, chips, sodas, packaged foods, and pre-prepared foods. All of those things can cause us to experience some health concerns in the long-term. Attending some of the classes will definitely assist you with developing good eating habits."

"I'll give it a try. I think Laura has signed me up for the class. Right?" Leslie asked.

"Tomorrow, remember?" Laura interjected.

"Great," Leslie responded.

Leslie, Laura, and Trevor completed the cool-down phase and made it back to their cars.

"Well, thanks again, Trevor," Leslie said while unlocking her car door."

"I'll send you the training schedule, and we'll correspond back and forth via phone and email. I'm generally in Houston the second week of each month. I'll let you know what days I'm available once I get back and review my schedule."

Leslie was excited about changing her unhealthy habits, losing weight, and the possibility of getting off her high blood pressure and cholesterol medications.

Laura had gone to her car to get Leslie a bottle of water for her drive home. "Leslie, hold up, here's another bottle of water. Also, have you given any more thought to helping me with Mom and Dad's medical care?" Laura asked.

"When's the doctor's appointment?" Leslie asked.

"It's on Monday."

"Let me think about it," Leslie replied.

"Leslie, I know you've got some emotions you need to work through, but it's a fact of life that we're going to encounter some troubles that need solving, we're going to face some issues that need managing, we're going to stumble upon some fears that need controlling, and we're going to tackle some threats that need confronting. You can't just tuck the pressures of life away in a box," Laura paused before continuing. "I'm just going to say this and let you go. You have some tough choices to make. The longer you continue to feed your mind with hate, unforgiveness, and revenge, the more contaminated it will become. Worst of all, you will rationalize your conduct—"

Leslie cut her off, "Thank you, Laura."

"Also, I want you and Hunter to go to church with us on Easter Sunday," Laura said, walking quickly to her car. "I don't mean to rush off, but I've got to get home and spend some time with Jessica."

"Let me check with Hunter," Leslie said. "I'll talk to you later. Thanks again."

Leslie sat in her car, saddened by the words Laura had spoken. Deep down, she knew she needed a change of perspective. She knew her struggles with unresolved anger would continue to eat away at her soul. It was time for her to take control of the emotional disorder that had obstructed her from living a life filled with love, peace, joy, and faith.

CHAPTER 4

A Change of Perspective

*I*n the midst of rekindling their bond, Laura and Leslie were both struggling with the challenges surrounding their families. Laura had convinced their father to undergo a combination of hormonal therapy and chemotherapy for his cancer. Meanwhile, it was time for Leslie to confront the reality about the state of her marriage.

Hunter came into the bedroom while Leslie was reading. Ignoring her presence, he headed straight for their closet.

"Hi, honey. I didn't realize you'd be home early this evening."

"I forgot some paperwork that I need for a meeting tonight," Hunter responded. He walked into their huge walk-in closet with built-in cabinets and drawers. Leslie had organized his garments in a systematic manner. From formal to informal, and darkest to lightest, his suits, sport coats, dress shirts, and slacks hung on special hangers. His ties and belts hung on custom-made racks, and his shoes sat on custom shelving. Other essentials and accessories were neatly arranged in cabinets and drawers.

"A meeting tonight?" Leslie asked, surprised. She got out of the bed and followed him into the closet.

"Yes, a meeting," Hunter said. He switched out his suit jacket for an Armani Collezioni plaid jacket and abruptly left out.

Leslie followed him. "When do you think you'll be back?"

"It'll be late, so don't wait up for me," Hunter responded, heading down the hallway to the staircase.

"Before you leave, my sister wants us to go to church with them this Sunday. It's Easter, remember?" Leslie asked, walking quickly to catch up with him.

Hunter entered his study, sat down at his desk and began entering some information into his computer. "Don't plan on me going. I'll be out of town this weekend."

"You hadn't mentioned anything about going out of town. Where are you going?"

"I'm going to Baltimore to see my parents and to check on the girls and Casey. Dad has a business deal he wants me to look at, and Courtney needs some money for rent," Hunter replied.

"Courtney hadn't mentioned anything to me about needing money," Leslie said.

"That's probably because she knows I'm the one with the money," Hunter said, his anger evident.

Ignoring his comment, Leslie responded, "Do you need to go this weekend? You can put the money in Courtney's account — or I could go with you." She walked closer to his desk.

"Leslie, you know I'm looking at confidential information, and yes, I need to go this weekend. No, you don't need to go with me; like I said, I have to do some stuff for my dad. I'll be back Sunday night."

After printing out some information and shutting down his computer, Hunter began preparing for his departure. "I'll see you in the morning. It'll probably be late when I come in. I'll probably sleep in one of the guestrooms."

"Are you going to be home early tomorrow? I attended a healthy living class the other day. The instructor guides the participants on how to cook healthy dishes. Since one of your favorites is gumbolaya, I wanted to experiment with how to make a healthy version. I was going to cook it tomorrow."

"Not interested in being your test subject. Anyway, I'll be home late tomorrow. I'll call you tomorrow from work," he said, slamming the front door behind him.

Leslie walked in the kitchen and contemplated what she would eat for dinner. *It's so depressing being in this big house alone night after night. Always having to eat by myself. I know what would make me feel better, and that's the sampler of my breaded favorites at McMurray's Grill — boneless buffalo wings, catfish strips, steak fingers, popcorn shrimp, fritters onion rings, and fried okra. Or, I could stay home and eat my freshly made tuna salad on top of the mixed greens with my fruit medley — which sounds boring. Trevor says 'It's all about choices.' I can't allow unhealthy food choices to be my reaction to feelings of loneliness and unhappiness. Okay, I'm not going to succumb to these feelings; tuna salad it is.*

Since they'd moved to Texas, Leslie rarely saw Hunter. He was always working late or just never at home. She knew he wouldn't call her. Their interactions with one another were virtually non-existent. She knew he never loved her and that whatever feelings he may have had for her in the past were dead. The time had come for her to re-invent herself. She had always lived in the shadows of her husband and children, but now she was ready to move to the forefront.

It was Easter Sunday, and Laura was excited that Leslie had finally decided to attend her church service. Leslie was to meet Laura and Marti at the church since it was mid-way for both.

"Hi, Laura and Marti," Leslie said while standing in the vestibule. "And baby Jessica."

"Hi, Leslie," Marti and Laura responded.

"Where's Hunter? I thought he was coming with you to church," Laura inquired.

"Actually, he went to Baltimore on Friday. He needed to help his dad with some paperwork," Leslie said, reaching for Jessica.

Laura was growing concerned that Hunter was never around. She could discern from her conversations with Leslie that he was never at home and that they never spent any time together.

"Well, I'm glad you're here," Laura said, hugging Leslie.

"So am I," Leslie responded, admiring the crowd of people walking into the sanctuary.

"Let's go inside so we can get good seats," Marti suggested.

"He means so he can get *his* seat," Laura laughed.

Leslie enjoyed the praise and worship. The pastor's message for the morning was *Basic Training for the Spiritually Unfit*. As the pastor spoke from a variety of scriptures, Leslie began to think about her life — spiritually and emotionally. She continued to listen to the pastor and his message, stating that no one was exempt from the troubles of life, that storms will always come from different areas. He stated that one's connection to the right source would provide strength, courage, and perseverance. He also stated how God uses trials to reveal and restore. Leslie's spirits were lifted by the pastor's message.

"Leslie, did you enjoy the service?" Laura asked.

"I sure did," Leslie responded.

"Hopefully, you'll be coming back to visit," Marti said.

"Most definitely."

"Are you coming out to the house for dinner? We're having baked chicken, macaroni and cheese, and a vegetable medley," Laura said.

"You're having macaroni and cheese? I know that's not healthy — Is this a splurge day for you?" Leslie asked.

"Don't get excited; it's a healthy version of macaroni and cheese. We use whole-wheat elbow pasta. Although we use traditional products like cheese and butter, our version is much lower in fat."

"I think I'll follow you all home," Leslie said. "Since Hunter is gone, I hadn't thought about what I was going to eat."

"Great! Just follow us."

Walking through the front door, Laura made Leslie feel welcome. "Do you want a T-shirt to put on, Leslie, so you can be more comfortable?"

"I'm okay. I'll watch the baby while you and Marti get situated," Leslie said.

"Great. I'll go in the kitchen and get things ready. Jessica will probably be asleep in a few minutes. Marti has to go to the grocery store."

"It was a great turnout at church. Is it normally that crowded?" Leslie asked, while playing with Jessica.

"We generally have a good crowd, but there's always going to be more people on holidays like Easter and Mother's Day."

"It's been so long since I've been to church. The pastor's message got me to thinking about some things," Leslie admitted. "Hey, I've really gotten into working out." While holding Jessica, she walked into the kitchen to be closer to Laura. "Since I've been going to the living healthier classes, I've learned so much in a short period of time. Last week, we learned about foods that are supposed to be healthy but aren't."

"What are those foods?" Laura asked.

"Salmon was one," Leslie stated.

"Oh, yeah, I know about the farm-raised salmon and how they're loaded with antibiotics and get their color from dye."

"You're absolutely right," Leslie said. "Hunter has always loved salmon. For years, we've eaten it two to three times a week. Now, I'm finding out that what we may have been eating is unhealthy."

"Wild salmon is the way to go. It's more expensive, but if you're going to eat it, it's better to be safe and make sure you're eating the version with nutritional value. Wild salmon get their red color from krill, an antioxidant that's in their natural food source," Laura said. "What was another food?"

"Granola bars," Leslie said. "Looks like Jessica is fading away."

"I figured so. You can take her in the living room and lay her down beside you on the sofa," Laura said. "What's wrong with granola bars?"

"Vanessa, the registered dietician Trevor mentioned says a large percentage of granola bars are like candy bars, offering no nutritional value. They contain the processed carbohydrates you hear so much about. She says they have minimal fiber, and, just like a candy bar or soda, they have a lot of sugar."

"I can see how that's probably true," Laura said.

"Vanessa says you can make your own healthier version from products like raw oats, coconut flakes, chopped almonds, raisins, and a spoonful of raw organic honey."

"I'm going to try that."

"Living healthier is quite a journey. I'm comparing it to putting together a jigsaw puzzle: when you look at the cover on the box of the puzzle, you see a pretty picture that'll hopefully represent the results of your efforts. Then, you open the box and see the tiny pieces you need to assemble to form the picture. If you're inexperienced at puzzles, the notion of fitting the right pieces together can be overwhelming and discouraging. Well, in our scenario, we see a picture of eating healthier and exercising. Just like with assembling the pieces of the puzzle, you can become overwhelmed by the thought of what it takes to fit together the right lifestyle pieces to be healthier."

"All while trying to face the daily obligations, problems, and distractions of life," Laura interjected.

"It's okay. I'm ready to put forth the effort because now I understand the end results," Leslie replied excitedly. "Another class I attended was really fun. We played a game where we had to pick out the foods with the most calories and fat."

"Which foods were they?"

"Okay, which one do you think is the lowest in fat — a donut, bagel, or breakfast sandwich from your favorite fast food restaurant?"

"Let's see. I don't eat donuts because I know they're high in fat and sugar. Before going healthy, I loved to stop by The Breakfast Club, my favorite breakfast spot, to get the egg, sausage, and cheese sandwich. But, of course, I stopped because I found out it was high in calories and fat. On the weekends, I'd go order their catfish and grits, or wings and waffles," Laura chimed.

"It's a good thing you've gone healthy," Leslie commented.

"On the days where I was rushed, I'd stop by my favorite bagel shop and get a honey, whole-wheat bagel," Laura said. "So, I'm going to go with the bagel. It's lower in fat."

"You're correct in the traditional sense. The bagel is the lowest in fat. The other day, though, I saw a donut company advertising donuts that contained three to four grams of fat; nevertheless, bagels are the better choice, especially the whole-wheat without the cream cheese."

"Do they talk about the sodium in foods? I know bagels are high not only in carbohydrates but also sodium — something you can't overlook."

"You're right. Vanessa did talk about sodium. She even gave us a handout with a listing of the different terms used for sodium, terms that people don't generally associate with salt and sodium."

"When you get home, email me that list. I'd love to see it. I think I'll attend the next class with you," Laura said.

"That would be great. Vanessa has started a series called *The Ten Essential Habits for Living Healthier*."

"That sounds pretty powerful," Laura replied. "Do you know the ten habits?"

"So far, we've covered numbers one and two: 'Be Physically Active Each Day' and 'Eat Nutritious Foods Each Day.' Vanessa says that in order to be successful with physical activity every day you have to find one you enjoy."

"Sounds like what Trevor said the other day," Laura said.

"Right. She and her partner Alley have exposed us to a variety of activities to consider, different stuff like your belly dancing. They talk about traditional activities like walking, riding a bike, registering for swimming lessons, or taking yoga, Pilates, or jazzercise classes, and non-traditional activities like pole dancing."

"Pole dancing? That's too funny. I saw a special about that on the news the other day. They said it's a great aerobic workout!" Laura shouted. "Oops! I don't want to wake Jessica."

Leslie started laughing, "The ladies say it's a great way to strip off the pounds. They say there are a couple of places in town that offer classes. Supposedly, the activity creates a lean, strong, and flexible body."

"Are you going to take a class?" Laura asked.

"I think for now I'm going to stick with what Trevor has me doing. I'm not that adventurous yet."

"I'd better get everything set up before Marti gets back. Just stay in there and watch TV while Jessica's asleep."

"What about your birthday party? Do you need any help planning it?" Leslie asked.

"I think I'm okay. We're gonna keep it simple. I don't want to do anything, but Marti has insisted on something. We're kind of watching our cash flow, with having to contribute to the prom, graduation, kids' camp, and college."

"Whew! I'm glad those days of graduation and college are over for me."

"I think I hear Marti driving up. Let me hurry and get finished."

Both Laura and Leslie were embarking on a new season of growth and change. Laura wondered if her life would have been easier if she had married and had children in her twenties, and Leslie was forging ahead to live her life in the midst of uncertainty.

In a telephone call to Laura a few days later, Marti said, "Hi, Honey. Sydney called and said Jr. is sick. Can you go get him from school? I can't get away from work."

"Why can't Sydney go get him?" Laura asked.

"She says she's at the hair salon and has perm on her hair."

"Perm on her hair?!" Laura shouted. "You ought to get tired of her dog and pony shows."

"Can you pick him up, Laura? Wait, hold a minute; it's her on the other line." Marti clicked over to answer Sydney's call.

"Sydney, I'm trying to see if Laura can pick Jr. up from school."

"Laura?!" Sydney shouted. "She doesn't have any legal authority to get my kid out of school."

"First of all, he's our kid," Marti said abruptly. "After I married Laura, I put my permission in writing to give her authority over the kids when I wasn't available."

"You had no right to do that without my approval."

"Sydney, I have Laura on the other line."

"Hang her up!" Sydney shouted.

"No, Sydney, I'm going to hang *you* up. I know you. I knew this day would come. You've tried over and over to punish me for our failed marriage. I tried to be what I thought you needed me to be, but you rejected me over and over. Now, your hold over me to keep me in check is the kids."

"I'm going to have that piece of paper removed. Any involvement with school, medical, financial, or anything else concerning the kids is between you and me. At her age, I know that new baby is more than enough for her to handle."

"Sydney, don't bring Laura into this. She loves our kids, and all I want is to have regular visits, overnight stays, and a good relationship with them."

"Whatever. Jr. is waiting at school for you," Sydney said, hanging up on Marti.

Feeling sandwiched in, Marti took a deep breath before returning to Laura. "Laura, I'm so sorry for keeping you on hold for so long. She was ranting and raving about you picking up Jr. Can you go get him? I need to get back to work."

"Sure. I'll take the rest of the day off and take him to the house."

"Thanks, honey."

En route to pick up Jr., Laura received a call from Leslie.

"Hi, sis. You're not at work?"

"No, I'm not. I'm on my way to pick up Jr. He's sick and his mother can't pick him up."

"You sound irritated," Leslie said. "Is everything okay?"

"Where are you?"

"At home. I just accepted a job. I called to give you the good news," Leslie said.

"A job? I didn't know you were looking for a job," Laura replied, sounding surprised.

"You've forgotten, but I mentioned my interest in finding a job during our initial visit. Anyway, it's time for me to branch out and start doing some things differently. I've relied on Hunter for so long, financially and emotionally, even though he's never been there for me emotionally. Other than having you, I'm always at home alone. The girls and Casey are off living their lives, and Hunter is never around for us to do anything together, so, it's time."

"So what will you be doing and where's the new job?" Laura asked.

"I'll be doing clerical work in the forensic lab for Harris County. Listening to you talk about your job and the field of forensics made me interested in working in that environment. I'll be assisting in all aspects of daily specimen processing."

"I am so happy for you, Leslie. When do you start?"

"I start working for them on Monday," Leslie said, laughing out loud. "Can you believe it? Me working full-time, making my own money? There's something else I need to tell you."

"What?" Laura asked.

"I'm going to train for the three-day breast cancer walk," Leslie informed her, continuing to laugh.

"What?!" Laura shouted.

"Yes, me. In three days, I'm gonna walk sixty miles."

"How did you come to that decision?"

"With Trevor's training program, I'm up to six miles of walking and running. During our last two living healthier classes, Vanessa talked about the walk and its cause. You walk approximately twenty miles a day for three days, camping out each night in a tent. The only drawback for me is that I've got to raise a minimum of $2,200 in donations."

"Don't worry about that. I'll help you raise the money. I'll talk to my minister. Maybe we can do something at my church to raise money and awareness."

"Thank you so much, Laura. I love you," Leslie said.

"I'm here for you. Well, I'm at the school. Let me go in and get Jr., then, I've got to pick up Jessica from daycare."

"Alright, I'll talk to you later."

To avoid a confrontation with Sydney, Laura took Jr. home with her. She never diminished the fact the Sydney disliked her. A few weeks after she and Marti were married, Sydney showed her disapproval when she drove down their street screaming profanity about Laura and Marti. Laura had accepted the fact Sydney would never like her, so she focused on Marti, her child, her step children, and their lives together. She knew they were most important and subdued any negative thoughts about Sydney.

"Hi, Honey, where are Jessica and Jr.?" Marti asked, walking into the kitchen from the garage door.

Laura was standing over the oven cooking the chicken for her tasty Chicken Fajita Roll Up.

"They're in Jessica's room," Laura said.

"I thought Jr. was sick. Is it okay for him to be around Jessica?" Marti asked.

"Actually, Jr. is fine. I took his temperature, and everything else seems okay. His teacher didn't know he was sick. She said Sydney called and said he needed to go home and that his father was picking him up early. Since he was standing right there, I decided to bring him on home with me."

"I can't believe Sydney," Marti said, leaving the kitchen. "Let me go say 'hello' to the kids."

"Marti, before you go, I need to talk to you about something else," Laura said. She placed the cooked chicken in a bowl and covered it with a lid.

"What is it, honey?" Marti asked, turning around.

She motioned for Marti to have a seat at the kitchen table. "Dad's treatments are taking a toll on him. I'm going to start paying someone to give him and Mom ongoing care day and night. Mom's eyesight is failing probably due to the advance stages of her diabetes, so I need to act quickly. It's gonna cost us around $22,000 a year, but I have no choice."

"I understand, Laura. I'm gonna hold off on school for now. After the company kicks in their portion, it's gonna cost around $15,000. We just got over the prom, and now, with monthly childcare expenses, Tisha's college tuition, and camp for the boys coming up next month, we just can't take on any additional expenses. With the way the economy is right now, we have to be cautious with our spending. With the rising costs of gas, food, utilities, and everything else, we just know we'll be on a strict budget."

"We'll be okay. We know about making sacrifices. I know you wanted to take the kids somewhere this summer since we didn't get a chance to go to Corpus Christi for spring break, but I think we just need to stay at home," Laura suggested.

"You're right," Marti agreed. "Do you need any help with the meal?"

"I've pretty much finished everything. I just need to roll up the chicken mixture, mixed greens, and diced tomatoes in the whole-wheat tortilla."

"Okay. I'll be back. Let me check on the kids."

Laura knew she and Marti were facing the same struggles as other families going through tough times and trying to seek the American dream. She was confident that if they exercised good judgment and controlled their spending, they could weather the challenges ahead of them.

Marti came into the kitchen to check on Laura.

"Where are the kids?" Laura asked.

"They'll be down in a few minutes. They're watching the end of a show on the Disney channel."

"I forgot to tell you, Leslie's started a new job," Laura said. "I think something must be going on between her and Hunter."

"Maybe she'll be able to contribute to the expenses for your parents," Marti hinted.

"Maybe... We'll see," Laura responded.

"Oh, yeah, Tisha is interested in studying criminology in school. Do you think Hunter could get her a part-time job with the District Attorney's Office this summer?"

"I'll ask Leslie to talk to him," Laura said. "I'll see her Thursday for our girls' night out."

"What's this about a 'girls' night out'?" Marti questioned.

"I'm sorry, baby. I forget to mention that Leslie and I had designated Thursdays as our day to spend some quality time together — a movie, a concert, or a restaurant. But for now, since she's going to start training for the three-day breast cancer walk in November, we thought we'd walk at Hermann or Memorial Park together."

"What a way to find out about your special day — What if I want to do something on a Thursday, like take you to a movie, out to dinner, or rent a video and cuddle up with you?" Marti asked, not entirely pleased.

"Marti, I am so sorry. Normally, if we do something, it's on a Friday. However, if you want to do something on a Thursday, I'm there," Laura said, trying to reassure Marti that *he* came first.

"Is Sydney throwing Tisha a graduation party?"

"What she wants to do is invite all her relatives to some expensive restaurant and pay for their food."

"How many people, and how much money is she asking for, Marti?" Laura asked with frustration.

"About fifty people at approximately $25 per person, and she's asked for $750."

"What! You need to start saying 'No' to her, Marti!" Laura shouted. "You're letting her walk all over you. Did you tell her we could use my boss' clubhouse, which is really nice and plush? We can prepare an assortment of dishes ourselves."

"Yes, I did," Marti responded calmly.

"Tell her that's the only way we're contributing any money, and that's if she has it at the clubhouse."

"I hear you — Let me go and get the kids," Marti said, walking briskly out of the kitchen.

Laura and Leslie met at Hermann Park, a popular park in the heart of Houston, for their first official girls' night out. Hermann Park, best known for its zoo, museum district, planetarium, outdoor theatre and beautiful landscaping, also had a designated jogging trail.

Laura liked the trail at Hermann Park because it was an easy loop around the Hermann Park Golf Course. It also had tall oak trees that provided shade along the route. They had agreed to park near the Spanish Colonial-style Old Clubhouse.

Standing in the parking lot near their cars, Laura commented on the changes in Leslie's body. "Hey, lady, aren't you looking good?"

"I've lost around twenty pounds in two months. I'm eating healthier, eating less, and following my training program for the walk. Thank you for helping me with the donations," Leslie said, putting on her walking shoes.

"You are definitely looking leaner."

"Trevor has shown me how to use the home gym exercise equipment at home. I'm actually having fun doing the strength training exercises," Leslie giggled.

"Not my sister — the woman who couldn't 'fathom having to look at her body while trying to exercise'? Let's get started. Here's a bottle of water. How's the job going?"

They headed south, following the crushed granite trail, which curved around the golf course.

"It's great," Leslie replied. "Everyone is so nice, but they definitely have some unhealthy habits around the workplace. The other day one of the ladies went to the break room to eat fried chicken strips, mashed potatoes, and broccoli for breakfast. I overheard her saying she was hungry and the only food she had to eat was her lunch. Another day, the lady I share a cubicle with ate three slices of leftover meat lover's pizza — and it wasn't thin crust. Yesterday morning, when I walked into my supervisor's office, he was sitting at his desk eating crab salad and crackers for breakfast."

"They just totally bypassed the traditional unhealthy breakfast, like the egg, bacon, and cheese croissant or blueberry muffins. Hopefully, once you get comfortable with everyone, you'll be a role model."

"We'll see," Leslie replied. "I remember the days when I bragged about asking for an extra serving of meat, beans, and rice to go in my burrito bowl. Now I understand how those extra helpings contributed to my unhealthy size and health problems."

"Now, it's your responsibility to help others come to that same understanding. How's Hunter?" Laura asked.

"He's doing good," Leslie hesitated. "Casey is moving here with his girlfriend, Marilyn, and their baby. He's hoping to find a job here."

"I know you'll enjoy having your son here. Does Marilyn work in Baltimore?"

"No, she doesn't. Hopefully, she can find something here, too. They'll be living with us for a while. At least that big house Hunter bought will be filled with life. I never figured out why he bought a house with 5200 square feet."

"When will they be here?"

"In a couple weeks," Leslie said.

"Do Casey and Marilyn plan to get married?" Laura asked.

"Casey wants to, but for some reason Marilyn keeps putting him off, saying she's not ready," Leslie replied. "Let's speed up our pace so we'll have time to get a bite to eat."

"How many miles are we walking and/or running?"

"We need to do four miles. Today we're just going to walk."

Laura looked at her watch and sighed; she preferred jogging to walking. "Marti wants you to ask Hunter if he can find Tisha a summer job at his office," Laura stated.

"Sure, I'll ask him."

"She's interested in studying criminology. Working at the District Attorney's Office might give her some ideas about career choices. Plus, it'll put some money in her pockets. Her mother is killing us."

"It must be tough having to consider his children when you're making decisions about your family," Leslie said. "I was always glad that we didn't have any outside children."

"It can be overwhelming, but we manage. The kids are not the problem, it's their mother."

"So what are you doing for Mother's Day?"

"After church, I'm gonna spend some time with Mom and Dad. I'm sure Marti has something of his own planned. What about you? Are the girls coming this way?"

"No, but I'm sure they'll send me something," Leslie responded softly. "I forgot to mention that I've been going to one of the women's bible study groups at your church on every other Thursday."

"Why didn't you tell me? I usually go to the general bible study on Wednesdays."

"No reason," Leslie said. "I know I've embraced a lifestyle that's not characteristic of my upbringing. I know God is not pleased with me. If I'm looking for greater things to happen for me, I know I've got to do things differently, and that includes my spirituality. On the Thursday women's bible study group, maybe it can serve as our girls' night out. I know I'll start attending bible study on Wednesdays."

"Sure," Laura agreed. "I am continuously amazed at how you're growing, Leslie."

"God has blessed me with a sister who's a good role model," Leslie said. "How's work going? What happened with your manager who was accused of harassment?"

"I had to fire him about a month ago. Dealing with employees poses one problem after another. Now, I'm dealing with an employee who's sharing confidential information about another employee. Then, I have a client who doesn't want to work with one of my managers. To top it all off, I have an employee who tried to commit suicide at work last week."

"Wow! How do you manage to get work done in the midst of all of that employee drama?" Leslie asked.

"It's a challenge. I love my job, but managing staff is the worse part of it. My bosses want me to resolve outstanding employee issues they should have taken care of months — and in some cases, years ago. If I could make the kind of money I make and not manage — that would be ideal," Laura said.

"It's been about fifteen minutes; let's take a water break," Leslie suggested.

"Okay."

"I love this park," Leslie said, admiring the scenery. "How's Dad?"

Laura was shocked that Leslie asked. "He's weak from the treatments, but he's a strong man. He'll beat the cancer. I had to hire someone to come stay with him and Mom around the clock. Mom's eyesight is failing, and they need more attention."

"How much is it costing you?" Leslie asked.

"It's around $1,800 a month," Laura responded.

"Let's start back walking," Leslie said. "Once I help Casey get situated, I'll start giving you something toward their care."

"That would be wonderful," Laura replied, sounding grateful.

"I know you have it hard right now, and I do want to help lighten your financial load," Leslie said. "I have some decisions of my own to make."

"What sort of decisions?" Laura said frowning.

Laura hesitated before continuing. She then replied in a gloomy voice, "Mainly about my marriage. I believe Hunter has someone else."

"What do you mean 'someone else'?" Laura asked.

"It's complicated and difficult to put into words; I think that's the first time I've ever said it out loud. I don't want to burden you."

"We're sisters, right?"

"Right."

"Well, then you can't burden me. Tell me what's going on. During your first visit with Trevor, I overheard you mention something about your intimacy with him."

"Right. I've known about his women for years. I've overheard him on numerous occasions talking to them on the phone. I know I probably shouldn't have, but on numerous occasions I've retrieved the text messages on his cell phone when he was asleep. They were pretty explicit. And for years I've sneaked around and read his credit card statements, outlining the elaborate gifts and hotel stays, which I knew were not business related. He comes home smelling like perfume, alcohol, and smoke. I've had more than enough evidence to ruin his noteworthy name and impressive career. But, knowing about his indiscretions, I looked the other way," Leslie said, teary-eyed. "What was I supposed to do? As someone with a GED and limited work experience, I couldn't face being a single parent of three, trying to survive on a clerk's income. Thoughts of living in low-income housing with my kids, losing the privilege of driving my Lexus, and shopping at discount stores caused me stay with him."

"I know this must be hard for you to talk about," Laura said. "Let's sit for a moment. There's a park bench. Has he ever been physically abusive toward you?"

A sadness overshadowed Leslie's face. "There have been times that I've made him angry. I can be a nag," Leslie replied in an apologetic tone.

"You didn't answer my question. Has he ever—"

Leslie interrupted her. "The time has come for me to stop feeling sorry for myself. Years of rejection and not feeling comfortable in my own home must come to an end."

"I guess you just did," Laura suggested. "I can help you leave. You don't have to take his abuse."

"Can we move onto something else?" Leslie pleaded.

"Leslie, don't be like I was for years, trying to pull the covers over my head so I wouldn't have to deal with reality. And you don't have to put on a brave face for me. You're right, you've got some tough choices to make. Just know that I'll support whatever decisions you make."

"I love you."

"I love you," Laura responded, hugging Leslie. "Listening to you has made me think about my relationship with Marti. Since the birth of Jessica, and all of the other stuff surrounding Sydney and the kids, we hardly ever just sit back and focus on us. Would you mind watching the baby for us sometimes?"

"Absolutely not. I'd be honored to look after my niece."

"Marti and I need to find time for us. I heard someone on TV the other day say, 'The success of a relationship depends on how you navigate the highs and lows.' "

"That's true. That's why love must be the foundation for your union. There'll be good times and bad times. Hopefully, you'll have more good times than bad. Nevertheless, your response to the bad times will determine your survival."

"I want us completely focused on making sure we're fostering an environment filled with love and security for Jessica."

"You have to work at making sure you never lose what you have, Laura."

"Do you love Hunter?" Laura asked.

"In high school, he was the love of my life, and I believed he loved me. Then, I got pregnant, and we were forced to get married. Looking back on it now, I know I wasn't his preference; he got me by default. Things really got bad when the girls left for college. He began starting arguments — trying to provoke confrontations so he'd have an excuse to leave the house. Now, he just comes and goes as he pleases, without any explanation of his whereabouts. He stopped kissing, hugging, and touching me years ago. When I'd try to be affectionate toward him, he was cold and callous. We haven't been intimate in years."

"You've been living in a bad environment for a while," Laura commented.

"I'm glad you'll never experience that kind of pain in a marriage. I know you're overwhelmed with the remnants from Marti's previous life, but the two of you fit together like a couple of bookends. You're really a good match," Leslie said with sincerity. "Let's start back walking. I know you want to get a bite to eat."

"Do you think the pain from your marriage has affected your ability to move beyond the hostility you feel toward Mom and Dad — mainly Dad?"

"Yes, I do believe so, but I'm working through that. In our bible study class, Pastor Wallace is going through a series on forgiveness. It's really helping me. For years, I've obsessed over a past that I can't change. The emotional baggage has caused me to wage a lifelong battle with anger, loneliness, self-doubt, and low self-esteem. As a result, those battles have disturbed my pathway to fulfilling God's purpose for my life."

"It's all happened according to His purpose. Look at you now, though: you're talking different, you're acting different, and you're thinking different. God is at work in your life."

"I didn't want to overwhelm you with the details of my marriage, but it's been very difficult lately. For some reason, I thought by moving to Texas..." Leslie paused, "...that things would be different. I guess I thought the women would be left behind in Baltimore; nonetheless, I'm moving beyond the worry that he'll leave me someday."

"Sis, you're on the right road to piecing together your brokenness. I know God brought you back to Texas."

Laura and Leslie finished their session and went to a nearby Whole Foods Market to get a bite to eat; Laura favored their selection of healthy prepared foods.

CHAPTER 5

A Resurrected Lifestyle

A month later, Laura had enjoyed another birthday and her second Mother's Day. She and Marti had survived the prom and Tisha's high school graduation and were preparing for Drew and Jr.'s visit for the summer, while Jessica was learning to speak more words. Instead of going to her father's house for the summer, Tisha had decided to stay at home with her mom before leaving for college so she could work with her Uncle Hunter at the District Attorney's Office. Tisha's mother had agreed to drop her off in the mornings, since it was on her way to work.

Meanwhile, Leslie's life had taken a turn for the better. She loved her job and increased her mileage steadily for the three-day breast cancer walk scheduled for November. Her son, Casey, his girlfriend, Marilyn, and their baby daughter had moved to Texas. Life for both Laura and Leslie was seemingly headed in a positive direction.

A few weeks later, Leslie had started helping Laura with the financial aspect of caring for their parents, and their father's condition was showing signs of improvement.

"Hey, baby," Laura said, walking into the kitchen with Jessica in tow.

"Hi, my two favorite girls," Marti replied, kissing Laura and Jessica.

"What are you cooking? It smells great," Laura said.

"We're having chicken, sausage, and shrimp jambalaya wraps," Marti said.

"What?"

"Chicken, sausage, and shrimp jambalaya wraps," Marti repeated. "I got the healthy recipe for jambalaya from Leslie. She had a recipe for gumbolaya, but I'll try that one some other time."

"What in the world is gumbolaya?" Laura asked. "And a jambalaya wrap?"

"Gumbolaya is a combination of gumbo and jambalaya. I'm sure it's good, but I decided to keep it simple this evening. The jambalaya wrap will be good," Marti said. "Don't worry. It's low-calorie, low-fat, and low-sodium. Aside from the chicken, sausage, and shrimp, I'm using celery, red pepper, low-sodium chicken broth, no sodium whole peeled tomatoes, and some of our favorite seasonings — oregano, thyme, and ground allspice. I'm also using brown rice instead of white rice, and whole-wheat tortillas."

"Sound goods," Laura said. "Watch Jessica for me while I go get the mail and put some clothes in the washing machine, please."

"For sure," Marti said, picking Jessica up off the floor. "How's Daddy's little girl?"

While Laura stood outside on the porch looking through their mail, she noticed a hospital bill addressed to Marti. She walked back into the house to show him.

"Open it and see what it's all about," Marti said.

"It's for an emergency room visit to Baylor Memorial Hospital in Dallas," Laura replied.

"It must be a mistake. We haven't been to Dallas," Marti said. "What are the details? How much is the bill?"

"It's for $1,500. It says that Tisha Renee Mason was treated on April 26th," Laura said.

"Treated for what?"

"Looks like it was related to an infection," Laura stated. "Didn't she go with her Aunt Clara to Dallas around that time?"

"I think you're right, but why would she need emergency care?" Marti asked. "And why wouldn't I know about it if she did?"

"Marti, call her. This is a $1,500 bill. Find out what this is all about."

With Jessica sitting on the floor playing with her building blocks, Marti walked into the living room to call Tisha. Listening from afar, Laura could hear the stress in Marti's tone as he questioned Tisha about the bill.

He walked back into the kitchen, where Laura was steaming some vegetables, and shared his conversation with Tisha. "Apparently, when Tisha went to Dallas with her aunt, one of her cousins convinced her to get her tongue pierced."

"A tongue piercing? What was she thinking? People have died from getting their tongue pierced."

"You're right. After six hours, she said her tongue was swollen and bleeding, and she was having a hard time breathing. Her cousin rushed her to the emergency room without her aunt knowing anything about it."

"So, what? Did she think they'd just treat her for free? What do you plan to do about it?"

"She was really sorry. Sounds like the whole ordeal really scared her," Marti said.

"That's fine and all, but what about the $1,500 bill? Who's going to pay for that?"

"I'll take care of it."

"I don't believe you should let her off that easy. Make her help pay for the bill from her earnings at her new job," Laura said. "You've got to teach her that when she makes a mistake, she has to pay for it."

"I'll see," Marti responded. "Let's eat so we can take our evening stroll before it gets dark. It's fun watching how excited Jessica gets in the baby jogger."

Tired of casting herself as the perfect wife and mother, Leslie was on the brink of making some tough decisions about her future. She knew her marriage had run its course. Rather than settle for the status quo, she'd searched and found the antidote for conquering a life of defeat, worry, and bitterness: she joined Bethany Missionary Baptist Church, which proved to be a place of refuge for her hurting soul. Her life was finally moving in the right direction because of her partnership with God, through Jesus Christ.

Laura and Leslie were meeting at Hermann Park for another girls' night out. For a change of scenery, they started near the park's reflection pool. They had planned to walk the perimeter of the reflection pool from Sam Houston Monument to McGovern Lake, then to the Miller Outdoor Theatre and other various parts of the park.

"Hi, li'l sis," Leslie said, walking up to Laura's car in a nearby parking area. "Are you ready to rock and roll?"

"Hey, lady, I'm ready. Give me a second to make sure my walking shoes are straight."

"Did you get those blister control socks?" Leslie asked.

"I sure did. I'm glad you told me. I was starting to get this real ugly blister," Laura replied.

"I've learned so much from our training materials about all the things I hadn't considered for walking. They really stress making sure to have the right size and shape of shoe for walking or running," Leslie said, looking at her shoes.

"Before I learned all that, I figured any shoe would suffice, but that's not the case. I've learned that you can experience an assortment of feet, leg, and knee problems if you don't wear the right shoes."

"I didn't realize the importance of so many things until you sent me the information. Now I know more about chafing, how to treat and prevent shin splints, heel pain, plantar fasciitis, purchasing the right kind of bra, hydration . . ."

"I learned about chafing the hard way," Leslie interrupted. "On my first long-distance walk, I walked faster and sweated a lot. As a result, my arm motion caused increased rubbing. By the time I finished, my underarms were raw; that's a feeling I never want to experience again. Now, I lubricate the areas prone to chafe. Plus, I've invested in one of those shirts made from fabric designed to keep you dry during exercise. It's called dry-fit, or something like that."

"Girl, let's get started. I have to get home. Between Jessica and the boys, I know Marti is going crazy."

Walking along the perimeter of the reflection pool, Leslie glanced over at the ducks swimming in the water.

"So how is it having the boys around for the summer?" Leslie asked.

"Actually, it's great. The boys are going to the kids' camp at church. It's a great program. They do basic religious and academic studies, go on field trips, and participate in Trevor's fitness program. This year, they added Spanish classes. They love Jessica, so they keep her entertained in the evenings. Marti will generally play basketball or kickball with the boys. At least a couple evenings during the week, we'll go to the park. I'll jog with Jessica while they ride their bikes. What's really funny to see is all of them in the kitchen preparing the evening meal."

"Has Marti spoken with Tisha to see how she's doing at the District Attorney's Office?" Leslie asked.

"I believe so," Laura said. "Sounds like everything is going good. My main concern is her paying for that $1,500 emergency medical bill."

"I was just wondering; Hunter hadn't said anything about her working there."

"How's Casey and his family?"

"He's been going out on interviews. His girlfriend is content to lie around the house with the baby."

"How long are they going to stay with you?" Laura asked.

"Hunter told him that once he finds a job, he'll help them with rent for an apartment. He's really attached to our granddaughter. Whereas he didn't come home before, he's there on a regular basis, helping to feed her and all. The way he fusses over the baby, I'll be surprised if he let's them move out."

"He's probably like that since she's his first grandchild. What about the girls? Have you heard from them?"

"Yes. They're pretty busy with their careers," Leslie responded abruptly.

"Well, we're planning to grill some food for the Fourth of July at Mom and Dad's. Maybe you, Hunter, Casey, and the crew can come by. It would be a great opportunity for them to meet Casey and their great granddaughter."

"I'll see. Thanks for the invitation," Leslie said. "On a different note, I didn't realize you were the ministry leader of a career prep program at the church."

"Yes, I am. It helps kids identify career paths in the field of forensics."

"Is it for disadvantaged kids?" Leslie asked.

"Absolutely not. The kids are from a variety of backgrounds — two-parent and single-parent homes. They're a combination of good performers, low performers, and at-risk students."

"Did you actually start the program?"

"Yes, I did. After I pitched it to Pastor Wallace, he was sold on the idea. I got other professionals in the church involved, and we were set. We laid out the specifics of the program and what it would include in regards to career preparation: education and skills identification, application completion, interviewing preparation, and work ethnics training. Then,

I approached my boss about extending it to an actual work environment — job shadowing. So, now, the six-week program includes three weekends in a classroom setting, and depending on their ages, some go on to experience the opportunity to work with a forensic specialist."

"That's a great program," Leslie said. "Is it just for kids who are members of your church?"

"Absolutely not. Pastor is devoted to his members, as well as to the community. The program is open to all."

"Let's stop for our water break," Leslie suggested.

"The field of forensics is vast. Therefore, I wanted to create an opportunity for kids to learn more about it. They learn the importance of doing well in the hard sciences, such as chemistry, biology, or biomedical sciences. They become familiar with general forensic science literature to help them identify an area of interest. The best part of the program is the non-paid internship where they shadow a specialist in a crime laboratory to gain experience in the forensic application of science. There are so many occupations for them to consider: forensic psychologist and psychiatrist, fingerprint expert, crime scene photographer, forensic pathologist, forensic serologist, and forensic dentist and odontologist. Then there are the non-medical occupations, like forensic chemist and forensic geologist."

"That's great! It's a good opportunity for them to focus on a career rather than street life," Leslie said.

"Absolutely. Now, we're working on tracking the kids that have gone through the program. We plan to establish a way to keep them connected to us, like an annual career prep rally."

"Let's start back walking. Our water breaks are too long," Leslie said, laughing. "I'd like to explore doing something similar for adults. So many adults have settled into working on a job rather than pursuing a career. Because I spent all of my adult years catering to my husband and kids, I never took the time to explore having a career. I love my job in the lab, and now I'm thinking about going back to school. I want to be a role model for other women and show them that their options are not limited after forty."

"You go, girl!" Laura shouted.

"Pastor Wallace says God expects us to do great works with our lives, that we must make our gifts and talents available to the kingdom of God. The short time I've been working in the lab, I've gotten to know quite a few of the ladies. I've encouraged many of them to explore their ability to have a career and not settle on being a clerk until retirement. Most complain about not having enough money to support their families, money for daycare and higher education for their children, and the rising cost of gas, utilities, and food. Because a large majority of them are single parents and don't receive any financial assistance from their baby's daddy, saving is definitely out of the question, and we all know that because of our choices and our lack of planning for retirement, we'll have to work well beyond our sixties."

"Just more reasons why implementing healthier lifestyle habits are so critical," Laura said. "I'll help you develop a program. You can introduce it to our pastor. It's great seeing how your commitment to God has overflowed into other areas of your life."

"For the first time in thirty years, I've truly examined the many facets of my life. To be a part of a church where everyone has a genuine concern for others has been something wonderful for me to experience. It's caused me to shift the focus off myself onto helping others, and as a result, my life has changed dramatically."

"I can't tell you enough how proud I am of you."

"You know, for the past few weeks, Vanessa has been taking us through the *Ten Essential Habits for Living Healthier*.

"I remember you talking about them," Laura said.

"I told you about number one and two. The other eight are *Eat Breakfast Each Day, Drink Plenty of Water, Get Adequate Sleep, Set Goals for Lifestyle Modifications, Get Routine Exams and Screenings, Avoid Risky Behaviors, Examine Your Relationships,* and *Live Life with a Purpose.* The last two were probably the most significant for me. I didn't know how relationships could affect your body, thoughts, and behavior so negatively. Or should I say, how our reaction to things going on in our relationships can cause us to make poor lifestyle choices that ultimately affect our body, thoughts, and behavior. Vanessa gave us a handout illustrating the affects on your body — headache, chest pain, pounding heart, high blood pressure, shortness of breath, muscle aches, tiredness, and sleep problems," Leslie shared.

"I experienced some of those earlier in my life dealing with men," Laura said.

"Then, there are the effects on your thoughts — anxiety, restlessness, worrying, irritability, depression, sadness, anger, job dissatisfaction, forgetfulness, and burnout."

"Been there," Laura commented.

"And the effects on your behavior — overeating, undereating, angry outbursts, drug abuse, excessive drinking, and increased smoking. Vanessa emphasized how all of those things stress and weaken the body, making it easier for a disease or illness to surface."

"That's a lot," Laura said. "I know I've been affected in just about all of those ways."

"It was so appropriate for Vanessa to end the ten habits with 'living life with a purpose' — that we should position ourselves to recognize and accept God's purpose and plan for our existence. That's why I'm so excited about the program I want to start."

"Sorry, sis, but I've got to say it: you continue to amaze me."

"Thanks. Well, it looks like we're at the end of this session," Leslie said, drinking water from her bottle.

"We'll talk about the plan over the weekend. I've got to get home," Laura said, walking quickly to her car.

"I'll start writing down some notes. Talk to you later."

The day of restoration finally arrived. For nearly six months, Leslie had dismissed the idea of seeing her parents. Preparing for the Fourth of July celebration at her childhood home, she was now excited about their reunion.

Playing with Donna Gale, Casey's baby daughter, Leslie decided to call Laura to see what she needed her to bring over. Marti answered the telephone.

"Hi, Marti," Leslie said. "I was calling to see what you all may need me to bring over."

"I think we're okay, but I'll let you talk to Laura," Marti replied, handing the telephone to Laura.

"Hi, Leslie," Laura said.

"Hi. What's on the menu? Something healthy, I know. Probably a big change from my traditional sirloin steaks, hot dogs, smoked sausages, ribs, and burgers — and I know you're not making the mounds of potato salad, macaroni salad, and baked beans. What about dessert? Fudge brownies and ice cream is what I've been accustomed to eating."

"We're keeping it simple to minimize the damage, while still enjoying the holiday. Instead of eating high fatty meat, we're having meat lower in fat, like marinated chicken breast, and some seafood, like wild salmon, scallops, and shrimp," Laura said.

"Are chicken burgers on whole-wheat buns on the menu?" Leslie asked.

"Of course, and we'll have potato salad. It'll be a low-fat version using low-fat mayonnaise and less egg yolks. For dessert, we'll have a variety of low-calorie foods — blueberries and strawberries with angel food cake topped with low-fat whipped topping, frozen yogurt instead of ice cream, and fruit smoothies using a combination of fruits, low-fat milk, and ice. Marti has some physical stuff planned, like flag football, basketball, and volleyball."

"Sounds like fun," Leslie said.

"Who's coming with you?" Laura asked.

"Just Casey and Donna Gale."

"Casey's girlfriend is not coming?"

"She's a little under the weather," Leslie said. "Me, Casey, and the baby will be over in a couple of hours."

"What about Hunter?" Laura asked.

"He's going to stay home and do some work."

"Okay, I'll see you then," Laura responded. "We're on our way to Mom and Dad's."

Later that day, Leslie stood on the steps of their parents' home. Thirty years flashed by as she remembered her old blue and white, single-speed, pedal brake Huffy bike lying on the ground in front of the steps. She remembered using chalk on their driveway for a hopscotch design. Images of her and Laura hopping from box to box consumed her thoughts.

"Are you okay, Mom?" Casey asked as they stood in front of the house.

"I'm okay, son," Leslie responded. "There are a lot of memories here."

Just as they proceeded up the steps, Laura opened the front door.

"Hey, sis. I thought I heard you out here," Laura said, looking at Casey and Donna Gale. "Is this my nephew and great-niece?"

"Yes, it is," Leslie announced.

"It's so wonderful to meet you, Casey, and your baby daughter. I've seen years of pictures, but there's nothing like seeing you in person." Laura positioned herself to hug Casey and Donna Gale.

"It's great to finally meet my aunt. Mom has told us so much about you," Casey said.

"Where's Marti, Jessica, and everybody else?" Leslie asked.

"Marti and the kids are in the backyard. He's grilling some meat and vegetables. Mom and Dad are inside," Laura responded. "I must say you look fierce in that sleeveless wrap dress; so feminine and sophisticated. Absolutely fabulous. I know it's some designer."

Leslie was wearing a red sleeveless wrap dress, trim in white with a notched collar that included a belt at the waist. "It's a Neiman Marcus exclusive. This is the first time in my life that I've felt comfortable wearing something sleeveless. Gone are the days of big shirts, baggy pants, and warm-ups. Like you told me a couple of months ago, you can be a size twelve or fourteen and be just as sexy and elegant as someone who wears a size six or eight. I'm not interested in wearing some all-bearing shirt, showing my cleavage, but I do want to look sexy."

"You're definitely sporting your own *Sex In The City* look. By the way, we need to go and see that movie."

"Just let me know when you want to go."

Laura ushered them into the house to where their mom was sitting in the living room watching TV. She was listening to one of her favorite western shows, *Bonanza*.

"Hi, Mom," Leslie said, as she entered the front room.

"Is it really you?" her mother asked. She stood up slowly.

"It's really me, Mom," Leslie said.

"Come closer so I can feel you."

Leslie walked nervously toward her. Their mother began to use her right hand to trace Leslie's face.

"Mom, I have my son, Casey, and his daughter, Donna Gale with me," Leslie said, reaching her hand toward Casey and Donna Gale.

"Come give me a hug, Casey, with your baby," their mom said, reaching out.

"We love you, Grandmother," Casey said while leaning over with his baby to hug her. Standing nearly six feet and five inches, he overshadowed his grandmother, who was only five feet and four inches.

"It's so wonderful to meet you, and Leslie, I've missed you so much," her mother began to cry.

Leslie approached her mother, and began to hold her tightly. As they cried in each other's arms, Leslie asked about their father.

"Where's Dad?"

"He's in the bedroom. He had a treatment today. He's very weak," her mother said. "He's been waiting to see you."

Laura, who had been standing in the background watching the exchange with Casey, asked Leslie, "Do you want something to drink?"

"No, sis, but I would like to see Dad," Leslie stated.

"Come on," her mother said. Feeling her hands along the wall, she ushered Leslie back to their bedroom.

Walking down the hallway, Leslie admired the collection of photographs representing over fifty years of history. Casey followed close behind with Donna Gale.

"Olson, your daughters, Leslie and Laura are here, and your grandson and great-granddaughter."

"Is Leslie in here?" he asked, with his eyes closed.

"Yes, Dad, I'm here," Leslie confirmed, saddened by the sight of her father lying in bed.

"Come closer and give me a hug," her father urged.

Leslie drew closer. As her father reached up, she bent over and hugged him tightly.

"Dad, it's good to see you."

"Baby, I've been waiting so long for this moment. I've missed you so much. I've never forgiven myself for sending you away," he admitted.

"Dad, don't," Leslie begged.

"No. I've been waiting over thirty years to tell you how sorry I am. People make mistakes, try to fix them, and move on, but—"

"Dad—" Leslie said, trying to interrupt.

"Leslie, I can't forecast the future or make you any definite promises, but I'll spend the rest of my days making up for all the wrong . . ." Father Olson had deep lines in his face and passive torment in his brown eyes. His voice sounded tired. "I had a dream a few nights ago. I was dead, and you all hated me for the way I treated you. Laura has risked everything to help us out financially, and now you, too, and I know I'm not deserving of your compassion toward me. I know I wasn't there for you, but I will be there from now on. Can you ever forgive me? I love you all so much."

Typical of a dying man's confessions, Father Olson apologized for the hurt and pain he had caused his family. He admitted to accepting the truth about himself and his insecurities as a boy, man, husband, and father: that years of abusive and disruptive behavior had robbed his wife and daughters of happiness. The words of assurance coming from his mouth erased years of tainted thoughts and feelings shared among Laura, Leslie, and their mother, and the certainty in his eyes assured them that his words would result in action.

Everyone stood in shock. Flashbacks of the years of verbal abuse traveled swiftly through the minds of Laura, Leslie, and their mother. Laura turned around and motioned for Casey to leave the room with Donna Gale. Their mother began to walk slowly, feeling her way to the other side of the room to a nearby window. Laura looked intensely at her father, forcing her legs to move. She stood paralyzed at the entrance of the bedroom door, contemplating whether to leave or stay. Shaking her head back and forth, Leslie sat on her father's bed. Looking directly into his face, she said, "When I told you and mother that I was pregnant..." she paused, tears beginning to fall from her eyes. She continued, "Your reaction has haunted me for thirty years. I remember you telling me that I was a disgrace to the family, that you were ashamed of me, and that I had to leave your house. Because of you, I was forced to marry a man who didn't love me, has never loved me, and has condemned, embarrassed, and verbally humiliated me — like you did to mother. For years, I vowed never to see you in the flesh again. All my life, I've walked around angry and hurt, guilt and shame eating me alive, and I hated you for the way my life turned out. I blamed you for not knowing what normal love was. But, by the grace of God, I'm living in peace now. Someone recently told me that 'The longer I continue to feed my mind with hate, unforgiveness, and revenge — the more contaminated it would become, and worst of all, I would rationalize my conduct.' That's what

I've done for years: rationalized the hate, unforgiveness, and revenge. I'm in a different place now, and I probably wouldn't be here preparing to do the things that I'm doing if my past hadn't been as such. I know the events in our lives happened for us to get to this moment in time. Father, I forgave you awhile ago. Let's just take our healing process one day at a time."

After an hour of open and frank conversations, Leslie wheeled her father into the living room. The sight of his grandchildren and great-grandchild made him happy. They spent the remainder of the evening eating, chit-chatting, playing games, and viewing an array of photographs in the various photo albums.

CHAPTER 6

A Time of Resolve

As the weeks passed, Laura and Leslie's families merged as one — with one exception: Hunter. Although he was home more often, he had grown more distant toward Leslie. In the midst of ducking and dodging his mood swings, Leslie had taken on an active role in the care of her parents and was raising money for her three-day walk, participating in various 5K walks, working in her ministry at church, and preparing to enroll in her first semester of college.

The week before starting school, Leslie and Casey decided to take a trip to Baltimore to visit Courtney and Charlene. Laura took Leslie and Casey to the airport the day of their departure.

"Thanks, sis, for taking me and Casey to the airport," Leslie said.

"You are very welcome. Casey, I'm surprised Marilyn's not going. She didn't want to visit her family?" Laura asked.

"A lady from Hanson Electric is supposed to be calling her in for a job interview, and she didn't want to risk missing the call," Casey responded.

"I see. Your mom says you'll be starting your new job in a week or so."

"Yes, and I'm excited. It's a sales manager position with Rico Communications," Casey shared.

"He's gonna be a big-time communications sales manager," Leslie said proudly.

"I guess Hunter wasn't interested in going?" Laura asked.

"He has some huge federal case he's working on. He'll probably go to Baltimore around Labor Day. Casey and I wanted to go check on the girls. Once I start school in a couple weeks, I know my time will be limited."

"I still can't believe you're going back to school," Laura said.

"If I want a shot at moving up with the agency, more education and knowledge is necessary. Right now, I know I lack the skills to lead and be a part of management."

"How far along are you with the three-day breast cancer walk?"

"Actually, I'm up to eighteen miles in one session," Leslie said.

"Eighteen miles?" Laura shouted. "I didn't know you were up to that point. I know that's well over the sixty to ninety minutes you told Trevor you wouldn't do."

"That conversation seems like a lifetime ago. Motivation and inspiration is everything," Leslie said, smiling at Laura. "My group did eighteen miles last Saturday, and our schedule has us doing eighteen tomorrow, too. Since I'll be in the D.C. area, I've got to figure out how to get it done. I'll probably walk the National Mall area several times."

"That should be a nice walk going to and from the Lincoln Memorial, Washington Monument, The Reflecting Pool, and The Capitol."

"I'm looking forward to it," Leslie said, excited. "Oh, by the way, we've raised over $3,000. Between the monetary gifts from our church members and friends, along with the bake sales at work, I know I'll reach my personal goal of $5,000."

"Wow, $5,000!" Laura shouted. "Bake sale?"

"It was healthy stuff. I'm trying to help my unhealthy co-workers discover healthier food choices, and I'm also trying to get them to start exercising. I've started a walking group. So far, around five of us walk during our lunch break around the perimeter of the building or in the parking garage."

"We have quite a few employees who walk during their lunch break as a team. Right now, they have a contest going on where the team with the most walking miles will win a team prize," Laura said.

"I think I'll suggest something like that," Leslie responded.

"Looks like we're here," Laura announced, approaching the airport entrance.

"You can drop us off at the skycap area," Casey suggested.

"We were both scheduled to come back on Tuesday, but I'm going to change my day to Monday. I'm scheduled to be back at work on Tuesday. Hunter will probably be working late, so can you pick me up?" Leslie asked. "I'll pick Casey up on Tuesday."

"Sure. I'll see you on Monday."

"Thanks, Aunt Laura," Casey said, getting out of the car.

On her way home, Laura called Marti to find out if he wanted her to bring something home to eat.

"Hi, baby," Laura said. "I just dropped off Leslie and Casey at the airport. Did you cook something yet?"

"Hey, baby. No, I haven't. I was waiting on you," Marti replied. "Since it's the boys' last weekend here before going back to school, I was thinking about taking them out to eat, especially since we didn't get to take them on a trip somewhere. We haven't been out to eat in months."

"That sounds good. What are you thinking?"

"I was thinking *The Grill Market*. They've got reasonably priced home-cooked meals."

"Sounds good to me," Laura confirmed. "I should be home in about twenty-five minutes. What's Jessica doing?"

"She's playing with her brothers," Marti responded.

"Great. I'll see you soon."

Laura and Marti enjoyed their last weekend with the boys. Marti was proud that they were able to expose them to healthier habits. Before their departure back to their mom, he stressed the importance of not eating candy, cookies, and soda, and he encouraged them to play outside daily.

Lying in bed reading the newspaper, Laura remembered that she had forgotten to ask Marti about his conversation with Sydney regarding the kids' lifestyle habits. "Marti, did you talk to Sydney about the kids when you took them home? About implementing healthier habits? She needs to understand how the increase in calories and portion sizes, as well as the abundance of sugary beverages like soda and fruit juices, has had a major affect on the rise in overweight and obese children. Research shows that young people who are overweight or obese are facing health issues like diabetes and cardiovascular disease. As society moves forward with trying to reverse the hazards of unhealthy habits, it's going to be critical for parents to create an environment in the household where kids eat healthier.

"I know. Jr. and Drew told me about the kinds of foods they're accustomed to eating. Sounds like their refrigerator and pantry is routinely filled with high-calorie, high-fat, and high-sodium foods. They have no choice but to eat nutritionally deficit foods."

"Sydney, like a large majority of parents, has to limit sugar-sweetened beverages and get the kids to drink water. Parents have to get back to the basics and create time to get physically active with their kids. If kids see their parents being active, they'll get the message. That's why it was important for you to play with the boys while they were here for the summer," Laura said. "Did you talk to her, Marti?"

"Yes, Laura. I mentioned the changes we exposed the boys to. I told her it was important that we pay attention to what our kids are eating, increase their physical activity, and cut down on TV and other media use."

"What did she say?"

"Before shutting the door in my face, she said she was busy cooking fried fish, fried okra, and curly-cheese fries."

"That's a shame. What did you decide about buying *Wii Fit*?"

"I decided to wait until Christmas. When they come over here, I'll make sure we do some fitness stuff together."

"Marti, once a week or once every two weeks is not enough. They need to be engaging in daily fitness activities," she said, her frustration growing.

In a weary tone, Marti responded, "I understand that, Laura, but what am I supposed to do? I could go over there every other day and get them, but she'll find an excuse for them not to be available. My hands are tied. I can't make Sydney make them exercise. She keeps them cooped up in the house and doesn't let them play outside. Their only options for activities include video games or television. As far as eating healthier, I definitely can't make her buy healthier foods."

"That's why I thought the *Wii Fit* might be a good idea," Laura stressed. "At least if they're in the house, there's something available that gets them moving."

"Actually, I'm afraid that if she knows what it's for she won't let them play with it. She won't let me enroll them in any kind of organized sport, like basketball or football, because she's afraid they'll get hurt."

In a tone of indignant protest, she responded, "We'll figure out something. If you continued to encourage the boys to ask their mother to buy healthier foods, and also to do some sort of exercise each day, hopefully they'll continue on by themselves."

∞

The following Monday, Laura picked Leslie up from the airport. Leslie said that she had fun with her daughters but that she was excited about starting her classes. She would be taking an English, history, and math class.

As they pulled into her driveway, Leslie invited Laura inside, but Laura decided to go on home since she lived forty-five minutes away.

Leslie walked inside with her luggage and soon found herself surrounded by darkness. She thought to herself, *I wonder why Hunter has all the lights out. I know he's here because his car is out front. I wonder if Marilyn is here.*

Turning on the lights in the foyer, she proceeded up the spiral staircase that led to their bedroom. As she walked closer to the bedroom, she heard grunting and moaning. Opening the door, she saw both Hunter and Marilyn nude, lying on the bed having sex. She stood paralyzed in shock watching Hunter on top of Marilyn, caressing and squeezing her breast, and her handling his private parts and putting him inside her.

After moments of watching them rapt in sexual passion, she screamed in disbelief, "What are you doing with her?"

Hunter turned around and jumped out of the bed, grabbing a sheet off the floor. "What are you doing home?"

Marilyn searched for some covering. "Mrs. Hamilton, I am so sorry."

"Hunter, I can't believe you're with your son's girlfriend, the mother of his child. How could you do this to me and your son?!"

Hunter approached Leslie. "Let's go downstairs."

"Go downstairs for what?"

"Mrs. Hamilton, let me explain—" Marilyn interjected, fumbling to say something.

"Honey, you can't explain anything to me. The only thing you can do at this point is get out of my house!" Leslie shouted.

Hunter began to push Leslie into the hallway. "Leslie, she's not going anywhere. Let's go downstairs. You need to calm down."

"Calm down? You're having sex with our son's girlfriend, in our bedroom, in our bed, and you want me to calm down? I can't believe you did this to us!" Leslie started crying and hit Hunter in the chest with her fists; she was devastated. "I'm gonna tear your reputation to shreds for this — and that's a fact, not a threat! You're gonna be sorry that you did this to me!"

"You did this to yourself! Consider this your only warning… if you make any effort to disgrace me, you *will* regret it. Any negative actions toward me will cost you your life!" Hunter shouted.

Hunter pushed and shoved Leslie from the staircase to their foyer, forcing Leslie out of their home. Before doing so, he stated that he never loved her and only stayed with her out of obligation — and that Donna Gale was his daughter.

Sitting in her car, Leslie called Laura on her cell phone. "Laura, have you made it home?"

"No, I haven't. I'm driving on I-45. What's wrong? Sounds like you're upset. Are you crying?" Laura questioned.

"I found Hunter in bed with Marilyn," Leslie screamed.

"What? With Marilyn?" Laura shouted.

"Yes, he kicked me out."

"Kicked you out? You're not making any sense. Where are you? I'll come and get you."

"I'm in our driveway in my car," Leslie said. "Hunter won't let me back in."

"Just get away from the house. Come on over to my house," Laura demanded. "Did he hit you?"

"No, he didn't hit me this time," Leslie admitted.

"Get away from the house. It's too dangerous for you to be near him," Laura said, sounding worried.

"After seeing the two of them in our bedroom, I feel like I've been kicked in the teeth. Laura, I'm sorry that I called you. It's too late to be calling you with my drama," Leslie said, looking at the clock on her dashboard.

"Don't worry about the time. I'll call Marti. Jessica's already asleep. Drive to my house, now."

An hour later, Leslie arrived at Laura's house. Laura greeted her at the front door and hugged her. Leslie stood crying on Laura's shoulder. Holding her tightly, Laura moved her inside.

"I'll get you something to drink," Laura said.

Leslie sat on the sofa. "Apparently, it's a relationship that's been going on for years. Casey was a decoy," she murmured. "Donna Gale is Hunter's child."

"Who told you Donna Gale was his child?" Laura asked.

"He did," Leslie replied, breathless, crying uncontrollably. "For years, I've flipped myself inside out trying to be a good wife. I pulled the cover over my head and ignored his infidelity. I loved him in spite of... Laura. I've been so out of touch."

"You *were* in touch. You knew exactly what was going on. You just didn't know it had spilled over into your family."

"I've experienced the ultimate in being beaten down and betrayed."

"I know it's devastating."

"What's devastating is that I haven't lived in the real world for quite some time. I've been living in a bubble where it was safer to ignore everything on the outside."

"Let's get you in bed, and we'll talk about it all in the morning," Laura said, trying to get Leslie to follow her.

Leslie shook her head back and forth. "I wasn't even worthy of the traditional appeal for forgiveness: no apology, no admittance of a mistake, no regrets, no excuses — nothing. He just kicked me out on the streets."

"Leslie, don't do this to yourself tonight. You've been through enough," Laura pleaded.

Leslie nodded. "It's not like I was asleep at the wheel and didn't have a clue that something was going on."

Amid the signs of infidelity she'd refused to confront for years, Leslie faced the sobering truth about her marriage to Hunter. It was over. She filed for divorce. The horrific images of her husband's infidelity served as a grim reminder of the betrayal, heartbreak, and humiliation she felt, but she vowed not to let a painful past delay or derail her plans to move on.

Leslie stopped by Laura's for her tasty banana and strawberry smoothie to celebrate the completion of her three-day breast cancer walk.

"Hey, sis, thank you so much for your support, financially and emotionally. By the way, I reached my goal of $5,000."

"Girl, you are amazing. After everything you've been through over the past three months, you emerged a victor in the fight against many odds. I can't believe you walked sixty miles in three days. The dedication and commitment; it's incredible."

"You and Trevor helped me stay focused on my goal, and I'm grateful to both of you for that."

"Plus, you'll be finishing your first semester of school."

"Next week is Thanksgiving, and I know I have so much to be grateful for," Leslie said.

"We all do. How's Casey doing?" Laura asked.

"He's getting through the hurt. His job at the communications company is going well. He gets to do some traveling, so that helps keep his mind off Marilyn. The hardest part of it all is his love for Donna Gale. Finding out she's his father's child was devastating for him," Leslie said. "His whole world has been turned upside down. The father he worshipped betrayed him. Had I been a mother in the

Word years ago, he would have been taught to worship God. I would have taken my children to church on Sundays."

"You're the right mother for him now," Laura confirmed.

"When I look back over my life, and I think about all the situations that I didn't know how would turn out — God was faithful. That's what I want my son to understand. There'll be trials and suffering, but God restores troubled situations and heals broken hearts," Leslie said. "The woman he loved used him. I told him that no matter how dark things look, there's always light and hope — and not to stop until he finds it."

"That's good. When I spoke with him last week, he was really beating himself up. How are the girls doing?"

"They love their dad. I haven't been able to talk to them. He has them believing everything is my fault," Leslie replied sadly. "I could have exposed his affairs a long time ago, but I didn't. At the time, my reasons for looking the other way were selfish, but if someone had told me back then my life would be shattered I would have done it in a heartbeat."

"Everything happens according to God's plan and His purpose for our lives. I remember times in my life when I had to put one foot in front of the other. Burdened down, I had to stand and act like everything was okay. I kept on giving God all of the glory. That's what you have to do. When you feel like you can't go on, your faith will bring you through," Laura said.

"I'm glad I had my life together when reality hit me in the face. Otherwise, I wouldn't have been able to help my son."

"Has a date been set for your day in court?" Laura asked.

"Next week. I'm trying to expedite everything so I don't get caught up in Hunter's legal problems," Leslie commented.

"It's amazing that he's been under investigation for misappropriation of funds in Baltimore County," Laura said.

"Some legal documents have been released, alleging that he was directly involved in a hot check scandal. All I know is that his leaving me is the best thing that could have happened. It definitely worked out in my favor," Leslie said.

"Everything and everybody is going to be okay," Laura confirmed.

"I went by to see Mom and Dad earlier," Leslie said.

"Is Dad feeling better?" Laura asked.

"Laura, I don't know if he's going to make it. While I was there, Aunt Edna called and told Mom that his cousin Pauline died."

"I didn't know she was sick," Laura said.

"Apparently, she went into the hospital for hip surgery, and the doctor discovered that she had congestive heart failure. For a couple months, they'd been treating her for the congestive heart failure, not realizing that it was caused by a rare cancer."

"How did they find out she had cancer?"

"The only thing I can make sense out of is that she wasn't getting any better, so her doctors ran more tests. As a result, they found the cancer. It had already spread throughout her body, though, and she died in hospice yesterday."

"That's so sad."

"I'm glad Dad is alive. I'd hate to think how I'd feel if he had died before—" Leslie said, beginning to cry. "I'm so glad God didn't give up on me — the sins I committed — the ungodly activities that consumed me — and now I know I can do all things and endure all things through Christ who strengthens me to forgive, love, and live differently."

"Sis, we're living in the Word, we're living our lives in the image of Christ, and that affords us the protection God extends to His children.

"How is Tisha doing?" Leslie asked.

"She's doing okay. I'm glad we were able to convince her to go on to college. After the ordeal with Hunter, we didn't know if she'd recover. Marti and Jessica went to visit her this weekend."

"I'm so sorry he tried to force himself on her," Leslie said. "For years, his followers were caught up in his talents and charismatic disposition, but now his supporters have left him standing alone."

"That's good to know," Laura responded.

"I know it's been crazy around your house, but what happened exactly, and how did she get away from him?"

"Well, it was Tisha's last day to work at the office, and Hunter asked her to stay late and help him with some cases. According to Tisha, from the first day she started working there he would make inappropriate advances and comments about her breasts and his private parts. She'd just ignore him. On the evening she stayed late, everyone in the building had left. Before she could react, he had grabbed her from behind, raised up her skirt, and proceeded to unzip his pants. While wrestling to get free, she was able to pick up a glass paperweight off his desk and hit him in the head with it. Apparently, she hit him hard enough that he staggered. She was able to get her purse and run out of office. Instead of waiting on the elevators, she decided to run down the stairs from the fifth floor to the garage level. Well, he caught up with her in the staircase around the third floor and tried to finish what he had started. She was able to kick him in the groin area, run down to the garage level, and get in her car. Of all the days that her mother had let her drive to work."

"She is a brave young woman," Leslie exclaimed.

"I just thank God she was able to get away from him and that she was brave enough to come forward. I don't know how Marti would have reacted if Hunter had raped her."

"When I think about the way he treated me for such a long time, I can finally admit that I was sleeping with the enemy. But, I would have never imagined the depths of his corruptive mentality."

"It all goes back to God's protection," Laura reiterated, handing Leslie a Kleenex.

"Thank you. I've reviewed the program you prepared for me. As I've gotten closer to some of the women at work and church, I recognize the need for it more than ever. Many of them are the heads of their household. They want to advance themselves and go back to school, but because of their obligations and financial constraints, it's hard to do. Even if they had opportunities made available to them, most have childcare issues."

"If the church can enter into a partnership with the local college, where basic courses are offered at the church during the evenings, we might be able to get women and men enrolled in a defined career program. I think the main hurdle will be convincing people to go back to school."

"I'm looking forward to exploring the possibilities," Leslie said.

"I'll set up a meeting with Pastor Wallace next week."

"Great. So what's on the menu next week for Thanksgiving?" Leslie asked. "How in the world are we going to survive the holiday eating frenzy?"

"Food and Thanksgiving will always be a major part of the holiday season, but a little planning and caution can go a long way in helping you maintain healthy habits," Laura replied. "Above all, we'll have plenty of vegetables, whole grains, and fruits available, and we'll stick to low-fat, low-cholesterol foods as much as we can."

"In Baltimore, Thanksgiving and Christmas were big eating events at Hunter's parents' home. It's one big potluck — a festivity with fried chicken, brisket, ham, turkey, dressing, and all the trimmings — potato salad, candied sweet potatoes, broccoli-rice casserole, and an array of desserts like German chocolate cake, pecan pie, apple pie, and eggnog."

"I go into the holidays with great caution. As people around the globe prepare for the upcoming holidays, they'll be surrounded by an array of sumptuous calorie-laden and unhealthy food from late November through New Year's Day. From office parties to traditional get-togethers at home, many look forward to their holiday favorites. If you plan to indulge in the holiday offerings, you have to do so with caution or else look forward to piling on an additional five to ten pounds. The only way to minimize the impact — expanding waistlines, bigger bulging bellies, and thickening thighs — is to exercise and make healthier eating choices," Laura said.

"From the discussions at work about our Thanksgiving luncheon next Tuesday, it's a pretty big deal," Leslie commented.

"There'll probably be food everywhere. Just focus on eating smaller servings of the high-fat, high-calorie foods you love, or eat them less often. You can also try healthier substitutes. Remember that a serving of meat, poultry, or fish is about the size of a deck of cards or the palm of your hands. If you have to fill your plate, fill it mostly with vegetables — and watch those carbs! Try to limit the amount of bread, pasta, potatoes, white rice, sugar, etc. The key is to fill up on healthy foods first. That means reaching for the veggies and black beans or smoked salmon instead of the sausage rolls, chips and dip."

"That helps out a lot."

"I'm looking forward to a healthy holiday season."

On the eve of New Year's Eve, while sitting on a park bench in Hermann Park, Laura and Leslie reflected back on an interesting year. Surviving the surprising and uncertain turns of life, Laura and Leslie looked forward to a new year. The waves of chaos, crisis, and distress in their lives had yielded order, victory, and peace.

"Leslie, my gut tells me next year is gonna be a year of abundance for us — spiritually, emotionally, financially, and physically."

"I believe so, too. God's power helped me rally from the depths of fear and overcome extraordinary challenges. I know He has great plans for our lives."

"I'm so glad Hunter consented to your divorce and the settlement," Laura said.

"With the state of his problems, he really had no choice," Leslie replied. "If the allegations of his involvement with the escort agency are true, it'll lead to his disbarment."

"What about the hot check scandal?" Laura asked. "What do you think caused him to go down such a tragic road?"

"I'm not gonna climb into his head and try to define his motives," Leslie stressed. "I just know his moral code of honor has been punctured. Considering the humiliation he subjected me to for so long, I'm just glad the charade is over."

"It's so sad," Laura said.

"What's sad is the lives of the young girls he has ruined — girls like Marilyn. He ruined the dreams her family had for her life."

"What do you think is gonna to happen to her and Donna Gale?" Laura asked.

"I have no idea. Casey has tried to call her, but she won't return his calls. He's having a hard time letting go of the baby. I know with time he'll get through it and abandon his thoughts of anger, resentment, and disappointment; feelings of betrayal."

"We'll be there for him to help focus his thoughts on a new beginning. You know Pastor Wallace's favorite statement is 'You can't cure what you won't confront; you can't get delivered from what you won't deal with; you can't fix what you won't face,'" Laura recited. "He'll be okay. At some point, we all have to rise above the trials and problems that face us."

"I know you're right," Leslie agreed.

"I'm glad you're finally in a better place."

"Yes, I am. No more planning my life around a man. I'm most excited about helping to inspire, mobilize, and motivate people to pay attention to what's going on around them, learn from past mistakes, exercise good judgment and control, and make decisions that foster positive changes."

"I know a decision we all must make at some point is whether or not to settle for the status quo or change. In my household, we're going for change. Marti is going to enroll in the program to obtain a Federal Aviation Administration Airframe and Power Plant Mechanic's License. For months, he's been saying we can't afford for him to do it, but I was finally able to convince him otherwise. We're able to manage our expenses related to the household, daycare, child support, and college. The excuses are no longer valid."

"I know I'm facing a tougher time now that I'm on my own. For the first time in my life, I'm having to develop and manage living on a budget. Hunter traditionally handled our money matters. I never had to worry about controlling my spending," Leslie admitted. "This is quite an adjustment — paying bills and all. I never would have thought twice about high gas and food prices or shopping at Neiman's for the latest pair of Manolo Blahnik, Jimmy Choo, or Prada shoes."

"It's amazing what you can live without when you need to," Laura said. "What are you gonna do with your divorce settlement? I'm surprised they didn't freeze all your accounts."

"Really, it was the timing of it all. Everything was settled prior to the official charges," Leslie said. "Filing that motion you suggested was truly a blessing. I found out about all of his money and his other assets. He had bank statements I didn't know anything about, a yacht docked in a marina in San Diego, and a surplus of stocks, bonds, and retirement accounts."

"He was really going to try and do you in."

"That's okay. I got the last laugh in the end. The settlement from the divorce is going into a savings account. It'll go toward my retirement and any unforeseen financial issues. I'll probably have to work well into my sixties, but it's okay. I love my job, and now that I've been promoted to an administrative supervisor I plan to do everything I can to move further into management. That's why I plan to continue my education and get my bachelor's degree. Management is also sending me to leadership seminars. Most people think you can go from employee status to a supervisor status and be successful, but that's not wise," Leslie said.

"It would have definitely been hard for me to go into management without preparation. There's a fallacy in thinking good employees make good managers. People don't understand that supervising and managing require a new way of thinking and a completely new set of skills," Laura confirmed. "How's your apartment?"

"Living in an apartment is a big adjustment for me and Casey after living in big houses for most of our lives."

"It's just temporary. Eventually, you'll be able to buy a home. Just be glad you've been able to get your blood pressure, cholesterol, and thyroid condition under control. Now that you'll have to work another twenty years or so, continuing good health habits will be paramount now and after your retirement."

"An understanding of our genetic predispositions will motivate me to continue healthy living. When I listen to my co-workers talk about disease and illness in their families, I can definitely connect. Seeing the effects of diabetes on Mom, and Dad's battle with cancer and its related complications encourages me to eat fresh fruit, vegetables, and whole-grain products everyday, along with everything else that I need to reduce my risks. Although I'm forty pounds lighter, it's more important that I'm healthier."

"The best thing we've done is change our reactive mentality about health to prevention. It's a whole lot easier to maintain good health than to regain it," Laura said.

Laura and Leslie made a pact to bury the pain and hurt that embroiled their history. The forgiveness Leslie extended toward her father and husband allowed her to let go of the past and walk in joy, peace, and faith. She had embraced God's plan and purpose for her life to impact the lives of others forever.

PART II

Preservation or Termination

CHAPTER 7

A Marriage Operating on Different Platforms

As she approached fourteen years of marriage, Brenda realized that the synergy between her and Billy had vanished. They were unable to agree on such matters as their children, household, money, and faith. Standing fast on opposing sides, Billy and Brenda were separated by their ideas, interests, and perspectives. Crippled by confusion, and paralyzed by a perishing plan, Brenda began to evaluate the stability of her marriage and family. Hovering on the brink of a break up, the challenge of finding their way back to happier times was ever present.

Brenda and Billy lived in Bradford Heights, a small rural community located west of Garland, Texas, with their three children, Claudia, Barbara, and Billy Jr., ages nine, seven, and four. The first five years of their marriage had promised eternal bliss. They communicated and showed respect for one another. They explored ways to mix spontaneity into their daily routine. To beat the odds of having a failed marriage or settling into unhappy survival mode, they were masterful at blending fun, adventure, excitement, and surprise to sustain the pizzazz and energy. Staying emotionally and physically connected was their X-factor to maneuvering smoothly through life's roadblocks, setbacks, conflicts, and adversities.

As with all things, though, the goods times were in jeopardy. Unable to manage the transition from a couple to parents, the spark in their marriage fizzled. Ten years later, their plan had become flawed: no communication. No respect. No emotion. No physical connection. Billy was no longer a husband, partner or a parent; instead, he began nurturing relationships with alcohol and his work buddies, a status change that had evolved as a consequence of Brenda's control over their lives and her ongoing recognition of his bad habits, shortcomings, and inadequate decisions. To escape her nagging, whining, and dominant demeanor, he spent his free time repairing his classic cars, gallivanting off to join his buddies on weekend fishing and casino excursions, and indulging his addictions to video games, car accessories, and electronic gadgets. His excessive spending on superfluous hobbies and bad habits, on top of a failed business venture, left them with a dwindling bank account and $80,000 in credit card debt.

Brenda was a courtroom clerk for Rockwall County. At the end of each day, she went home to serve as the household anchor; her husband had abandoned his parental duties. She provided direction, guidance, and wisdom to their kids. Shouldering the daily obligations and responsibilities — cooking, household cleaning, washing and folding clothes, household maintenance, and car breakdowns — Brenda negotiated her way through the challenges of sustaining a household while managing mounting money problems.

Billy was a plant technician for the Bartric Chemical Plant. When he wasn't working extended hours at the plant, he was cradling a bottle of beer with his friends at the neighborhood juke-joint nightclub or a glass of whiskey at their favorite sex club.

Although Billy accepted and accommodated the kids, he didn't play a significant role in their lives or upbringing. Brenda made and controlled all of the decisions about their education, medical, religion, and outside activities. Billy's response to Brenda's characterization of him came in the form of withdrawal and rejection. He had become less attentive, less complimentary, less affectionate, and he complained more about Brenda. He failed to recognize that his marriage was spiraling beyond the depths of restoration.

Thinking back, Brenda sat at the kitchen table, reflecting on the exact point when her marriage became inundated with increased conflict and less satisfaction.

Was it when Billy's mom died last year? Or when he lost the insurance money from her death policy because of that risky real estate deal with Ted? Or did it happen when he was laid off from the engineering firm two years ago? That layoff forced him to take a huge pay cut when he went to work at Bartric Chemical. What about me? Where did I go wrong? He's not attracted to me anymore. Am I one of those wives who whine and complain too much? Do I expect too much of him? Am I too hard on him?

Struggling for answers, the time had arrived for an examination of their lives. Brenda was committed to recapturing the life they once had. Dismissing thoughts of hopelessness for their marriage, she pressed on, knowing that the situation could change. She refused to accept defeat. Commitment to her faith landed her on bended knees at the end of each day, celebrating the goodness of God and praying for strength to handle life's challenges.

God, I celebrate Your goodness. Right now, I'm asking You to mend my marriage. Lord, I pray to You, asking for Your strength and Your power, to withstand all that I'm going through. If it's me that needs to change, then help me change, Lord. I lift You up and praise You, Lord. I love You.

Arriving home around eight o'clock in the evening, Billy slammed the front door and headed straight for the kitchen, carrying a new fishing rod and reel. Brenda was standing in front of the dishwasher placing dishes and pots inside.

"Where's my dinner?" Billy shouted, placing his latest acquisitions in front of the kitchen backdoor.

"How was your day?" Brenda asked, moving toward the refrigerator to retrieve his plate.

She couldn't help staring across the room at the rod and reel. She placed the plate in the microwave and heated the food to Billy's satisfaction. Taking the plate out of the microwave, she delicately arranged it on the dinner table with a napkin and eating utensils.

"Fine," Billy responded abruptly.

"You bought new fishing gear?" Brenda asked, avoiding eye contact with Billy.

She grabbed a cinnamon roll off the cookie sheet and a soda from the refrigerator to eat with her pork chops. Then, she sat opposite Billy and started to eat.

"Yep, I'm going with the guys up to Lake Lewisville for some fishing this weekend."

"You already have three or four fishing rods and reels. How much did all of that cost?" she said.

"If you must know, I got the reel on sale for $169.95. It's top-of-the-line. Ten double-shielded, stainless steel ball bearings, one-way clutch, instant anti-reverse bearing, and titanium line guide. The rod was on sale for $99.86."

"That's close to $300. How could you spend that much money without consulting me? We're barely making it as it is."

"Newsflash! I work like a dog everyday. I think I deserve a treat here and there." He started imitating the 'ruff ruff' sounds of a dog.

"I'm not gonna fight with you, Billy, but all of this spending has got to stop. Every couple of months you're making some major purchase. The credit cards are at their limits. With the high prices of gas and food, I'm doing everything I can to keep us afloat. We have virtually no money in our bank account, and you're still spending," Brenda said, frustrated.

"Are you finished?" Billy said, cutting her off.

"The 24-inch custom wheels you bought for your truck last month — for $3,400 — almost wiped us out. I'm afraid if your spending frenzy continues, we're gonna end up homeless. With the state of the economy, we need to be cautious — not frivolous — with our spending. I'm the one sitting at the kitchen table every week trying to figure out how we're gonna pay the mortgage, electricity, water, cable, telephone, and everything else when our income has gone down and our expenses have gone up."

Brenda stood up to go get another cinnamon roll.

"Brenda, I'm not gonna listen to your whining and complaining. Just shut up about those wheels! If you insist on sitting here with me, you'd better find something else to talk about. Anyway, I got those wheels at a discounted price."

To avoid a war of words, Brenda started talking about her day and the kids. Uninterested in her conversation, Billy silently ate his meal. Finishing quickly, he walked into the family room, leaving Brenda alone at the dining table. Aware that his father was home, Billy Jr., their four year old, rushed into the room, tightly clutching his favorite toy, "My First Robot," to hug his daddy. Reaching for the remote on a table, Billy pushed him away abruptly.

"I'm tired, Jr. I've had a long day. It's time for you to go to bed. Go up to your room now. I'll see you in the morning."

Billy Jr. proceeded to show him the features on his robot, but Billy sat motionless, surfing the channels. Billy Jr. silently sat next to his father on floor and flicked the switch on his robot to watch it turn, talk, and walk.

"Turn that thing off!" Billy shouted.

Billy Jr. flicked the switch on off and stood up to leave the room.

Eavesdropping from the kitchen, Brenda couldn't believe what she was hearing. In an effort to spare Billy Jr. from his father's insensitivity, she went into the room.

"Jr., go upstairs and put on your pajamas. Be sure to brush your teeth and wash your face. I'll be up to read you a story."

Unconcerned and detached, Billy sat in his recliner searching the listing of TV programs for a special wrestling event.

Soon it began; another heated discussion between Billy and Brenda regarding his selfishness.

"I can't believe you treat your son the way you do. He waits all day for you to come home. He wants you to play with him. He practices writing his alphabets so he can show you his progress in preschool."

From the top of the staircase, Claudia and Barbara listened, anticipating another intense argument.

"You should have him in bed by the time I get home," Billy replied, looking at Brenda with disgust. "When I get home, I don't want to be bothered with anyone. Those long days at work wipe me out, and the last thing I want to do is listen to a kid's rambling about a toy or writing."

"If you spent more time with him, you'd know he doesn't ramble. He speaks really well for a four year old, and he's really advanced for his age — nearly reading on a first grade level. He knows all his letters, and he's learned how to write his name. He also draws really well," Brenda said. She began to look in a desk drawer for a folder. "Here, look at this. It's some of your son's drawings. I know you work a lot of hours, but if you didn't spend your free time with Clyde and came home after your shift, —"

"Don't start with me!" Billy shouted, interrupting her. "I'm not interested in seeing that stuff."

Brenda continued, " — you might not be too tired to spend time with your family!"

"There you go again! Maybe you should get a life."

"My life is you and the kids."

"And that's your problem."

Saddened by the exchange of insults, Claudia and Barbara returned to their bedrooms. Brenda angrily went back into the kitchen to finish cleaning up.

Blinded by his compulsive control and belligerent behavior, Billy began to have flashbacks about his mother.

I sure miss my mom. I could talk to her about anything, Billy thought, as he sat watching the dirty tactics of wrestlers on cable TV. *Maybe I shouldn't have gotten married. Maybe I wasn't ready for it all. Now, I'm saddled with a wife and kids. Responsible for making sure they have a roof over their heads, clothes on their backs, and food in their bellies. Everything would be fine if I was still working at the engineering firm making $55,000 a year. How can I keep us in the lifestyle we're accustomed to on $30,000 a year?*

Defeat, worry, and fear fogged Billy's mind, impairing his vision on how to be a responsible, devoted, loving, caring, and supportive husband and father. His misplaced priorities of impressing his friends and keeping up a lifestyle of routine spending had his family on a train ride headed for destruction.

On her way upstairs to tend to the children and get herself ready for bed, Brenda paused and looked at Billy. "I was hoping you could say goodnight to the kids before they go to bed. Billy Jr. wanted you to hear him recite a Scripture he learned in Bible study, and he wanted you to hear him say his prayers."

Ignoring her, Billy was fixated on wrestling. He sat in his recliner until the early morning hours.

The next morning, Brenda woke to the sound of the Trip's Morning Show on the radio alarm at six o'clock. Turning over, she was startled by Billy's presence. He normally had to be at work by six o'clock in the morning and was typically out of the house by five o'clock. But, due to a recent schedule change, his hours had changed from six o'clock to eight o'clock, and he had neglected to inform Brenda.

"Aren't you going to work today?" she asked. "You're normally gone by now. Are you sick?"

He remained silent as he turned to face the opposite direction.

Brenda sat on the edge of the bed and thought about the state of her marriage.

What did I do to deserve this breakdown in my marriage? An internal broadcast sounded off, *Get up! Go on in the bathroom and take your bath! Get ready for work. He's not going to change. Your marriage is over. He doesn't love you or the kids. Just leave him. Quit subjecting yourself to his meanness. Get an attorney! Only a weak woman would continue to endure his hostility.* Deep down, Brenda knew her marriage would only survive if she blocked the negative thoughts and altered her outlook from pessimistic to optimistic.

Mornings were typically hectic in the Mishun household, which included getting the kids up and showered, dressed and fed, coupled with combing hair and making lunches. Barbara, the middle child, was easy. School always excited her enough for her to jump out of bed and move quickly to get ready in the mornings. Claudia and Billy Jr. were not morning people and needed more time to transition from sleep. Nevertheless, Brenda always managed to make sure she allowed enough time to get the kids ready, drop them off at school, and get to work.

"What's for breakfast?" Billy asked, entering the kitchen. "I don't smell any coffee."

"I just finished microwaving a stack of waffles, hash browns, and bacon," Brenda responded sharply. "I haven't had time to brew coffee."

"When are you gonna fix some real food? Every morning you microwave a bunch of that frozen stuff! When I was a kid, my mom cooked hot meals from scratch with real eggs, butter, and milk. She'd make homemade biscuits and gravy, pancakes, sausages, eggs, and grits, plus get six kids ready for school," he exclaimed proudly.

"Yes, your mother was a dynamic woman, but she didn't work outside the home. If you were just a little helpful around here, I'd have time to cook hot meals from scratch, too," Brenda responded. "Since my days are spent jockeying for time, those instant meals in a box — waffles, French toast sticks, croissant sausage, egg, and cheese sandwiches, and pancakes n' sausage on a stick — help me save time."

The kids bowed their heads and stared at their plates, pausing from eating.

Frustrated, Billy stormed out and headed back upstairs, shouting, "You're right: she didn't work outside the home, but she could have while running circles around you!"

Brenda ignored him and began making lunches. Billy Jr. loved the ham and cheese Lunchables, mainly because of the candy bar and fruit punch. Claudia preferred the nacho cheese chicken Lunchables because of their breaded nuggets, and Barbara's favorite was a ham and cheese Hot Pocket.

"Come on, kids. Get your lunch bags and backpacks. We've gotta go."

The following days were full of intentional acts of avoidance and hurtful comments. The situation worsened when Brenda became ill. She began to experience periods of shakiness and sweating, extreme tiredness, and unusual urination and thirst. Like a veteran super-mom, she managed to go to work, maintain household obligations, and care for the kids, but as the days went on she had difficulty finding the strength to continue. Drained of her energy, she felt as if all the air had been let out of her body. Unable to stem the tide of her illness through self-medication, she called her mother, Minnie. Hearing the distress in her daughter's voice, Minnie came over and stepped in to care for Brenda, help around the house, and take the kids back and forth to school. Minnie was not aware of the level of marital problems between Billy and

Brenda and thought she was helping out because of Billy's long work hours. Witnessing her daughter's agony, Minnie urged Billy to take Brenda to the doctor. Characteristic of a sheep in wolf's clothing, Billy imitated a caring and supportive demeanor when he responded favorably to Minnie's request.

"Baby, make an appointment for the doctor. Billy's gonna take you," Minnie said, sitting on the side of the bed, positioning Brenda's food tray.

"It that your homemade soup?" Brenda asked.

"Yes, it is," Minnie replied. "It has some powerful ingredients that'll make you feel better soon."

"They say soup is good when you have a cold. I don't have a cold. And even so, the theory is an old wives' tale."

"My mother believed in the healing power of soup, and so do I. Mine has boneless, skinless chicken breast, and onions, celery, carrots, tomatoes, clove garlic, bay leaf, fresh parsley, dried thyme pepper, and low-sodium chicken broth, served with whole-wheat angel hair pasta."

"Whole-wheat angel hair pasta?" Brenda said, surprised as she reached for her spoon. "What's up with that?"

"I've started modifying some of my traditional recipes with lighter substitutions and whole grains."

"It tastes great! And you can't really tell that the traditional white noodles have been substituted with the whole-wheat pasta."

"I've been trying to do better about my health. Since your Aunt Sally was diagnosed with diabetes, she's been emailing me information about eating better. Because our father died from complications with diabetes, as did his mother and my sister, Wilma, she says we're genetically destined to get it. She feels that if I don't implement some stall tactics I'm going to be next. I told her that I'll try some of her eating recommendations, but I'm not exercising."

"I've never even thought about the reasons why they died. I just figure everyone will eventually die from something."

"I'll start giving you some of the information she's given to me," Minnie said as she finished folding towels. "Reality starts to set in as you get older. You start thinking more about death and those who've preceded you. You start thinking about your time, leaving your spouse and children behind. I'd love to live to see your son and daughters finish college, get married, and have their own families. But, if I don't start making some noticeable changes, I know I won't be around to see those milestone occasions. I hate that my father didn't have a chance to enjoy his grandchildren and great-grandchildren. He would have really loved Billy Jr."

"I guess I just think about you being there for me and the kids," Brenda said. "With Dad off somewhere living a new life and my husband away all the time, you're my only constant."

"I know, honey. Don't worry. I plan on being around for a while. Don't give up on your husband, though; prayer does change things. Your faith will get you through this rough patch," Minnie said, walking toward the hallway to place the towels in the linen closet. "By the way, how's work going? Are you still having problems with your supervisor?"

"I'm really struggling with this new computer system they've implemented. It's far more complicated than our old computer system," Brenda explained.

"Why is it so much more complicated?" Minnie asked.

"The new computer system requires us to perform more steps to process our case judgments. The current system is much easier. If we had some sort of procedural guide, it probably wouldn't be so bad, but we're constantly having to write steps down, which slows down our processing. Management never thinks things all the way through from the design to the implementation stages. The whole training process is so unorganized."

"So are you working on the old system or the new system?" Minnie asked.

"The new system is expected to go live in a couple weeks, so we're training on it now. The current system has been turned off. Right now, there are no trials going on."

"Sounds like they're giving you all enough time to really learn the new system," Minnie commented.

"The old system was fine. Because of many extra procedural steps for each task we perform, the new system will not work nearly as fast as the current computer system. I'm not that good with computers, so having to switch to something totally different has been challenging. I'm afraid of getting poor ratings on my upcoming performance evaluation. The reason for implementing the new system was to create efficiencies — that is, reducing staff and shifting the responsibility of entering judgments to our judges. If my performance evaluation is low, then they have the justification they need to terminate me."

"If judges are entering case information, who's conducting trials?"

"That's the million dollar question," Brenda responded. "I think they'll find that clerks are still greatly needed."

"I'd suggest you take some computer classes. They're the way of the world. If you're not proficient with them, you're going to have difficulty excelling in the workplace."

"You're right," Brenda agreed. "I love the criminal justice system, and there are upper level positions in our courts that I'd love to pursue. With limited college hours, though, it's gonna be difficult for me to get promoted."

"Baby, just start taking a class or two per semester. Before you know it, you could have an associate's degree. If you want to move up, you have to make some sacrifices. Don't just expect to get a job because you've worked ten years as a clerk. The more education and job skills you get will enable you to make a real difference in your career and in your organization."

"Is that why you went back to school?" Brenda asked.

"Absolutely. I wanted to move up with my company, and I was having a hard time doing so because of my limited education. Although I was an exceptional worker, they kept hiring people with more college education and degrees above me. By taking a class here and there, I got my bachelor's at age 42. Baby, you can do the same."

"That all sounds good, but we don't have the money right now."

"Just don't lose the thought. When your money situation improves, start taking some classes. You'll be in a better position to move up."

"For now, I need to concentrate on getting better. The management team constantly nitpicks about the work hours and days off. One of the ladies was written up the other day for excessive absences, and her absences were all medical related, due to unexplained back problems. We told her that she'd better consider going on family and medical leave to protect her job. Mrs. Rainer, my supervisor, comes and goes as she pleases to take care of her sick mother. I guess that's a privilege of being the boss."

"You're right. As long as she has a qualifying medical condition and the qualifying work hours and time with the company, she's eligible for family medical leave, whether it's continuous or intermittent. The Family and Medical Leave Act is a great law because it helps individuals and families keep their jobs in the event of a serious medical condition. When I first started working years ago, if someone got sick and was out for more than five days, their job was gone when they came back."

"That's what I thought."

"Is your boss still picking on you about other stuff?" Minnie asked.

"Not just me, but everybody. We've had to remove our personal pictures, knick-knacks, quotes, and sayings we have pinned in our cubicle areas."

"Did she give you all a reason why?"

"She said it was too much clutter in the area. So, now our work areas are bare. She's always fishing for something to go off about. It's been like that for the past few months. I wish she'd put more effort into making sure our training for this new system is structured and organized. I'm getting so tired of it all. Trying to learn the new system and dealing with her is so stressful."

"Get back in school. I'll help you with the cost if you need me to. By all means, don't let her discourage you," Minnie insisted. "I need to get home before it gets dark. Stay in bed the rest of the evening. I've got the kids situated, so they'll be okay. I'll see you and the kids in the morning. Don't forget to make that appointment."

"I can drive myself."

"Brenda, you're too weak to be driving yourself anywhere. Let Billy drive you."

"Thanks, Mom, for all your help."

"You're my baby. That's what I'm here for."

CHAPTER 8

The Consequences of a Divided Household

A few days later, Brenda contacted the neighborhood clinic and made an appointment. More concerned with missing a day's pay, Billy reluctantly agreed to take her. The morning of the visit, Brenda awoke, dreading the 20-minute drive to the clinic with him; she feared another bruising argument.

Billy walked into the bathroom. "Your mother is here."

"Where is she?"

"She's in the kitchen fixing the kids something to eat. Do you need her to help you get ready?"

"I can manage. I'll be ready in thirty minutes."

"Just come on outside after you finish getting ready," Billy said, looking around for his wallet. "Where's my wallet? I sure hope your visit isn't gonna be long. We're losing a lot of money with me having to take off, and I'd like to get a few hours in this afternoon, if at all possible."

"Your wallet is on the nightstand," Brenda responded, disturbed by Billy's comments.

Billy grabbed his wallet and walked toward the door. Turning around abruptly, he reminded Brenda that he was going to the casino Friday after work. "I sure hope you're better by the weekend. I'm going up to the casino in Bossier City with Clyde and the boys. If you're not, maybe your mother can come over and take care of you and the kids."

"I thought you were going fishing. The new fishing gear, remember?"

"I do remember! We decided to go to the casino instead," Billy said sarcastically.

"Do you have to go gambling every weekend? We don't have any extra money, and you're wasting what little we do have traveling to Shreveport to go to the casino."

"I'm trying to win money to get us out of debt," Billy replied, slamming the bedroom door closed.

Brenda knew that their marital conflict would not be resolved without devotion to prayer. Kneeling down, she silently began to pray. She asked the Lord to remove the discord from her house and restore her family.

The mood in the car reflected the current state of their unhappiness; for Brenda, the 20-minute drive felt like hours of captivity on a deserted island.

Arriving at the office without incident, Brenda checked in at the front desk and was given a stack of papers to complete. Billy walked away to look for a seat.

The front desk clerk asked Brenda, "Do you have insurance?"

"No," Brenda responded in a whisper.

The nurse guided Brenda on how to complete the paperwork, and informed her that the cost of the visit would be $175 plus any blood work and related medical care. Brenda turned around to find Billy; he was sitting in a corner scanning the magazine rack.

"The doctor's visit is $175," Brenda said, as she sat next to him. Unresponsive, Billy started flipping through the pages of Time Magazine. "Do you have $175?"

"No, I don't! Just use one of the credit cards," he said with his head bowed.

Brenda completed the paperwork and returned to the front desk with her credit card in hand. Rotating credit cards was the only way they could still purchase anything.

They sat in silence with grim expressions on their faces. Their medical benefits had ended after Billy's layoff two years ago. Brenda was accustomed to having regular checkups performed for her and the kids, but when the benefits ended so did their ability to get regular physical examinations and dental checkups. The family coverage for medical and dental insurance on her job was extremely costly, and Billy's contract job at the chemical plant didn't offer it. Brenda had explored other options for medical coverage, including some of the government and discounted programs, but their household income exceeded the eligibility requirements. Brenda believed her only option was to wait until Billy became a permanent employee at the chemical plant. Until then, all medical expenses were out-of-pocket costs taken from the household budget. Fortunately, none of the kids had been seriously ill — just routine colds and allergies that time and over-the-counter medication helped to alleviate.

While waiting, Brenda thought, *I hope it's nothing serious. We just can't afford any major medical problems. We're barely making it as it is. Even with Billy's cut in pay, we'd be okay if he didn't spend all of our money drinking, gambling, and buying his toys. I still can't believe he spent all that money on those custom wheels — especially knowing we don't even have medical coverage for our family. How can he be so irresponsible?*

Brenda continued to think about the 8-inch LCD flip-down TV monitor he had added to the SUV to impress his friends. The video system with the built-in DVD player, wireless headphones, and remote control had cost them $650.

I don't know how long I can continue living like this. Our annual income of $55,000 is not going to sustain us and Billy's thoughtless spending. The kids are growing like weeds, needing clothes and shoes more often. We're drowning, and I can't continue keeping our heads above water if Billy doesn't change his habits.

Interrupting her thoughts, the nurse called her name.

"Billy, it's time to go to the back. Are you going with me?"

"Sure. Anything is better than sitting out here with a bunch of sick people."

They walked toward the nurse.

"Hi, Brenda," the nurse said, extending her hand. "I'm Clara, and I'll be getting some preliminary info for the doctor."

Brenda extended her hand. "Hi, Nurse Clara. This is my husband, Billy."

"Hi, Billy," Nurse Clara said, acknowledging Billy.

Billy nodded his head.

"Let's stop here," Nurse Clara said. There was an open area with a large stainless steel, digital, medical scale.

"I need to get your weight."

The nurse's jovial demeanor helped to ease the tension Brenda was feeling. She explained to Brenda that she would take her weight, blood pressure, pulse, and temperature first.

Sighing at the sight of the scale, Brenda proceeded slowly to step on it. She always hated having her weight taken. The number was an unwelcome account of how much her body had expanded. Deep down, she knew she had gained weight, but the scale was the official scorekeeper. She removed her shoes, socks, and jacket in an effort to reduce the digitized number.

It shouldn't be that bad. I don't feel any heavier, she thought, as she balanced herself on the scale.

Hesitant, she looked down. "This scale is pretty high tech."

In a matter of seconds, the number appeared. Horrified by the truth, she suppressed her emotions and stepped down. Nurse Clara retrieved a printout from the machine. Billy stood off to the side, watching and waiting.

"This is a reading of your body weight, body fat percentage, hydration level, lean body mass, and BMI. The doctor will discuss what the numbers represent during your visit," the nurse said, giving Brenda a copy to review. "I'll need to get a urine sample."

While Brenda was putting on her socks and shoes, Nurse Clara directed her to the restroom so she could get a urine sample. After she finished in the restroom, Clara escorted the couple to an examination room where she collected information related to Brenda's medical history and took her blood pressure, pulse, and temperature. Once she completed her portion of the examination, she informed Brenda that the doctor would be in shortly, and she left the room.

Moments later, the doctor walked in and introduced himself as Dr. Robert. He started by asking Brenda a series of questions. While conducting his examination, he noticed Billy in the corner reading. After he finished prodding and probing, he told Brenda that she had to go down the hall to the lab for some blood work.

"Doctor, is it something serious?" she asked. "I feel like I'm about to collapse. Getting around has become a daily chore."

"I can't really say at this point. We need to do some blood work to help us figure out why you're feeling so poorly. When was the last time you ate something?" Dr. Robert asked.

"Last night around nine o'clock," Brenda responded.

"Good," Dr. Robert said. "Nurse Clara will show you to the lab. We have an onsite lab; so, hopefully, you can wait for the results."

"I can wait," Brenda said, as she and Billy gathered their belongings.

Proceeding down the corridor, Billy asked, "What's the cost of the blood work?"

"I don't know, Billy. I just know I need to have it done," Brenda replied.

"I don't know; most of these doctors are just trying to rack up more money," he said with a skeptical attitude.

"Be quiet, Billy. I'll manage the cost somehow. I always do."

"I'll wait for you in the car. Hopefully, they won't take all day. You know I'm trying to get some hours in this afternoon," Billy said, observing the sign-in podium from a distance.

For Brenda, his behavior represented a form of cruel and unusual punishment.

∞

Billy needed an escape. He knew deep down that his uncontrollable spending habits were jeopardizing his family's future. Walking back to the car, Billy's mind filled with worry.

How am I going to get us out of this mess? We don't have medical insurance and I can't even reach into my pocket and get $175 to pay for Brenda's doctor's visit. She's right; my spending is out of control. But, I can't let Clyde and the guys think I can't hang. We do everything together. There's no way I couldn't get those wheels after everyone else was getting them. Even the rod and reel — I had to get them. I can't have them thinking I'm a henpecked husband. Things were so much easier when I worked at the engineering firm. I was on my way back to school to become a licensed engineer. Now, I'm stuck at the chemical plant in a dead-end job, with no future.

Pressing the remote to enter their SUV, Billy continued to think over his bad choices.

I didn't even have the sense to invest the money Mom left me. I let Ted talk me into that real estate deal that turned bad. I can't see clearly. I don't know what to do. I feel as if I'm backed into a corner with no way out. I just don't have a clue how to get us out of this mess, and I'm afraid of losing my family. I hate insulting and being mean to Brenda. It's like I'm using her as my personal punching bag. But, it's how I deal with the fear and shame of what I've created. I can't even look her straight in the face. I'm ashamed of the predicament I've gotten us into. What am I going to do? I need to get out of that casino trip this weekend. The only cash I can get is from the credit card, and the interest rate for cash on the credit *cards is killing us. Clyde expects all of us to have at least a $1,000 this weekend. I need to save whatever cash is left on the credit card in case Brenda's illness means more trips to see the doctor and more tests.*

Ten minutes after the blood work was complete, Brenda waited anxiously in the waiting area for the results. Nurse Clara finally came out to escort her to another exam room. When Dr. Robert entered and noticed Billy was gone, he inquired about his whereabouts.

Embarrassed that her husband was not by her side, Brenda responded by saying, "My husband wasn't feeling well, so he went to the car."

Puzzled by her response, Dr. Robert began to review the blood readings. He explained to Brenda that her blood sugar (glucose) levels were above the normal range. He went on to say she had pre-diabetes that could develop into Type 2 diabetes in the years to come unless she made noticeable lifestyle changes. He stated that he would recommend a course of action to delay or prevent a continuing increase in her blood sugar.

"What kinds of foods do you typically eat?" Dr. Robert asked.

"Because of hectic days, we eat foods that are quick and convenient. One evening, it might be Sunnyland's hot dogs. The kids love their chili-cheese hot dogs or corny dogs with tater tots. Another evening, it might be Pappi's Pizza. They have weekday specials like two large two-topping pizzas with their free cinnamon bread stixs or cheesy bread for $13.99. Wednesdays are buffet night at Daisy's All-You-Can Buffets. They usually have discount nights for kids, as well as free ice cream cones. On Fridays, I always fry a batch of catfish and fries, served with coleslaw, potato salad, and baked beans from the grocery deli."

"When do you ever get in some wholesome vegetables and fruits?" Dr. Robert asked, looking concerned. "First of all, I need for you to concentrate on modifying the types and quantity of foods you eat."

"Modify how?"

"You're taking in too many carbohydrates for starters," Dr. Robert stressed, taking a seat in his chair. "Let me rephrase that — the wrong types of carbohydrates. A high consumption of carbohydrates, sugar, salt, and fat leads to excess body weight and boosts insulin resistance, a precursor to diabetes. With your steady stream of processed food and fast food, it's a high probability that you're going to gain more weight and increase your risk of developing Type 2 diabetes sooner rather than later. Please keep in mind that we're not just talking about you, but your family as well. You can't fly solo on changing your habits. You need to take your family along for the ride, also."

"What is diabetes, Dr. Robert?" Brenda asked. "I know my Aunt Wilma and Grandpa Norman died from something related to it, and my Aunt Sally has it. But, I don't know what it means for me and my family. My Aunt Wilma was sixty when she died a couple years ago. She lived in Kentucky, so I don't know how long she had the disease. Seems like I'm a little young at thirty-six to have an old person's condition?"

"Pre-diabetes and diabetes are not confined to old people. There is a rise among people of all age groups because the diet of the average American has changed so dramatically over the years. Eating habits that consist primarily of high-caloric, high-carbohydrate, fatty foods like what you and your family eat — chili dogs, pizzas, and all-you-can-eat buffets — are causing waistlines, breasts, arms, hips, legs, and thighs to swell, and increase the risk of insulin resistance."

"Is that what diabetes is? Insulin resistance?" Brenda asked.

"Diabetes in adults develops if the body does not produce enough insulin or does not use insulin properly. To give you an example of why the body might not produce enough insulin — the breakdown can occur from an extended diet high in carbohydrates, such as breads, pasta, pastries, etc. Whenever we eat, our bodies convert the carbohydrates into sugar (glucose), which is the body's main source of fuel. This causes the glucose level of our blood to become elevated. The more carbohydrates we eat, the higher our blood sugar rises. Consequently, our bodies then need to metabolize this sugar and convert it to energy. Insulin, a hormone produced in the pancreas, allows the glucose to enter the body cells, where it's used for energy. It also helps the body to store sugar in muscle, fat, and liver cells for future energy needs. As blood sugar rises, our body produces more insulin to keep our blood sugar at a satisfactory level," Dr. Robert explained.

"So, as long as the body produces more insulin to contain our sugar, it sounds like we're okay?" Brenda interrupted.

"On the outside of every cell, we all have what's known as *insulin receptors*."

"What are insulin receptors?" Brenda asked.

"Insulin receptors regulate the amount of sugar that gets into your cells. Over the long run, as you continue eating a diet high in carbohydrates, you create the potential for health concerns. There become too much carbohydrates being converted to sugar. This causes the potential for your body to produce an excess amount of insulin. With all this excess insulin trying to push the sugar into your cells, the insulin receptors get tired. Some of the insulin receptors won't let the sugar into the cells. As a result, our blood sugar rises even more. Because your blood sugar is now elevated, your body thinks it needs to manufacture more insulin to get the excess blood sugar into our cells. This additional excess insulin causes even more insulin receptors to get tired, break down, and close their doors; thus, raising your blood sugar even further. As a result, your body is summoned to produce more insulin, causing more receptors to get tired. Therefore, the cycle goes on and on and on — more insulin causing more insulin receptors to fail, and there you go — Now the cells are insulin resistant. Ultimately, the body's inability to produce sufficient insulin to push the sugar into the cells leads to Type 2 diabetes," Dr. Robert explained further.

After listening to Dr. Robert's detailed explanation, Brenda looked out into the parking lot for Billy. Needing reassurance that everything would be okay, she realized that she needed him by her side.

"What does all this mean for me and my family?" she asked nervously.

"It means you've got to clean out the cobwebs of unhealthy habits."

Dr. Robert asked Brenda to review the printout the nurse had given her earlier. He pointed out that she had a BMI of 29.

"Body mass index (BMI) is a measurement of body fat based on height and weight," he clarified.

Based on Brenda's height and weight, she was overweight and now on the borderline of being considered obese. Being overweight was not news to Brenda, who was now thirty-six, and, at five feet, six inches in height, weighed 183 pounds. The reality of being considered obese and having diabetes was frightening, though.

Dr. Robert went on to explain the additional ramifications of having, as he defined, subcutaneous body fat — excess body fat. Not only was she at risk for diabetes, but also the associated complications like high blood pressure, high cholesterol, kidney disease, and depression.

"Is there some range for BMI?"

"Simply put, a BMI of 18.5 — 24.9 is normal, 25.0 — 29.9 is overweight, and 30.0 and above is obese."

"It all sounds so serious," Brenda responded.

"It's *very* serious. Our goal is to prevent you from inheriting diabetes. Like I've mentioned, with diabetes, you're at an increased risk for heart disease, stroke, and other complications, such as eye and kidney disease, nerve damage, and foot problems. Keeping your blood glucose, blood pressure, and cholesterol in a healthy range can reduce your risk of complications," Dr. Robert explained.

I have some belly fat, but it can't be all that bad. A lot of people are thick around the waist, she thought to herself.

Billy would always make horrible comments about her stomach, but she'd just ignore him. Brenda understood that her elevated blood sugar level was a warning sign that she needed to take notice of it. By no means did she want to end up with Type 2 diabetes. Brenda asked the doctor if her tiredness and fatigue were symptoms of the elevated blood sugar levels. Dr. Robert explained that being tired and fatigued occurred for many reasons; he didn't want to speculate on Brenda's state of tiredness and fatigue.

"Pre-diabetes doesn't always display symptoms, which probably accounts for the millions of people unaware they have the condition. The best method to detect pre-diabetes is the fasting plasma glucose test or the oral glucose tolerance test," Dr. Robert stated.

"It that the blood work you performed on me today?" Brenda asked.

"Yes, it is. We did the fasting plasma glucose test," Dr. Robert confirmed. "In addition to modifying your eating habits, I want you to start exercising at least thirty minutes a day. A weight loss of five to ten percent of your initial weight will help dramatically. Both will assist you in achieving weight loss. I'm going to write you a prescription for a medication that will help lower your blood sugar. Start thinking more fruit, vegetables, and whole grain products."

"Doctor, do you have any samples of the medication you're prescribing me?" Brenda asked, thinking about their limited financial resources.

"Unfortunately, I don't have samples of this particular medication," Dr. Robert apologized.

"What about side effects? Does this medication have any side effects?" Brenda asked.

"As with all medications, there are side effects: allergic reactions such as a rash, hives, itching, shortness of breath, wheezing, coughing, and swelling of face, lips, tongue, and throat. Be sure to read the printout from the pharmacist for extended concerns — and by all means avoid alcohol. Be sure to call me if you experience any of the things I've mentioned."

"Thanks, Dr. Robert."

"Our goal is to use the medication to help get your blood glucose levels on track. In a month or so, we'll hopefully see some improvements. If so, we can see about eliminating the medication. The lifestyle interventions I've prescribed will be more effective and cheaper than the medication in preventing the onset of Type 2 diabetes," Dr. Robert emphasized. "You might consider scheduling an appointment with our registered dietician, Mrs. Spencer, who's on staff here at the clinic."

"What exactly does a dietician do?"

"A dietician provides nutrition services that include nutritional screening and assessments, analysis of nutrient intake, nutrition counseling/education, and development of nutrition care plans and goals. She can develop an eating program tailor-made for you based on your identified needs and preferences."

"Thanks, Dr. Robert. I'll definitely start implementing the things we've discussed."

On the way home, Brenda explained the discoveries to Billy.

"If I get this disease, what will my quality of life be like? What about the children? How will it affect them?"

"Sounds like you just need to start doing some exercises like the doctor said. You'll be okay," Billy responded.

"It's much bigger than just exercising. We've got to change our unhealthy eating habits."

"You mean *you've* got to. I'm okay, and the kids are okay, too," Billy responded. "I told you to work on reducing your fat belly. You were fine back in the day, but now look at you: just fat."

"Billy, I'm so tired of your insults," Brenda said in a weary tone. "Right now, it *is* just me, but I don't want you or the kids to end up with some preventable health condition. The doctor recommended the services of a registered dietician."

"That sounds like more money."

"I didn't ask about the cost, but she could help us with establishing a nutritional plan."

A few days later, Brenda decided to do her own research on the Internet. As she began to search various keywords, she thought, *Dr. Robert explained glucose, but what is it really?* She found out that glucose was a type of sugar found in carbohydrate foods, and it was the main source of energy used by the body.

There's that word again: carbohydrate, Brenda thought.

After hearing all the hype about carbohydrates, she wanted to have a better understanding of what constituted a carbohydrate. She realized that she had to focus more on ensuring that Billy and the kids ate wholesome meals. She had to put the brakes on all of the refined and processed foods she had been preparing — frozen waffles, French toast sticks, bacon, sausage, or ham, and high sugar cereals and doughnuts for breakfast. She needed to stop serving the high-sodium Lunchable meals to the kids, and the frozen meatballs and spaghetti, chicken nuggets, tater tots, and fries for dinner. They definitely needed to curtail the Wednesday All-You-Can-Eat Buffet at Daisy's and the weekday specials at Pappi's Pizza.

Continuing her search on the Internet, she thought about the challenges of change.

The kids are so excited about Pappi's new sweetreats — very strawberry and apple-cinnamon twist. Even Billy likes to eat the cheesy bread and the Italian wings. How will I ever convince them that the foods they love so much may have deadly side effects?

Her research became too much to absorb.

There's so much to consider, but one thing is clear: I've transferred my bad habits onto the kids. Pastor Calvert always says the habits of the parents become handcuffs for the children.

After reading an article about carbohydrates, she quickly concluded that not only was she headed for trouble, but so was her whole family. First things first, she needed to move the entire family toward a healthier style of eating. If she wanted to improve the family's chances of a longer, healthier life, things had to change.

CHAPTER 9

Listening to Words of Wisdom

*A*s she sat thinking in the study, Brenda decided to call her Aunt Sally. *If I expect to have a shot at ending a history of bad habits, I need some help filling in all the blanks.* Her Aunt Sally had diabetes, and Brenda believed she would be a good source of information.

"Hi, Aunt Sally. This is Brenda. How are you doing?"

"Hi, Baby, it's good to hear from you," Aunt Sally responded, elated to hear from Brenda. "I've been asking your mother about you. How are you and your family? When are you going to bring the kids by to visit with me?"

After playing a bit of catch-up due to months of not speaking, Brenda admitted to her aunt the real reason for the telephone call.

"My doctor says I'm borderline obese and a candidate for diabetes."

Aunt Sally encouraged her to do whatever her doctor recommended to avoid the disease. Although she herself was managing the effects of having Type 2 diabetes, she wished it had never happened to her. Aunt Sally discussed the hardship of having to administer insulin injections everyday after being diagnosed. She also described her father — Brenda's grandfather, Norman — and her sister, Wilma's, long-term struggles with the disease.

"After my initial diagnosis, I tagged Daddy as the common denominator, the root of the family's diabetic curse. I blamed him for me inheriting the disease." Aunt Sally now understood that their family had a predisposition for diabetes, and she stressed to Brenda that she had options for offsetting its entry into her own life.

"All I can tell you is that the trigger has been pulled — Now I've got to figure out how to dodge the bullet," Brenda said, sitting at her kitchen table.

"If only I'd been more informed about the disease — knowing more about the impact of my bad habits might have prompted me to make better choices, and things could have turned out differently," Aunt Sally confessed. "Nevertheless, at sixty-two years of age, I know God has plans for me."

"Didn't you go for regular checkups, Aunt Sally?" Brenda asked.

"Sure I did, and for years my doctor pleaded with me to eat better and exercise. He didn't tell me enough, though, about the long-term impact of the foods I ate. I guess I could have done some research like you're doing, but my generation is not into computers like yours," Aunt Sally said regretfully. "Plus, I always thought I needed to reduce my sugar intake. I didn't understand the connection between sugar and carbohydrates. We grew up on syrup and biscuits, hot water cornbread, and the like."

"Yeah, as a kid, I remember Grandpa Norman's love for cakes and pies," Brenda recollected.

"Yes, your grandpa was a big man who loved his sweets — along with his alcohol," Aunt Sally said. "Since I got the disease, I've learned the horrible consequences of what we've traditionally eaten and drank for generations. Our family is genetically predisposed to being large, which increases the risk of diabetes. It's so important that you train your children while their young to practice good nutritional habits."

"Aunt Sally, sometimes I drink a glass of wine. Do you think that contributed harm to my body — my cells?" Brenda asked.

"You should ask your doctor, but from what I've heard others say, alcohol can be toxic for a diabetic. Your grandpa was a heavy bourbon and beer drinker, and both beer and sweet wine contain carbohydrates, which may raise blood sugar. I remember drinking as a young person years ago and how my drinking led me to eat more. Now, I know that alcohol stimulates your appetite, which can cause you to overeat and consequently may affect your blood sugar. Because I take insulin, I know alcohol can interfere with the positive effects."

"Because of the medication the doctor has me on, I can't drink any alcohol. It's not a big deal, though; I don't drink every day. But, when I put the kids to bed, I sometimes relax with a glass of wine."

"I understand, but follow your doctor's recommendations."

Months after Aunt Sally's diagnosis, she admitted her failure to adhere to her doctor's advice. She just couldn't bring herself to exercise and apply his recommendations. After the death of her sister, Wilma, though, she started making a conscious effort toward adopting a healthier lifestyle. Aunt Sally talked about how she started walking with her friends at the local park and changed her eating habits.

"How did Aunt Wilma actually die?" Brenda asked.

"She died of a heart attack, which was a consequence of the diabetes."

"Did she die at the hospital? I was around fourteen at the time, but I remember the telephone call Mama got, letting her know that Aunt Wilma had gone into a coma."

"The day after Memorial Day, May 27th — I'll never forget that date — I had to take her to the hospital for a regular doctor's visit. During the visit, the doctor checked her blood pressure, did some blood work, got his money, and sent her on her way. I wheeled her back to the car, and as soon as she got inside she slumped over. I gave her some Coke and told her we'd be home soon. She kept saying how tired she was. So, I decided to go back into the hospital to get a nurse. They immediately got a gurney, rolled it to the car, and got her back into the hospital; four hours later, they came out and told me they couldn't revive her."

"Sounds like there were no warning signs," Brenda said.

"Well, the weekend before Memorial Day she ate a slice or two of ham, and afterwards her amputated leg swelled up pretty bad. We called her doctor that Saturday, and he told us to get some sort of compression wrap to place around her leg. When I got her to the doctor's office on Tuesday, the doctor treated her. Throughout the visit, she kept saying how tired she was."

"Hearing the details are so disturbing," Brenda commented.

"Wilma battled the disease for most of her adult life, and her refusal to change unhealthy lifestyle habits led to the amputation of her right toe and eventually her right leg. Cataracts led to her blindness, and toward the end of her life I remember her mental instability — hallucinations that people were after her, placing snakes in her bed. I really do think it was the medication. And on that Tuesday, her life ended in heart failure." Aunt Sally recalled the events as though they happened yesterday.

"Sounds like Aunt Wilma had a terrible life."

"She didn't have a terrible life. She loved the Lord and her kids. She just couldn't commit to making the necessary adjustments because of her love for food, especially sweets and carbs. Plus, she earned her living as a cook, and that alone placed her on the shores of temptation all day, every day."

Aunt Sally's voice began to tremble as she described Wilma's inability to eat better, trying diet after diet.

"One of her favorite foods was a peanut patty. To counteract the effects of eating a peanut patty — the ingredients that made it super sweet like sugar, corn syrup, and artificial vanilla — Wilma would drink a glass of vinegar to cut the sugar. Plus, she used the vinegar as a weight loss tool."

"Did the vinegar work?"

"I really don't know. I just know she tried everything to lose weight. I didn't know much about the disease at that time, so I never questioned the impact of her perpetual dieting. When one of us tried something new, we all tried it," Aunt Sally said. "But, I never did the vinegar."

Although she had been diagnosed two years prior to Wilma's death, Aunt Sally had made a choice not to live her life as her sister had. She had grandchildren and wanted a quality of life that would enable her to enjoy them.

"To help me get on track, I sought the guidance of a registered dietician to get recommendations on preparing healthier foods. After reading a newsletter circular from my community recreation department, I took advantage of free exercise classes for individuals fifty and over. We have a fitness expert, Trevor MacElroy, who comes in twice a week to coach us. His classes focus on increasing muscle tone, improving the cardiovascular system, building endurance, and maintaining balance. For someone who had never exercised, going from complete inactivity to full-on activity was challenging — but Trevor makes it fun! Now, I wish I would have started exercising much earlier in my life."

"My doctor suggested exercise and recommended I see a registered dietician. I don't have time to exercise, and we can't afford a dietician's services."

"You definitely want to do all you can, and don't say you don't have time. You can start by simply walking in place in your living room or in your neighborhood for fifteen minutes or during your lunch break. Each week, add on five minutes. As far as eating healthier, you could start by reducing your intake of sweets and other unhealthy foods you crave. It just takes small changes to make a difference."

"I know. It's just so hard," Brenda admitted.

"You know, your cousin, Larry, was diagnosed with pre-diabetes seven years ago," Aunt Sally announced. "Now he has diabetes."

"Larry has diabetes? He's only thirty-two," Brenda said.

"How did he end up with diabetes so young?"

"Over the years, he's never been able to make adjustments to his eating habits. As a child, his mother let him eat anything he wanted, and those habits followed him into adulthood. He was diagnosed with diabetes in his mid-twenties. He started out on pills, then insulin injections, and most recently, insulin pump therapy."

"What's insulin pump therapy?"

"Through your doctor or own research, you'll learn that all people, with or without diabetes, need insulin for two reasons: a background amount of insulin for normal body functions without food, and a burst of fast-acting insulin when food is eaten. People without diabetes can rely on their pancreas to produce the required insulin for them, but people with diabetes have to take insulin as similar as possible to the way their pancreas would produce it if it could."

"My doctor told me that insulin was a hormone produced in the pancreas, and that it lets the glucose enter the body cells, where it's used for energy. He said it helps the body store sugar in muscle, fat, and liver cells for future energy needs."

"Good! Just like a pancreas, an insulin pump releases small, uninterrupted amounts of insulin into the bloodstream. In pump terminology, it's called "basal" insulin. Just like the pancreas produces insulin quickly to counteract carbohydrate intake, an insulin pump allows its recipient to click a button to deliver insulin to cover the amount of carbohydrates ingested. This insulin is called a "bolus" of insulin. The combination of correct basal insulin rates with additional bolusing allows the person with diabetes to have the closest thing possible to a working pancreas."

"How was it determined that he needed a pump?"

"He kept having episodes where his blood sugar would drop, causing him to become confused and incoherent. Right before getting the pump, he stopped in the middle of the freeway during rush hour traffic one day, confused and in a daze. It was a blessing that a trucker saw him, stopped, and called 911."

"I thought you said he did the daily injections?"

"He did multiple daily injections, but because of his sporadic eating habits and inability to control poor choices he kept running into problems. He's a software salesman who tends to go all day without eating, and when he does eat it's not good food. The pump offered him a flexible way to monitor, control, and deliver insulin to his body for normal functions."

"How does the pump work?" Brenda asked.

"I don't know if there are different types of pumps, but his insulin pump is made up of some sort of pump pool comparable to a regular needle. The pump pool is filled with insulin, and with a small battery-operated pump and a computer chip the device allows him to control exactly how much insulin the pump delivers. The insulin is housed in a plastic case about the size of a beeper, and the pump pool delivers it to the body by a thin plastic tube; all he has to do is click a button to inject it when it's needed. The insulin then keeps his blood glucose in the desired range during and in-between meals and overnight. It's a nifty device, but he still has to count carbs. He enters in a number — a number he believes represents the amount of carbs he's gonna eat, and the machine helps him determine the amount of insulin."

"It sounds wonderful."

"The only thing is, even though he has the pump, he still doesn't understand the error of his ways. He still keeps eating poorly," Aunt Sally said.

"How can you eat poorly with a device controlling the way the food breaks down in your body?" Brenda asked.

"Here's an example: we were first introduced to his pump on Christmas at his mother's house. Because I understand the impact of carbs, I ate moderately. But Larry had hefty portions of everything — cornbread dressing, hen, turkey, ham, fried chicken wings, sweet potato casserole, broccoli and rice casserole, collard greens, green beans, potato salad, pink salad — everything."

"Seems like the pump lets you eat what you want?"

"I don't think it's being used the way it was intended to. It's like Larry will never learn the concept of denial and control. He was also encouraged to exercise, but he doesn't."

"I wonder if the equipment is expensive."

"I don't know, but Larry has good insurance, so he doesn't pay anything."

"Wow!"

"Then I had a friend diagnosed a few years ago with diabetes. She's now on dialysis because of her refusal to make changes to her diet."

"What is dialysis?"

"Dialysis is a kind of therapy that rids the body of toxic wastes when the kidney fails and can't do away with the wastes itself. Her sister has to take her to the facility three times a week to get treatment."

"How does the treatment work?"

"From what I understand — but don't quote me on this — there's two types of dialysis: hemodialysis and peritoneal. In hemodialysis, blood is pumped from the body to a filter made of tiny plastic capillaries, where it's then purified when the waste products scatter from it across the membrane of these tiny capillaries. The purified blood is then returned to the body. In peritoneal dialysis, the body's own membrane is used as a filter, and the fluid drained in and out of the abdomen replaces the kidneys' usual function of getting rid of the body poisons."

"You know a lot about diabetes and its complications."

"I *should* know a lot; I've had enough friends and relatives affected by the disease. Just seeing all the other stresses and risks associated with their illnesses has been an eye opener for me."

"How does diabetes damage the kidneys?"

"Like we've been talking about, diabetes affects the body's ability to produce or use insulin. When the body turns the food you eat into energy or glucose, the insulin moves this sugar into the cells. Just like we've talked about Wilma and Larry, whose bodies produce little or no insulin or can't use the insulin (insulin resistant), their sugar remains in the bloodstream instead of going into the cells. Over time, high levels of sugar in the blood can cause damage to tiny blood vessels throughout the body, including the filters of the kidneys. As more damage occurs to the kidneys, more fluid and waste stay in the bloodstream instead of being removed."

"This is all so depressing for me. I've been so accustomed to eating what I want, and now I've gotta deny myself. It's like you're the sick kid on the playground who has to stand on the sidelines and watch the other kids have fun playing."

"The kid on the playground can play; he or she just can't do it to the same extent as the others."

"Okay, Aunt Sally, that was a good comeback."

"What's gotten your generation out of whack is the quick and convenient, ready-to-serve lifestyle; just plain laziness, if you ask me. Everything my daughter and her family eat is fully cooked, ready to serve. The only time her kids get a real meal is when they come over to my house. Otherwise, it's the ready-made, breaded, country-fried chicken with rib meat, breaded country-fried chicken nuggets, crispy chicken strips, breaded chicken breast patties, or sweet, barbecue-seasoned breast chunks."

"Aunt Sally, my kids eat the same kind of food," Brenda said, taking the opportunity to explain her reasons. "You don't understand: when I get off work, I make three stops to pick up the kids, and then go to the grocery store, cleaners, or mall. Once I get home, I get the kids some snacks, put a load of clothes in the washer and dryer, straighten up around the house, and help the girls with their homework assignments. After all that, I'm basically looking for whatever loophole I can find to fulfill food requests, and that's usually something requiring minimal effort to prepare and serve, or some fast-food joint like Sunnyland's, Pappi's Pizza, or Daisy's All-You-Can-Eat."

"Believe me, I understand; I raised four kids. Somehow, though, you have to figure out how to get back to basics. All that processed, ready-to-serve stuff is not benefiting you or the kids. Those foods you gravitate to for convenience are usually high in fat, cholesterol, sodium, chemicals, and offer no nutritional value. Try to bake a fresh chicken, mash some real potatoes, and steam some fresh broccoli sometimes. Learn how to slow down your pace and think about what you're putting inside your body and the kids'. Your spin cycle habits of ready-made, ready-to-serve, ready-to-eat will eventually stop on diabetes, high blood pressure, high blood cholesterol, and who knows what else. So many health conditions come as a result of poor lifestyle habits."

"Mom said you've been emailing her some health information. She's even started using whole-wheat pasta in her homemade soup."

"I love my sister, and I don't want her to end up with diabetes. If I keep up my healthier lifestyle, there's a chance I'll be able to stop my insulin injections."

"That's great, Aunt Sally."

"Baby, start *now*! Today! Take a good look at the foods you and your family eat. My daughter loves to feed her children nachos and pizza. After I told her about the amount of calories, fat, carbohydrates, sodium, and chemicals in nachos and pizza, she's learned how to prepare healthier versions of nachos and pizza using whole foods. I told her that their choices have my grandchildren much larger than they should be, and as a result she has increased their risks for disease and illness, like heart disease and diabetes. She's just like Larry's mom, who allowed him to eat everything he wanted as a child. During one of my fitness sessions with Trevor, he talked about how research continues to reveal that a large number of kids don't eat healthy, nor do they engage in physical activities. He gave us a handout from the U.S. Center for Disease Control illustrating the effects — a growth in health issues, and how the number of overweight and obese children is growing at an epidemic rate."

Brenda thought how she allowed her kids to eat everything they wanted and responded, "My kids love pizza."

"She and her kids had gotten hooked on the cheesy bites pizza at Jay's Pizza. One slice of their pizza ranges from 340 to 460 calories, 950 to 1340 milligrams of sodium, 22 grams of fat, total carbohydrates averaging around 45 grams, and so on. The highest calorie, sodium, fat, and cholesterol deliverers are the meat lover's and pepperoni lover's pizzas. Her girls, ages 12 and 15, can each eat 3-4 slices apiece — not including the soft drinks and hot wings."

"Holy cow! I never imagined that pizza contained all that," Brenda interjected.

"When you add it all up, it's scary," Aunt Sally said.

"What about the frozen pizza?" Brenda asked.

"There's not much difference. Just start checking the nutritional labels before you buy an item. Back in the day, I loved Sicilian's Frozen Pizza. One slice was 380 calories, total fat 22 grams, cholesterol 15 milligrams, sodium 870 milligrams, and total carbohydrates of 34 grams. Most of the time, I'd eat a whole pizza," Aunt Sally confirmed.

"Then there are the nachos my kids love to eat," Brenda said. "Are nachos bad? It's just tortilla chips and cheese."

"Even if you don't smother your nachos with meat, refried beans, sour cream, guacamole, and salsa, and just stick to the tortilla chips and cheese, you're still left with too much fat and sodium on any given day from the deep fried chips and cheese. Plus, it has the hidden, bad carbs you want to avoid."

"If the nachos are my primary source of fat and sodium for the day, and I cut those out, I eliminate the harm, right?"

"More than likely, they're not the primary source. Start looking at what you eat for breakfast — the calories, fat, sodium, and carbohydrates — and what you eat for lunch. Also, pay attention to your intake of snacks, like chips, cookies, pastries, and soda. The spin cycle of unhealthy contributors can potentially be harmful to your cells, which can lead to disaster. I learned that an order of nachos with all the trimmings at my favorite restaurant had 1420 calories, 87 grams of total fat, of which 31 grams were saturated fat, 175 milligrams of cholesterol, 2690 milligrams of sodium, and 113 grams of total carbohydrates."

"Aunt Sally, you weren't eating nachos everyday, were you?" Brenda asked.

"No, I wasn't, but the combination of my other food favorites was adding up to the same or more. Start checking those food labels! Look on the Internet! Some of your favorite restaurants probably have the nutritional value of their foods online; that's how I found out about Jay's Pizza. Start adding up what you're putting in your body. It would also be a good idea for you to contact Trevor, my fitness guy. He'll give you a free consultation."

"We don't have money for fitness experts and the like, Aunt Sally," Brenda admitted. "We're kind of in a financial crisis right now."

"Don't worry about the money. Just call him. You can even email him for advice. He will respond. I'll email you his contact information as soon as we get off the phone," Aunt Sally said. "Brenda, baby, you are destined to live healthier. You're in a position of significant transition. Start visualizing the benefits of healthy lifestyle changes. Then, start implementing the steps necessary to achieve progressive and positive results. I'm a believer and know everything happens according to God's plan for our lives, but I can't help thinking about all of my relatives that died in their thirties, forties, and fifties. I believe their deaths could have been delayed had they done things differently. My first cousin, Scott, died at forty-four from a pancreatic disorder. Before his death, he hadn't been sick and didn't have any major health concerns. He was rushed to the hospital one night and never came out. Even though his wife never disclosed his true cause of death, the family figured that his pancreatic disorder stemmed from diabetes that he wasn't aware of."

"I remember my mother saying Cousin Scott was a heavy drinker."

"Yes, he was. Unfortunately, he didn't understand the relationship between the pancreas, alcohol, and his diabetic gene. As I mentioned before, alcohol can be very harmful for a diabetic."

Brenda was glad she had contacted Aunt Sally because she needed an attitude adjustment, and the information she received was enlightening. She had children that were depending on her, and, now that it was confirmed that she was in that large percentage of overweight and obese Americans, she had to go to work on reducing her body fat. She was at risk not only for diabetes, but also heart disease, kidney failure, and other major illnesses. Aunt Sally directed her to the American Diabetes Association's website, which stated that people with pre-diabetes develop Type 2 diabetes within ten years.

Brenda started thinking about Claudia and her weight gain over the previous two years. Although Claudia's pediatrician talked about her weight during a visit two years ago, Brenda dismissed her excess weight as baby fat. Aunt Sally mentioned that an increasing number of children are being diagnosed with pre-diabetes and Type 2 diabetes, so Brenda knew she needed to improve the eating habits of Claudia, Barbara, and Billy Jr.

Saddened by her revelations, she left the study in search of the children. Peeping into each bedroom, she saw Billy Jr. playing with his action figures, Barbara playing a video game, and Claudia watching television. Retreating to her bedroom, she sat on her bed contemplating whether or not to share her medical condition with the kids.

I don't want to worry the kids; they're too young, she thought.

She proceeded downstairs to discuss her concerns with Billy, who was reclined in his chair watching a basketball game in the family room.

"Billy, I think we need to talk about my doctor's visit and what we should share or not share with the kids," Brenda said. She stood firm in front of Billy, waiting for an answer. "We've got to make some changes around here."

Aggravated that she was talking to him during the game, he replied, "Not now, Brenda. We've got plenty of time to discuss that. It's not like you're really sick or anything. You make such a big deal out of everything. I'm so sick and tired of all the drama..." Billy said, his voice fading.

The tone of his voice was horrendous; the man she had shared her life with for fourteen years had turned into someone she didn't recognize. She couldn't believe what she was hearing. It felt like she was talking to a stranger, but even a stranger would have responded more favorably than Billy did.

Standing in shock, she thought, *What happened to the man I married? The man who was gentle, caring, and supportive? Where is my hero? Someone has taken my husband away and invaded his body.*

It was clear that Billy didn't share her concern for her health, so she realized that she had to be strong for herself and the kids. *I'm going to email Aunt Sally's Trevor for some advice on how to get started with eating healthier. I know that's going to be the biggest hurdle to overcome, especially since the prices of groceries have increased so much that I don't know if we'll be able to eat healthier. The good deals are with the fast foods.*

Despite the common misconception, shared by many, that eating healthier is more expensive, Brenda would soon learn that planning her weekly meals, redistributing the household dollars to buy fresh or frozen fruit and vegetables, buying the ingredients to prepare and cook healthy and nutritious meals from scratch, and substituting bad products with good products was not as expensive as she thought.

Brenda sat at the computer in a corner of the family room to email Trevor. *"Hi, Trevor. My name is Brenda. My Aunt Sally, a participant in one of your fitness classes, referred me to you. She said you can offer me some advice on implementing healthier lifestyle habits. My biggest concern is my eating habits."* Brenda continued by sharing information about her recent doctor's visit and the discovery of her pre-diabetes.

CHAPTER 10

From Rescue to Recovery

*I*t was a crisp, spring Saturday morning, and Brenda felt better than she had in weeks. She envisioned a new beginning. She woke before daybreak and started outlining a course of action for the family while sitting in bed.

Time to get up and get prepared for a fresh start. My life has been in a holding pattern for far too long, but it's all about to change. I'm ready to move forward. As Aunt Sally said, I'm destined to be healthier. Let me see if Trevor emailed me back.

Brenda went downstairs to the computer in the family room. Trevor had indeed emailed her, and he also included his telephone number for her to call him. *I'm going to call him, Brenda thought to herself, her excitement growing.*

Brenda called and was able to connect with Trevor. They spent the first few minutes talking in general about Brenda, her family, and her nutritional goals.

"Despite a tougher economic outlook, there are some tricks of the trade for eating healthier without busting your budget," Trevor stated. He wanted to assure Brenda that she and her family could eat healthier in spite of their financial problems. "The key is to have a plan that'll help you stay afloat while you face the challenges of continued rising gas and energy costs, as well as everything else that's rising right along with them, like food."

"Trevor, I'd love to eat fresh fruit and vegetables every day, but right now they're just too expensive. With my current financial status, I just can't afford to buy fresh fruit like oranges, blueberries, and cantaloupe. The other day, I priced one orange at $1.50 and a small container of blueberries at $4.98. When I consider our usual bills, which include paying the mortgage and related expenses, buying gas, and everything else that goes along with having three children, I can't pay those prices."

"Your concerns are shared by many. The challenges that many people face every day require difficult decisions. So, when it comes to food, they're looking for what's affordable. Although making better decisions can be challenging, it can be done. It's really important to take a deeper look at the distribution of your money toward food — but, before we get down to the nitty-gritty, did you get the two documents I emailed to you? One is related to the Food Guide Pyramid and the other has tips for eating healthier on a budget."

"Yes, I did."

"Great. The Food Guide Pyramid illustrates the type of foods you should be eating every day. A large majority of people plan their meals around meat and leave out the essentials like grains, vegetables, and fruit. According to the Food Guide Pyramid, the bulk of your diet should consist of grains — bread, pasta, and rice — and fruits and vegetables. Meats and dairy foods, which are shown high on the pyramid, should be the least consumed."

"I must admit that I'm a big meat eater, and I've transferred those same habits onto my children," Brenda admitted. "When you really think about it, society's failure to seriously consider and conform to healthier habits is the fault of the food manufacturers and the restaurant industry. They make it hard for us; their tasty and affordable menu items can often be irresistible."

"As adults, we are responsible for our decisions and actions," Trevor said frankly. "Even with the state of the economy, various restaurants manage to offer great specials, possibly due to their ability to purchase low quality food products in bulk; nevertheless, I have clients tell me all the time how they can buy a BBQ Bacon Sirloin Burger and upgrade to a combo. With the combo, they can get a small fountain drink and a small fries for free. The total meal is less than $6.00. Or, they can get eight pieces of chicken — legs and thighs — for $5.99 and add two large sides and four biscuits for an extra $4.00. Or, they can get three pounds of a new creamy chicken Alfredo pasta from their favorite pizza place for $11.99 — a price that includes five breadsticks."

"Wow! Those foods sound a lot like what me and my family eat."

"All the items I just mentioned are far beyond where you need to be with respect to the Food Guide Pyramid. The main things they offer are a cargo load of calories, saturated fat, trans fat, cholesterol, and sodium — not to mention that they're loaded with chemicals — all of which will have you and your family on the road to heart disease and an array of other health problems," Trevor stated. "You'll find that if you plan your daily meals and snacks you can do a much better job of redistributing your dollars to eat healthier. Let's take a look at the next handout."

"I have it," Brenda responded.

"Like a lot of people, you're traveling an unhealthy road, and it's time to change directions. You don't have to fall victim to the food manufacturers' or fast food industry's attempts to lure you in with their elaborate portrayals of cheap and tasty food items. The only requirement is that you have to be willing to put forth some effort. With simple ingredients not requiring a lot of fuss, you can make your favorite foods healthier while staying within your economic guidelines," Trevor stated. "Unfortunately, I can't help you create a healthy version of the BBQ Bacon Sirloin Burger, but you can create a modified version like a turkey burger."

"Somehow your turkey burger doesn't have the same appeal," Brenda admitted.

"It's important to understand that a continued cycle of unhealthy food items will wreak havoc at some point in your life," Trevor suggested. "You're getting your warning with the pre-diabetes."

"It's hard to face that fact, but I know you're right," Brenda agreed.

"Number one: if you reduce or eliminate unhealthy foods like soft drinks, candy, chips, baked goods, specialty coffee drinks, and other high-calorie items, you can invest in a whole orange or container of blueberries during the week," Trevor said.

"You want me to give up my comfort foods," Brenda commented. "I need that soda and candy bar at work during the afternoon to energize me and help me deal with a crazy supervisor, and I enjoy having a pint of ice cream while watching Grey's Anatomy."

"Brenda, that's *exactly* what I'm asking you to do: give them up!" Trevor continued with his initial points. "Food stores like Wal-Mart and Sam's typically offer better prices. Their prices for a box of brown rice, a package of whole-wheat pasta, a box of whole grain cereal, or a loaf of whole-wheat bread are better than those typically found at smaller grocery and convenience stores," Trevor said, reading from the handout he emailed Brenda. "Once you plan your meals and make your grocery list, look for sales on the items you have to buy. But, I do have a word of caution: make sure the food you pick is fresh. Sometimes the sale items are starting to get old, so be sure to check the dates."

"A lady at work uses coupons and saves a lot of money. What are your thoughts on those?"

"Absolutely, you can also look for coupons for the food items you plan to buy. Just make sure you're not cutting out coupons for unhealthy foods. Other options might include checking the websites of the different food manufacturers for coupons, and even buying fresh fruit and vegetables from your farmer's market. And remember, when vegetables are too expensive, frozen is the next best thing," Trevor advised. "If you eat out for lunch everyday, set a goal of bringing your lunch at least three times a week. Small steps to change life-long habits will help you achieve your ultimate goal, which should be to prepare more meals at home. One of my clients cooks on Sunday, Tuesday, and Thursday. The meals he prepares for his family will usually last them about two to three days, which is a lot cheaper than eating out."

"I don't eat out for lunch at work. I usually bring a frozen dinner to eat. I can buy those on sale at my neighborhood grocer for $1.50 to $3.00, or I may just have a package of popcorn or a pack of Ramen noodles," Brenda stated. "For my kids, it's the Lunchables for lunch, and Sunnyland's hot dogs, pizza, or a nice buffet for dinner. The kids love Sunnyland's chili-cheese hot dogs, corny dogs with tater tots. Pappi's Pizza have weekday specials like two large two-topping pizzas with their free cinnamon bread stixs or cheesy bread for $13.99. On Wednesdays, it's buffet night at Daisy's All-You-Can-Eat Buffets. They usually have discount nights for kids, and free ice cream cones. On Fridays, I usually fry a batch of catfish and fries, served with coleslaw, potato salad, and baked beans from the grocery deli."

"Many frozen dinners and soups, as well as pre-packaged meat like hotdogs, are high in sodium, which can be a stepping stone for heart disease. And above all, they offer no nutritional value."

"I guess I need to change some things," Brenda confessed.

"First things first: plan healthy meals that are in line with the Food Pyramid Guide. Once you've figured out what your daily meals will consist of, stick to them when you reach the grocery store. Based on your meal selections, for example breakfast, you and your family could plan on having a bowl of whole grain cereal with low-fat milk and fresh fruit, or a slice of whole-wheat toast with a carton of low-fat yogurt and fresh fruit, or a bowl of homemade oatmeal with low-fat milk and fresh fruit," Trevor stated.

"There's no meat in your scenario," Brenda stated, hesitating to continue.

"You're right. None is needed. Organizations like the American Institute for Cancer Research are urging people to cut back on their consumption of red meat, like beef, pork, and lamb, and to eliminate processed meat from their diets. They suggest that there is strong evidence supporting a link between red meat, processed meat, and cancer. I don't know if the evidence has been validated, but my clients eat entirely too much meat. Their day may consist of a slice or two of bacon, a sausage pattie or link, or a slice of ham for breakfast, a burger, or a slice or two of meat lover's pizza, or a roast beef or bologna sandwich for lunch, or a pork chop, steak, meatloaf, pork roast, or brisket for dinner. To make matters worse, if you've cooked a meat like roast or brisket for the Sunday meal, you typically spend the following two or three days being creative with and eating leftover beef — that is, making beef stew, beef stroganoff, roast beef sandwiches, or a beef burrito," Trevor responded.

"So, are you suggesting I become a vegetarian?" Brenda asked.

"Not at all, I'm just saying you don't need to consume meat at every meal. And when you do eat a meal, it's better to have poultry or fish. Other times it's really okay to have spaghetti and substitute the meat in the sauce with vegetables, or to have a bean burrito with a whole-wheat tortilla, or to have a serving of pinto beans with brown rice and steamed vegetables, or to have tuna salad on mixed greens."

"I hadn't thought about those meatless options," Brenda commented.

"Remember that the goal is to adhere to the guidelines recommended in the Food Guide Pyramid. As you continue to review your options, think about meals you and your family can eat for lunch and dinner like spaghetti, stir-fry, tacos, and jambalaya — all of which can include a host of vegetables like zucchini, squash, and broccoli; meals that can last a couple days and don't have to include meat."

"I like those suggestions," Brenda commented. "My children would like the stir-fry, and definitely the tacos."

"Great."

"On the weekends, I spend a large majority of my days running errands with my kids, and I usually end up having to buy something while we're out and about," Brenda interrupted.

"I can't say it enough: planning is the key," Trevor stated. "More than likely you know what your day will consist of before you leave home, so pack some healthy snacks and water so that when hunger sets in you and your kids won't be forced to stop at a fast food restaurant or buy snacks from a convenience store."

"Trevor, you've definitely provided me with some great information to start developing a strategy of redistributing our dollars to eat healthier. I really appreciate you taking time out of your busy schedule to talk with me."

"You're welcome. Now, I'm on my way to teach your Aunt Sally's class at the community center."

"Tell her I said 'Hi.' Have a great day!"

Brenda was excited and ready to move in a different direction. Her first stop would be the grocery store; her goal was to cook more meals at home.

She had started considering ways to be creative with their favorite foods. *We've got to start eating more vegetables. If I start with subtle changes, they won't notice too much of a difference. Using creative substitutions, I can make healthy versions of their favorites, like improvising the contents of a cheeseburger — a whole-wheat bun instead of a white bun, ground white turkey instead of ground beef, spinach or mixed field greens, fresh tomatoes, honey mustard or low-fat mayonnaise instead of regular mayonnaise, and a low-fat mozzarella cheese. For healthy snacks, I could make one of those fruit shakes or smoothies Aunt Sally talked about during our conversation. It would be easy to whip together a banana and a handful of berries with yogurt or soy milk in our blender.*

Brenda knew it was critical to include more whole grain products in their diet. *Whether I'm cooking a hamburger or turkey burger, spaghetti and meatballs, chicken and rice, or making a sandwich or wrap, I just need to develop a habit of choosing brown over white for breads, buns, pastas, rice, tortillas, and pita pockets.*

She left the family room to go get dressed. While curling her hair, she wrote down a list of items to buy at the grocery store. Since Billy was at home, she was glad she'd be able to take her time shopping alone. His planned casino trip with his friends was canceled because of a death in Clyde's family. Brenda believed he was sulking in the garage. But, unbeknownst to her, the canceled trip was a sigh of relief for him. He knew he didn't have the $1,000 Clyde expected the guys to have, nor did he want to get another cash advance. After months of listening to her complain about the clutter in their garage and her car not fitting inside, he had decided to organize it and put more of his lawn and garden equipment in their storage shed.

When Billy noticed Brenda walking toward her car in the driveway, he yelled out, "Where are you going?"

"I'm going to the store and around!" Brenda shouted out.

"Did you fix breakfast? What about the kids? Who's gonna watch them?"

"I'll be back in a few hours. You and the kids can eat cereal for breakfast," she responded, getting into her car.

She hated to leave in such an abrupt way, but Billy had to start taking on some of the parental responsibilities.

"What about the birthday party Jr. is going to?"

Brenda had forgotten about the birthday party, but she responded, "Jr. knows how to get to Trustin's house. He needs to be there at noon."

"It's eight o'clock. You should be back long before noon."

"I've got errands to run, and I don't know what time I'll be back. I trust you'll do the right thing!" Brenda yelled from her window as she drove off.

Walking down the aisles of the grocery store, she recited in her mind, *Okay, we need to eat more fiber. Aside from not drinking enough water, I know I'm constipated all the time because I'm not getting enough fiber. I'm tired of having to take laxatives to prompt a bowel movement when all I've got to do is eat healthier. Plus, Dr. Robert says researchers believe the beneficial effect of soluble fiber may be the slow absorption and digestion of carbohydrates that lead to a reduced demand for insulin. Let me look at my grocery list so I don't miss anything.*

Dr. Robert warned her about picking true whole grain products. He had explained that refining involved a process of removing certain parts of the grain that contained the nutrition — the fiber, vitamins, and minerals.

I have to start reading the ingredient lists on food labels. He says to look for whole as the first ingredient listed on the food label, she thought. *Dr. Robert says wheat flour and enriched flour are not whole grains.*

After leaving the grocery store with a host of healthy foods, Brenda finished the remainder of her errands. Spending time by herself without screaming kids was a rare occasion. This Saturday would be the start of a new era; Brenda saw more days like it in her future. She loved her kids more than anything, but a few more opportunities for time alone would be wonderful. She wanted to get back to the weekend excursions with her mom, but with three kids such excursions had become extinct — especially with a husband stranded on his own mental island of self-absorption.

What about exercise? Trevor was really nice about giving me tips for eating healthier; now, I need his advice about exercising, but I'm sure I've used up all the minutes of my free consultation.

Brenda knew she had to factor exercise into her schedule of activities at least three times a week, not only for her but for the kids and Billy as well. With every evening packed with things to do — homework and dinner, Bible study on

Mondays, etc. — she thought about ways to add exercise to the mix.

We bought the kids those bikes during the Christmas holiday. Billy and I could get out our bikes from the shed. There's a park nearby with a wide path for us to ride — no traffic or red lights or stop signs to worry about. I need to get us some protective gear — helmet, knee and elbow pads. Billy will need to make sure the bikes are in good working condition, fit properly, and that the brakes and tires are okay. Riding bikes will be an enjoyable way for the family to spend time together — but the challenge will be getting Billy to agree to go along for the ride, Brenda concluded.

When she arrived back home, the children heard the sound of their mother's car pulling into the driveway and ran out to greet her. Eagerly anticipating their usual goodies, they each grabbed a bag to carry inside the house.

"Hi, kids. Did your father take Jr. to the birthday party?"

"Yes, Mom," Barbara answered.

As they reached the bottom of the bags, there were no chips, cookies, or soda — signs of disappointment came over their faces.

"We should have gone to the birthday party with Billy, Jr.," Claudia sighed. "I know he's eating cupcakes, nachos, hot dogs, hot wings, and birthday cake."

"Hopefully not," Brenda mumbled.

"Where are our favorite chips? What are natural chips? Fig Newtons?" Claudia asked looking disturbed. "I don't like Fig Newtons. What about my grape juice, Mom?"

"I want us to start eating more fresh fruit. There are some oranges, bananas, and strawberries in Barbara's bag. Help Mommy out and finish putting away the groceries. I'll be back."

Brenda went upstairs to straighten up the bedrooms.

I think I'm going to email Trevor and get his thoughts on bike riding and other activities. How am I going to explain healthy eating to the kids? They looked so disappointed with not having their favorites. Am I going about this the wrong way? Trying to go from A to Z without the upgrades? Going from no fast food, no sodas, and no processed foods to fruit and vegetables? Aunt Sally did say that small changes would make a difference.

Outside her bedroom window, Brenda heard the closing of car doors. *I guess Billy and Jr. are home from the birthday party.*

Moments later, Brenda heard Billy Jr. running up the stairs yelling for her. He ran into her bedroom.

"Mommy, I had a great time at Trustin's birthday party. Can I have Spiderman cupcakes at my birthday party? He had Spiderman *everything!* We played games — Stick the Spider on Spiderman and Web Walk. It was FUN!"

"It sounds like fun," she responded. "Where's your father?"

"He's in the garage. Trustin got a basketball goal for his birthday. Can I get one?"

"We'll see when you get a little older. Let's go downstairs."

She felt this would be the best opportunity to talk to the kids. Claudia and Barbara were sitting in the living room watching a *That's So Raven* DVD.

"Hey, Jr., what did you eat at Trustin's party?" Claudia asked Billy Jr. as he reached the end of the stairs.

"We had Spiderman cupcakes, chili-cheese nachos, chili-cheese hotdogs, and soda pop. It was great! We played games and won candy," Billy Jr. responded. "We played with Trustin's basketball goal."

As Billy Jr. rambled on about the party, Brenda visualized all the unhealthy foods he had eaten. The nachos, hotdogs — all the things Aunt Sally had talked about avoiding.

"Kids, come into the kitchen with me," Brenda said. Seating Claudia, Barbara, and Billy Jr. around the kitchen table, she started by saying, "As you all know, Mommy has been a little sick—"

Billy Jr. shouted, "You're not going to die, are you?"

"No, baby, Mommy is not going to die," Brenda responded quickly.

"Did the fighting with Dad make you sick, Mom?" Barbara asked, looking worried. "He always yells at you."

"No, honey." She began to explain to the kids about her condition. "I have a condition called pre-diabetes."

"What is that?" Claudia asked.

"When we eat, our body takes the sugar from the food and turns it into fuel. The sugar fuel is called glucose."

"What is glucose used for?" Barbara asked.

"Our body uses glucose for energy, so it can do everything from blinking our eyelids to reading a book to washing dishes. In order for our bodies to use the glucose, we need a hormone known as insulin to transport it into our body's cells."

"What is a hormone, and where does insulin come from?" Barbara asked.

"Hormones are special chemicals your body makes to help it do certain things — like helping it grow. Insulin primarily comes from the pancreas, an organ near the stomach," Brenda said, touching Barbara's stomach. "Now, back to the pre-diabetes: my sugar fuel is higher than normal and will make me sick if I don't start eating better."

"And Grandma will have to come and take care of us again," Barbara said, standing up to hug her mother.

"Right. I could get much sicker if I don't start eating better. I also need the three of you to eat good with me so you don't get sick, either. Instead of nachos, chicken nuggets, hotdogs, cookies, chips, candy, and soda, we need to drink more water and eat more fruit and vegetables. I promise to make the food good so you'll like it," Brenda explained, motioning for Barbara to sit beside her.

"We can't eat anymore chocolate chip cookies, cheddar cheese potato chips, peanut butter candy bars, or cherry vanilla soda?" Barbara asked.

"I'm not saying we can't ever eat those foods again. I'm saying we need to reduce the amount that we eat. Those foods contain a lot of bad stuff, and we can't keep eating bad stuff everyday."

"What's the bad stuff, Mommy?" Claudia asked.

"Sodas, cookies, chips, and ice cream sandwiches. Between the five of us, we go through a large box of chocolate chip cookies, a 12-pack of soda, and a box of ice cream sandwiches in a day. Eating like that at such a young age can increase your chances of getting sick with a disease."

"Turner, one of my classmates, must have diabetes. He doesn't drink soda and has to check his blood sugar after lunch. When he takes medicine, he also has to eat foods called GI or something. What does that mean, Mom?" Claudia inquired.

Brenda explained that Turner was probably talking about foods on the glycemic index (GI). "The glycemic index (GI) provides an estimate of how fast a food item affects our blood sugars. When certain foods enter our bodies, go through the digestive processes, and enter the blood, they cause sudden and drastic spikes of sugar in our bloodstream. This makes the insulin have to work harder."

"Are they foods we like to eat?" Barbara asked.

"Yes. They're donuts, muffins, candy bars, popcorn, potato chips, fruit juices, white bread, and white rice. Foods that don't cause spikes include broccoli, sweet potatoes, apples, and cherries."

"Mommy, I don't want you to get sick again. I'll eat my vegetables," Billy Jr. said, sounding frightened as he hugged her.

Brenda reassured the kids that she and their family would be okay.

Eavesdropping from the garage door, Billy listened to their conversation. He realized that he had taken advantage of his wife for far too long. He made Brenda, Claudia, Barbara, and Billy Jr. victims of his unhappiness with self. To hear his children proclaim their love for her caused him to take a hard look at himself. The kids were willing to do whatever was necessary to protect and save their mother; he remembered feeling that same way about his mother.

I have to get my act together. Mom would be so disappointed in me. I squandered the money she left me. She made me promise I wouldn't end up like my dad. He caused her so much pain and hardship with his gambling addiction — trying to get rich overnight.

Remembering the past, he was finally able to admit to himself that he was desolate in spirit because of the impact his decisions had on his family. His boredom and dissatisfaction with his job at the chemical plant consumed him. When he worked as an engineer assistant at the firm, he enjoyed the exciting challenges of helping design roads and bridges. In his current job, he had to work twice as many hours just to earn a fraction of the pay. His family had no health insurance, and their financial debt was out of control — his isolating and unaccommodating behavior was like poison flowing through their lives.

After thirty minutes of listening to Brenda's conversation with the kids, he bowed his head next to the door and knelt down to pray.

Lord, what have I been doing to my wife and family? Your Word says a man who finds a wife findeth a good thing. I'm praying for Your guidance and direction as I try to repair the damage I've caused and restore love and happiness in my household. Lord, before I got married, I didn't expect each day to be a bed of roses, but I never imagined the kind of challenges I've faced. I'm confused, lost, and hurt, and the pain I feel is unbearable. When I took my vows, I meant them. I was committed to my wife, our marriage, and our love. I need Your help, Lord. I don't know what to do. I feel like I'm backed into a corner and don't know how to get out. I know I need to be released from my compulsion to spend. Help me, Lord. Help me be the man You'd have me to be, which is a loving and devoted husband and father.

Billy realized it was time for him to reclaim his status in the family and prove to Brenda that the man she married fourteen years ago still existed. He thanked God for His faithfulness and for answering his prayers. Billy knew that it was because of God that the course of the casino trip was altered.

He nervously entered the kitchen. "Kids, let me have a moment with your mom," he requested while closing the door behind him.

"Dad, Mom was telling us about her pre-diabetes. Did you know about it?" Barbara asked. She stood up slowly and walked forward, stopping in front of him. Claudia and Billy Jr. remained seated.

"Yes, honey, I know about it. That's what I want to talk to your mom about," he said touching Barbara on her shoulder.

A concern and uncertain look overshadowed Brenda's face. She frowned in confusion.

"Okay, Dad," Claudia said. She stood up and proceeded to direct her sister and brother out of the room.

Brenda watched the kids leave the room, looking at their father intensely. In a concerned tone, she asked, "Is everything okay, Billy?"

"I just needed to talk to you alone." He walked sadly toward her.

She hurried across the kitchen to put up the remainder of the groceries. "How was your day with the kids?" she asked.

Billy grabbed her hands and held them tightly. To her surprise, Billy broke his silence, suddenly professing his love for her. He apologized profusely for the way he had treated her for such a long time. Brenda stood frozen, hanging onto every word he was saying.

He drew her closer to him. "From the moment I met you fifteen years ago, I knew I'd spend the rest of my life with you. I knew you'd be the mother of my children. I knew we'd have a wonderful life together. What I didn't know was that there would be turbulence along the way. I didn't really understand how my decisions affected you and the kids. I've made so many mistakes financially, and now we're barely making it because of them. It's just... when I lost my job and had to settle for lower pay, I couldn't handle it. We had reached this higher standard of living, and I couldn't fathom not staying there," Billy said, his eyes tearing up.

"Where is all this coming from, Billy?" Brenda asked, pulling away from him in shock. "Just give me a moment to process this—"

Grabbing a hold of her, he continued, "Hearing you and the kids. I'm so sorry. To hear Barbara talk about me yelling at you — the worry in her tone. If only I'd been more conservative with our spending when the money was good. Instead, the larger home, the larger SUV, the new furniture, the plasma TV, the real estate risks, and the cost of refurbishing my old cars has slaughtered our bank accounts and created a cargo load of credit card debt. Now you're sick, and we barely have enough money to pay medical expenses," Billy said, trying to hold back tears. "My selfish acts — I never thought enough of my family to prepare for the future or uncertain times. That layoff put me in a state of depression; it's hard being saddled in a job with no future."

"Billy, if you are serious about turning things around, our lives can be much different. Phony comments and promises will only make matters worse," Brenda said, unsure about how to proceed.

"Baby, I'm not lying. I am serious," Billy said trying to assure her. "I know you're not going to believe me, but I've spent some time reevaluating those things I've given priority to in my life. And God has revealed some things to me. He has answered my prayers."

"God! What about the way you've treated me? Do you think God approves of that?" she shouted, staring him in the face. "Do you have any idea what it's like to have your spouse make intentional and hurtful comments toward you? Do you know what it's like to have a spouse whose actions and decisions wreak havoc on the family both emotionally and financially? Do you know what it's like not to have your spouse's concern or support when you're facing a potentially serious medical condition? Of course not!"

He hugged her tightly and pressed her head into his shoulder, as she cried. "Baby, there's no excuse for my behavior, and I want to apologize for how I've treated you and neglected you, and for hanging out with my friends and putting them before my family. I'm sorry for always unleashing my anger on you, for being negative and irritable, and for my explosive temper."

"What we shared in the beginning — I never would have

imagined you turning your back on it," Brenda said, wiping her face.

"I know... I know…" Billy admitted. "I hope you haven't given up on me." He grabbed a kitchen towel to help her wipe her face.

Admitting the inexcusable trauma he had put them through with his drinking, gambling, and spending, Billy vowed to reconcile his relationships with Brenda and the kids. He confessed to owing money to several of his friends, stating that he was worried about their safety. While opening up about his many indiscretions, though, he conveniently omitted his secretive weekend excursions with his friends to party houses, where he'd had sex with exotic women.

"Billy, I love you and will always love you," Brenda stated, embracing him.

"I've just been feeling so depressed and helpless," Billy said. He buried his head in Brenda's shoulder and began crying uncontrollably. "I just can't see a way out of the depths of our financial debt. All I ever think about is how I wanted to go back to school to get my engineering license. That license was supposed to secure our future financially."

Billy's confession brought more tears to Brenda eyes. She had longed for peace between them. She admitted to Billy that she felt as if she were being eaten alive — the life being sucked out of her. While expressing the pain and hurt she had endured for so long, Brenda reached for another kitchen towel to wipe Billy's face.

Ignoring their parents' discussion, the kids ran into the kitchen one by one.

"Mom, Claudia won't let me look at That's So Raven," Barbara said, looking at her parents for intervention.

"Jr. and I want to look at something else," Claudia said, pushing Barbara to the side. "Mom and Dad, have you been crying?"

Billy told the kids to settle down and have a seat at the kitchen table. Unsure about his reason for telling them to do so, they walked reluctantly to the table. Billy explained to the kids that things would be different in their household and that they would be spending more time together as a family.

"I love you guys so much." He kissed their heads one by one and hugged them tightly.

For nearly thirty minutes, he talked to them about their mother's medical condition and the reasons for his unkind behavior, apologizing and assuring them that things would be different. After he finished, Brenda ushered the kids out of the kitchen so she could have more time alone with Billy. Continuing their conversation, Billy shared with Brenda that the chemical plant had a management position available and that he was going to apply for it.

"Baby, sit down," Billy said, positioning the chair for Brenda. "Our lives are going to be better. No more contract work. The position is a permanent job with benefits — benefits for you and kids. And no more overtime!" he shouted.

Brenda was excited about the news, especially since she was facing the unplanned costs of routine doctor visits and medication. The cost associated with her recent visit — the office visit, blood work, and medication — had drained their household budget for the next three months. The thought of having to pay $175 for future doctor visits and other related costs overwhelmed her.

"See, there *is* the possibility of a future at the chemical plant. What are the chances of you getting the job?" Brenda asked.

"I have a pretty good chance, considering my background. Actually, the plant manager encouraged me to apply for the position," Billy replied.

"Great, baby. I know you'll get it," Brenda said, thrilled about the possibilities. "I've been thinking about applying for positions in other departments."

"What's wrong? I thought you liked your department."

"I like the type of work I do, but the bosses are becoming hard to work for; they ride the employees for no apparent reason. If I could just go to work, do my job, and not have to deal with the petty stuff, it would be ideal; unfortunately, that's not the case. My supervisor spends most of her day walking around trying to find things to complain about. If it's too noisy, she complains, not realizing that she's causing the most noise. The communication is bad. No clear direction about anything. They're not trying to provide us with any instructions on the new court system they recently implemented. People are getting fired for job performance issues, most of which are not valid. One lady at work has been in and out caring for her husband, who had a heart attack. He eventually had to go on dialysis and has been pretty bad off for a while. After her family and medical leave ended, they terminated her for job performance. Anyway, I might be able to get a promotion to another area. I'm gonna start looking around. First things first, I need to get my health status under control. I don't want my illness to be the reason for me getting fired."

"You've had to deal with drama at work and at home."

"Well, at least home back is on track now."

"I've got so many things running through my head," Billy said. "I'm gonna get us out of debt. First, though, I've got to get these guys off my trail."

"What guys?"

"Just some guys I've borrowed money from," Billy said, reluctant to share any additional information.

"How much money do you owe?"

"Baby, don't worry about the details. I've got everything under control."

"I can borrow some money from my mother."

"No, I don't want to borrow from your mother. I got us into this mess, and I'll get us out. I've first got to learn how to restrict and restrain myself from my spending compulsion. I need for you to trust me. I need for you to allow me to be in control. I need for you to believe in me. Please don't give up on me. When we exchanged our vows fourteen years ago — to love and to cherish, for better or for worse, for richer or for poorer, in sickness or in health, till death do us part — I meant them."

"I know you did, honey. A lot of our problems have to do with your relationship with Clyde," Brenda suggested.

Holding her hands tightly, Billy hesitated before continuing, "Baby, I can't solely blame Clyde. I'm the one who's allowed outside relationships to come before my family. The other day we were hanging out, and the guys started talking about Carl: he and his wife had to file for bankruptcy."

"Carl and his wife are filing for bankruptcy?" Brenda said, surprised. "They just bought that big home in Glen Estates. Those homes start at $350,000."

"With a combined income of $85,000, they should have never bought that house; still, hearing the comments Clyde, Dwight, and Stanley made as they talked about Carl's troubles was disturbing. That information should have been confidential. There was no sense of loyalty, compassion, or support. It was a clear sign for me that people by your side aren't necessarily *on* your side. I realized that I've wasted so much of my time trying to please and accommodate folks who couldn't care less about me, time that should have been focused on my family. Please forgive me, Brenda. Forgive me for using you as my personal punching bag. Forgive me for transferring my anger, guilt, regret, confusion, and shame onto you. I know that my actions now must seem like some miraculous return from the dead, but I'm truly sorry, and I want to make things right between us."

As Billy continued talking, Brenda thought about his hobbies and the cars. She wished he would consider selling the three classic cars, which he inherited after his father's death and had spent so much money on restoring. Then there were the jet skis they never rode and the boat that sat idle at Joe Mann's Lake, both of which were costing them exorbitant storage fees. While he was confessing, Brenda wished he would mention selling those items, but she remained silent as he kept talking.

"I know some guys who are interested in buying the cars, and the money would give us an opportunity to pay down some of the debt and have some emergency funds in the bank," Billy said. "Also, I don't need the boat. The storage and maintenance is killing us. I could run an ad for the boat and jet skis on eBay. They're over ten years old, so I don't know how much they're worth — Baby, I need to make up for so much. When I made a vow to you, it included loving, protecting, and providing for you. I apologize for drifting away and leaving you to fend for yourself."

Jumping up and down inside, Brenda supported the idea of selling the cars, the boat, and the jet skis. She said a quiet prayer as he continued talking, *Thank You, Lord, for answering my prayers.*

CHAPTER 11

Facing the Dawning
of a New Day

*H*appier times in the Mishun household returned, and Brenda was ready to erase their past and embrace their future.

"Are we going to church this morning?" Barbara asked as she entered her parents' bedroom. She always looked forward to Children's Church — particularly the singing, reading Bible scriptures, and the worshiping experience. "We've got to ask God to make you better again."

"Yes, baby, we're going to church. Go wake up your sister and brother," Brenda said, tired but motivated by Barbara's enthusiasm.

Brenda was a Sunday school teacher and participated in many church events. She liked her church because they had educational offerings specifically designed to help kids grow in their relationship with God. Recognizing the importance of modeling her spiritual life for her children, she expressed her love for God and the church routinely. She made sure they prayed at home and read scriptures;

Billy, on the other hand, had rarely gone to church with them.

"Are you going to church with us this morning?" Brenda asked, nestled in Billy's arms.

"I think I will go with you this morning," Billy replied, after a significant, silent pause.

"Honey, I really need your support in a huge way," Brenda said.

"Anything — What is it?" Billy questioned.

"We've got to start eating healthier and exercising."

Billy held Brenda tight. "Don't worry about the healthier eating; I'll support whatever changes you make. I understand just how bad things can turn out if we don't change our habits, and, hopefully, the changes will allow me to eat a steak occasionally."

"I think it's time we pulled out the bikes. My Aunt Sally connected me with a fitness person, Trevor, who gave me free a consultation. He gave me some great advice on eating healthier."

Billy responded, "Nothing is 'free', baby. 'Free' usually turns into a package deal."

"I know we don't have a lot of extra money, but even if he charges us for additional advice on exercising, it'll be worth it. Plus, it's his business, and I don't want it to seem like we're trying to take advantage of him."

"It's okay with me."

"Great! I don't want to put off getting active. I think I'm going to email Trevor after church and get his thoughts on bike riding and other activities."

Overwhelmed with happiness, Brenda leaped out of bed and headed toward the bathroom. Smiling in the mirror, she thanked God for all He had done for them.

Lord, I know You're aware of all things — our pain, suffering, and despair, but did You allow my illness to mend my marriage? I trust You and Your Word, and I know everything happens for a reason to fulfill Your destiny for us. I'm just glad You're in the business of reversing adverse situations, and I thank You for reversing mine.

On their way to church, the children's voices filled the car with laughter and songs of praise. It was important to Brenda that the entire family attend church to learn more about God and develop a relationship with Him. Because Brenda had grown up in the church, she looked forward to the religious training they received each week. She always read the Bible, attended worship service regularly, and had an active prayer life. She looked forward to fellowshipping with other believers, and she relied on her spiritual foundation to equip her with discovering new ways to handle daily challenges more appropriately.

The pastor's sermon about relationships and God's expectations brought tears to Billy's eyes. The pastor stated that it was time for men to step up and be good spouses.

"Men, I'm concerned about our role as husbands and fathers. If we invested the kind of time, energy, and money on our relationships with our spouses that we do on ourselves — I'm talking about hanging out with the guys, going on weekend excursions alone, buying expensive gadgets and electronics — then the divorce rate would go down dramatically."

The pastor shared passages in the Bible that illustrated how loving relationships are the key to healthy family values. He stated that those values included treating each other responsibly with respect and pride, respecting the differences of others, and being truthful and caring to others. He continued by adding, "The core of family values is not about the number or gender of parents; it has to do with loving relationships that encourage our kids to be kind, caring, respectable, and productive adults who love and worship our Lord and Savior Jesus Christ."

Walking to their car, Billy commented on the church service. "I really enjoyed the message. You've gotten to know quite a few of the members."

"Yes, everyone is warm and inviting. I like Pastor Albring because he's humble and devoted to teaching the pure Word."

Brenda was hoping Billy's attendance was a sign of a new beginning. Since joining Bethel Community Church, she had met a large number of the members. Genuine concerns regarding the whereabouts of her husband often left Brenda feeling guilty and shameful when she made excuses for his absence. She tagged this day as a day of resurrected rituals for their family, a day of hope and promise. No more feelings of being abandoned, ashamed, embarrassed, or guilty because Billy was at home and not with his family at church.

"Are we gonna eat at The Soul Food Kitchen?" Claudia asked as they walked to the parking lot after service.

"I think it would be fun to go back home and experiment with cooking some of the healthy foods I bought yesterday," Brenda said.

"Do we have to start today? We always go out for soul food on Sundays," Claudia replied, disappointed.

"I know, sweetie, but the food at the restaurant really isn't good for us. Remember what we talked about yesterday?"

Brenda explained the unhealthy attributes of sweet potatoes swimming in sugar and butter, collard greens swimming in salt pork, macaroni and cheese made with seven different cheeses, chicken and fish fried in unhealthy oils.

"All those foods are high in calories, sodium, cholesterol, carbohydrates, and fat, which are all the things we want to reduce and learn to cook healthier at home. Yesterday, I bought some chicken, so we're going to start with that first. Don't worry, kids. We're going to figure out how to make our favorite foods healthy and tasty. I also bought a healthy cookbook that'll help us," Brenda said.

Brenda encouraged the kids to pretend that they were completing a homework assignment to develop a plan for eating healthier and living longer without depriving themselves. Her goal was to promote an appreciation of better health, which she had learned was paramount for developing a legacy of lifelong healthy habits.

Turning into the driveway, Billy Jr. and Barbara were eager to help in the kitchen. They ran upstairs to change their clothes. Claudia remained downstairs, making it known that she wasn't particularly interested in participating in the cooking adventure.

"How long will all this take? We could be eating right now — had we gone to The Soul Food Kitchen like we always do," Claudia said in an impudent tone. "Right now, I could be eating their Grandma's Meatloaf and famous banana pudding."

"Claudia, we're all gonna take part in cooking the family meal today," Billy replied firmly.

"Don't yell at me like you do Mom!" Claudia shouted out.

Shocked and disturbed by her reaction, Brenda walked toward her. "What did you say, Claudia?"

"It's okay, Brenda," Billy said, trying to intervene.

"No, it's not okay. We don't talk to grown-ups like that in this house. Now, go to your room. I'll be up to deal with you in a minute."

Claudia ran out of the kitchen, shoving Jr. out of her way as he and Barbara entered the kitchen.

"I'd better go," Billy said. "Barbara and Jr., help your mother."

Brenda interrupted him as he began to leave out. "She'll be okay. Let's start with the chicken."

"Brenda, remember my role with the kids," Billy said, staring at her before he left out.

Billy had shared with her how for years he felt like he had

no say so in the rearing of his children and how he expected to be an integral part of their lives. There would no longer be solo decisions related to their education, medical, religion, outside activities, or discipline.

"How can we make fried chicken and macaroni and cheese healthy?" Barbara asked.

"First, we can take the skin off the chicken and use egg whites and bread crumbs to add the crispy texture for taste. Then we can bake it in the oven rather than frying it in oil. And for the macaroni and cheese, we'll use the whole-wheat elbow pasta, with 1% milk and the reduced-fat cheddar cheese," Brenda explained.

"What about the collard greens you bought? The only way to cook collards is with salt pork like Dad's mom use to use," Barbara suggested.

"Your Aunt Sally gave me a recipe that excludes meat; the meat we traditionally use, like salt pork, ham hocks, or even turkey legs are either high in fat or sodium or both," Brenda said.

Moments later Billy and Claudia came into the kitchen, and Brenda asked them to prepare the collard greens. Claudia remained silent while helping her father cut out the tough stems of the collard greens and wash them thoroughly. The recipe received from her Aunt Sally included fresh tomatoes and 'no salt added' tomato sauce. Billy and Claudia rinsed the torn leaves, placed them in a large pan, and watched them wilt over a medium-low heat. Billy stirred them constantly and asked Claudia to add the combination of basil, oregano, rosemary seasonings, and chopped tomatoes to the large pan. He continued stirring about five minutes longer. He instructed Claudia to add the 'no salt added' tomato sauce. Minutes later, they had created a healthy version of collard greens.

∞

The family sat in the dining room eating and enjoying their time together. Brenda couldn't remember the last time they sat down together as a family at the dinner table; Billy usually ate his Sunday meal in the family room while watching football or some other sport. The kids sat at the dinner table long enough to down their food hastily. This day was the first of many for them to share their lives and enhance their relationships with one another.

While at the dinner table, Brenda had the perfect opportunity to introduce the idea of exercise to the family. Exercising as a family was an added bonus for strengthening their connection, but it could also serve as the chance to lay the foundation of making regular physical fitness a priority for a lifetime.

"What do you kids think about us exercising? You all have new bikes that you've barely ridden." Brenda said.

"I think it's a great idea. We can ride at the White Rock Lake," Billy interjected.

"Do we have to?" Claudia questioned.

Claudia avoided outdoor activities like the plague. Brenda figured it was because she was self-conscious about her weight. Rather than expose herself to the ridicule of the neighborhood kids, her free time was spent watching TV shows and music videos and playing video games.

Brenda blamed herself for the kids' unhealthy habits. Without any thought of recourse, she accepted the fact that physical education had been cut from their school curricula due to tight budget cuts and to make room for academic programs. She was one of the millions of parents neglectful in promoting physical activities at home.

"I was thinking we could pull out the bikes and start riding at least two or three evenings every week. I bought some protective gear for all of us yesterday," Brenda said.

"I don't want to ride. Are you gonna make me?" Claudia reiterated.

"Your brother and sister would really like to go, and we can't leave you at home by yourself, Claudia," Billy said.

"I promise you we're gonna have fun. You know I love you, don't you?" Brenda said. "I wouldn't ask you to try anything that wasn't good for you."

"Yes, I know," Claudia replied solemnly.

"Great! Who wants to help me wash the car after we finish eating?" Brenda asked, anticipating the participation of all the kids.

"I want to help!" Billy Jr. yelled out.

"Me, too, Mom!" Barbara shouted.

"What about you, Claudia?" Brenda asked, unsure about her response.

"I'd rather go back to my room," Claudia said grudgingly.

Billy and Brenda looked at one another, then Billy responded, "Claudia, you don't have to go out with us, but I do want you to start thinking about some activities you might want to do."

Billy and Brenda recognized that they needed to be patient with Claudia; they would work with her to find an activity she liked. The first step was for them to be role models; if Claudia saw them having fun while being physically active, she would be more likely to participate and develop an appreciation for being and staying active. They didn't want to push her into an activity that she wouldn't enjoy, possibly turning her off to a lifetime of fitness.

Everyone trotted outside to engage in the family's first official group physical activity — except Claudia. A month ago, Brenda never would have considered washing her own car, a chore she normally left for Don's Car Wash. The kids were excited about doing something new, though, and Brenda was excited that they were spending a different type of time together. It wasn't about cooking, cleaning, doing homework, or listening to disgruntled kids; it was about having fun. Brenda instructed the kids on how to gather the essentials: the bucket, cleaning solution, towels, and water hose. Unable to contain themselves, Jr. and Barbara began pushing and shoving one another to get the products.

"Okay, kids. Billy Jr., you get the bucket. Barbara, go ask your father for the cleaning solution and towels off the shelves," Brenda instructed. "I'll get the water hose."

Brenda explained everyone's role in the car washing process. The children took pride in washing their respective sections of the car, enjoying the warm sudsy water. The activity took two hours longer than Brenda expected, but a behind-the-car-door view of their reactions to the new experience was worth it.

Later that night, while they were lying in bed, Brenda shared with Billy the joy she felt watching the kids that afternoon.

"Baby, we've gotta stay on track with healthier habits to make up for the bad habits we've fostered and let linger in our household for so long. I emailed the Trevor for some fitness advice; I need to see if he's responded back to me."

"As their parents, we should have been setting a better example of what's right and what's wrong. But, considering our upbringing, it's no wonder," Billy said. "Is this fitness expert gonna charge us?"

"Aunt Sally says he's generous with giving free advice," Brenda replied. "You're right, though: we've basically eaten like our parents did."

"Yeah, my mom probably could have lived longer. But, a lifetime of homemade biscuits and gravy, pancakes, sausages, eggs, grits, pork chops, and beef may have shortened her lifespan," Billy said.

"Don't worry, things will be different for us and the kids," Brenda said with assurance. "We're not gonna jump on the 'blame wagon.' We're adults — parents — and we're responsible for the standards we establish for our kids."

"I'm sorry you got sick — but, if you hadn't, we probably would never have changed our unhealthy habits," Billy said, hugging her. "With your research and the information from Aunt Sally and Dr. Robert, we know so much more about what it takes to be healthier. Even when my mother died, I didn't ask questions. I just accepted that she was gone and that she died from a series of ailments. I should have sought more answers about the cause of her death. There are probably some hereditary factors I need to consider — not only for me, but also for the kids."

"We're gonna be more active and get the kids more active. I'm thinking we can stop paying for lawn service and start doing it ourselves. We can rake and blow our own leaves, dig and plant our own garden. Our lives have become so saturated with what's quick and convenient — remote controls, push button appliances, and paying others to do what we can do ourselves, like washing the cars," Brenda said.

"Right," Billy agreed. "Back in the day, it was easier for us to get exercise. Number one, we didn't have all these modern-day luxuries. I remember walking everywhere — to and from school, the grocery store, the library, and the park. Of course, it was much safer to do it back then, plus, the places we went to were closer."

"My mom made us walk everywhere. In this new day and age, we don't have the luxury of nearby stores and other places to keep us physically active," Brenda said. "I'm gonna start getting the kids more involved in the household chores. Plus, it's important that we teach them the principles of sharing and accepting responsibilities."

"I want to make sure you get the break you deserve from all the responsibilities around here," Billy said apologetically.

"Let's go downstairs and see if Trevor's emailed me," Brenda said, grabbing Billy's hand.

The two of them went to the computer in the family room, and Brenda signed on to her email account.

"He did. Let me print out the information so we can see what he's saying." Brenda printed the document and scrolled down the page, looking over Trevor's comments. "He says he teaches an aerobics class at the recreation center on Crossland Drive."

"I've seen that rec center; one of the guys at work lives near it. It's about twenty minutes from here," Billy said.

"I'd love to take an aerobics class," Brenda said. "He's listed some classes for the kids, the times, and their costs. When I spoke with Aunt Sally, she mentioned participating in exercise classes at her local recreation center."

"And?..."

"They have classes for dance and gymnastics, exercise, aquatics, and youth sports. It looks like they offer a wide variety at this center, too."

"How much?" Billy inquired, getting a chair so he could sit next to her.

"The costs are not that much. We can reallocate the money we save from the lawn and car wash services to a fitness account."

"How much?"

"The prices vary. The aerobics class on Mondays from 6 P.M. to 7 P.M. is free, but the one on Mondays and Wednesdays from 7 P.M. to 8 P.M. is $3 per session."

"What's the difference between the free one and the one that costs $3 per session?"

"I don't know. Let's check out the center's website," Brenda said, clicking on the website link Trevor provided. "In the free one you work out to a video; the other one has an instructor. The one with a cost says it encompasses the three components of physical fitness: cardio-endurance, flexibility, and strength. There's also a youth/teen nutrition and fitness program. They evaluate diets and show the kids fun and effective workout techniques."

"That might be fine for the girls, but what about my boy?" Billy asked. "I need him involved in sports."

"Okay, they have junior NBA basketball and karate/tae kwon do."

"That's more like it. How much is the basketball?" Billy asked with excitement.

"I believe it's around $40 per player. Barbara's expressed an interest in dance and gymnastics, and I'd like for her to take one of the two."

"How much?"

"The dance class is $30 per month, and the tumbling class is $30 for four weeks."

"What about Claudia?"

"I don't know yet. I'll ask her," Brenda said, sounding distressed. "I'm so worried about her. The likelihood of high blood pressure, high blood cholesterol, stroke, diabetes, and other diseases are greater because of our lifestyle and her size. I've read that a major consequence of overweight and obese children is a lack of confidence and self-esteem."

"Instead of letting our kids spend their free time watching TV, surfing the Internet, and playing videos, we'll start helping them lead healthy lifestyles. Let's figure out the costs," Billy responded, retrieving a calculator. "Okay! The costs of all these activities we're talking about will be — if you do the aerobics class, that's $30 a month. The basketball for Billy Jr. is $40 per player. The dance class for Barbara is $30 a month. And we're just gonna guesstimate that Claudia's activity will be around $30 a month. That's around $130. Wow! Anything cheaper?"

"We do a lot of wasteful spending. I'm sure when we start evaluating the things we need to eliminate, like the lawn service costing us $90 per month, the $130 won't be a huge undertaking. The annual family membership for the recreation center is $300, with no enrollment fee, and it includes access to the fitness center with all the cardio and strength training equipment, swimming pool, and basketball and volleyball courts. The additional costs stem from the various specialized activities that generally have instructors, like the dance, gymnastics, aquatics, tumbling, and aerobics classes," Brenda said.

"There's a group of guys at work that play basketball on Thursdays. I probably need to get some better shoes, but I'd like to do that with them."

"Are you talking about Clyde and the boys?"

"No, honey! I'm talking about some other guys — ones with family values."

"Okay! Again, what about Claudia? I'm hoping she'll follow our commitment to exercise," Brenda paused. "She needs a lot of encouragement, Billy."

"There are a lot of activities at the rec center. Hopefully, she'll agree to something. Plus, when we go bike riding, I'll stay with her. You can concentrate on Barbara and Billy Jr."

"Can you work on the bikes tomorrow?"

"Yeah, I'll make sure they're all working fine."

After a few months, the Mishuns' journey to a healthier lifestyle had paid off. Trevor played a pivotal role in their lives, often providing valuable fitness tips. Brenda's blood sugar levels were within the normal range. By simply making changes to her diet and increasing her level of physical activity, she was able to remove herself from the perilous path to diabetes. Best of all, she didn't have to take the medication; better habits had become their vehicle to a longer, healthier life.

The kids emerged from the captivity of life's conveniences and technology by fostering healthier hands-on options: stovetop cooking rather than microwaving. Hand washing the dishes rather than machine washing. Hand car washing rather than the automatic drive through. Raking the leaves rather than using the blower. Manually changing the television channel rather than using the remote. The vicious cycle of eating junk food and fast food were replaced with a creative style of eating fruits and vegetables. They were no longer couch potatoes; they played outside on the driveway, jumped rope, played hopscotch, and reinvented that old familiar *Tag! You're It*, a game Billy and Brenda remembered playing as kids. Although Brenda and Billy were focused on the kids being healthier, they were pleased that Claudia was looking a size healthier; she had taken an interest in gymnastics.

As for Billy, the cargo load of anger, regret, shame, selfishness, disappointment, and unworthiness that he'd hauled around for years was finally unhitched as he excelled in his roles as husband and father. He and Brenda put together a realistic plan that maintained open channels of daily communication, respect for one another, staying emotionally and physically connected, and managing their stresses. They were united in fostering a marriage built on love, honesty, and stability, and the days of secret getaways, gambling excursions, and spending escapades came to an end.

Billy was finally promoted after several failed attempts at moving up, and the family's health was protected by the insurance coverage granted by his new job. Because of their lifestyle transformations, Billy and Brenda were able to reduce their accumulated debt and start saving. Billy sold his classic cars, the boat, and jet skis on eBay and was able to pay off his gambling debts. Those, as well as other major lifestyle changes, financed their first official family vacation trip to Florida.

After being promoted to senior courtroom clerk, Brenda was able to escape the confinement of an unhealthy work environment. She started classes at the local community college so she could move closer to her goal of being promoted to courtroom supervisor. In her heart, she knew her faith had everything to do with the progress of her health and her relationship with Billy and the kids. The family was a cohesive unit with a solid foundation, able to withstand and overcome the adversities of life. Furthering her commitment to raise selfless, caring kids, they entered and walked in various charity fundraisers. Billy committed to attending church regularly, and he also volunteered at many 'Keep the Neighborhood Clean' programs.

Brenda's life wasn't just about her husband and kids; she was experiencing the freedom of being fit and living her life the way God had planned.

With a deeper understanding of the importance of lifestyle changes, Brenda was moved to approach Pastor Albring with her idea to have the church sponsor a Fall community health fair to increase health awareness. She shared with him her previous health concerns, particularly how for a long time neither she nor her family had medical insurance. She was concerned that a large number of their members, as well people in the community, did not have medical insurance, which affected their ability to get the necessary health screenings. Pleased with her initiative and comprehensive plan, Pastor Albring supported her idea and approved her to work with the church leadership staff to plan the event. As the committee chair, she worked for several months with various individuals and organizations to coordinate a series of health screenings, activities, demonstrations, and information. For individuals without medical insurance, the committee invited several local, state, and federal organizations to provide information about their various services and resources.

The health fair was spectacular and greatly appreciated by the community. Brenda's church received many favorable comments and compliments about the variety of services offered — blood pressure, blood cholesterol, blood glucose (sugar), body mass index (BMI) and prostate screenings. They also had a mammogram unit. Brenda put a tremendous amount of work into planning and was pleased that it was well attended. Pastor Albring praised Brenda for her efforts and expressed his appreciation for her commitment and dedication to the church and the community.

On the eve of New Year's Eve, Brenda knelt to pray, *Oh God, my Lord and Savior Jesus Christ. Lord, I want to thank You for all of the things You brought me through this past year. I knew if I remained faithful and walked in Your Word, You would fix the situation with my marriage, my job, my finances, and my health. I thank You for being what I needed in my life in a time of trouble. And, Father, thank You for giving me the strength to forgive my husband and the supervisor that treated me so badly for so long. Thank You for helping Billy to turn his life around. I ask You to continue to lead and guide me so that I can help him to grow in Your knowledge. Father, I give You all the honor, all the praise, all the glory that You so richly deserve. All these blessings I ask in Your name, for Your namesake, I pray. Amen.*

PART III

The Heel and Forefoot
of the Golden Years

CHAPTER 12

Remembering
a Friend's Journey

*A*s Maurine listened to the expressions of support, encouragement, and tribute made by Beth's family members, friends, and co-workers, her attention was interrupted by thoughts of her lifestyle habits.

Could my eating habits cause me to get cancer or face an untimely death? What if the health reminders I've been ignoring sabotage my dreams of living better and longer after retirement?

Fighting to regain her focus, she zoomed in on the minister's final words of tribute commemorating Beth's life. Unable to concentrate on the minister, she faded in and out of the eulogy. Her thoughts were filled with celebrations of Beth's energy and passion toward the countless number of patients and families she'd served over a career that lasted nearly three decades. She recalled Beth's excitement as she talked about retiring from Methodist Memorial Hospital.

As the minister concluded his message, a cloud of sadness came over Maurine as she stared at the premium stainless steel casket. The funeral directors approached the front, opened the casket, and arranged the tailored gray velvet interior with matching pillow and throw. The old familiar hymn "We're Marching to Zion" led the recessional, and those in attendance stood and began marching around the casket for a final viewing. A week before her retirement, Beth had succumbed to breast cancer at the young age of fifty-four.

Whispers about Beth's sudden death spilled over from the sanctuary to the church corridors as family and friends awaited the processional to the burial grounds. Praises of a person who loved life, family, and the purpose she was placed on Earth to accomplish resonated in the minds of those assembled for the going-home celebration. The last order of business was a twenty-minute drive to Beth's family burial ground, where she and her husband would rest in peace together, just as they were in life. Upon approaching Beth's earthly resting place, Maurine admired the silhouette of cedar and maple trees that surrounded their graves, which were blanketed in peacefulness.

At the conclusion of the graveside service, Pastor Searly spoke an unforgettable prayer. "In sure and certain hope of the resurrection to eternal life through our Lord Jesus Christ, we commend to Almighty God our sister, Beth Miers. We commit her body to the ground, earth to earth, ashes to ashes, dust to dust. The Lord bless her and keep her. The Lord make His face to shine upon her and be gracious unto her and give her peace. Amen."

Back at the church, those who returned to fellowship with the family displayed an emotional mixture of joy and sorrow: joy stemming from the end of Beth's suffering mixed with the sorrow surrounding her absence. No one outside her immediate family was aware that Beth had been sick — at least not sick enough to die. A cancer survivor for nearly five years, Beth knew it had returned, and, as the staggering news of her death reached the multitude of individuals Beth encountered throughout her life, most were shocked.

Groups stood around in the church's cafeteria, chatting and waiting to partake of the lavish spread of generational delights. Moving swiftly, Carey maneuvered her way through the crowd, excited to see Maurine, a longtime friend of Beth's.

"It's good to see you, Maurine. I can't believe Beth is dead. Everyone on my floor is in shock. Did you know she was sick?"

Maurine, still disturbed that Beth hadn't shared the news that her illness had returned, replied, "No, I didn't. I found out the morning she passed. Her daughter-in-law called me at work. Bob, over in radiology, says she found out that her cancer was back about seven months ago."

"Seven months ago? I thought the two of you were close friends," Carey said, surprised.

"I thought so, too. I saw her two weeks ago at the hair salon, and she was excited about her retirement."

"I heard she had breast cancer a few years ago and that it went into remission," Carey responded, surveying the food selections.

"Yes, she did. This time, according to Bob, it attacked her liver. From what I've heard, she started chemotherapy treatments after the doctors found it this second time around," Maurine said. Becoming teary-eyed, she began to look through her purse for some tissue. "Two months ago, I noticed she had lost weight, but it didn't register with me that she could have been ill. She mentioned working out with Trevor, the fitness consultant that comes to the hospital to facilitate healthy living classes on Thursdays. She talked about how she enjoyed his walking session. Then, when I saw her two weeks ago at the hair salon, we talked about her grandchildren and how fast they were growing. I just thought to myself that she looked great."

Looking around at the multitude of family, friends, co-workers, and church members in attendance, Carey said, "That's sad. She was always a petite lady, so why was she working out? Had she been at work?"

"I guess she was working out to be healthier, which is something we should all be doing," Maurine responded. "We worked in different buildings, but I heard she was at work last week. One of our old friends on her floor said she suddenly became ill during her shift. Apparently, she went home early but never returned to work after a visit to her doctor. The saddest part is that her birthday is next week, and her retirement was scheduled for the following week."

"That *is* sad," Carey said.

"I received the invitation to her retirement party a little over a month ago," Maurine said as she hovered over the food table, contemplating her choices. "Are you gonna eat something?"

"Yes, I am. Could you hand me one of those plates? I think I'll just get some of the ham, brisket, macaroni and cheese, and potato salad," Carey said, extending her hand. "Wow! They have a lot of food."

"I know," Maurine replied, handing Carey a plastic plate. "The church bought the catered meat. I think Georgia's Country Kitchen cooked the sides and pastries."

"You know, death at such a young age is heart-wrenching, and I say young because you know fifty is the new forty," Casey said, smiling.

"I've heard that," Maurine responded.

"Retirement is a time we all look forward to: traveling, watching our grandchildren grow up, and doing what we want when we want. Volunteering, exploring new activities, and looking forward to everyday being Saturday," Carey said, picking up a serving spoon to dip into the potato salad. "During the service, her children looked as if they were at peace with her death."

"I'm sure they were hopeful about the treatments, but I think they were probably prepared for the worst," Maurine replied. She picked up a couple pieces of barbecue and fried chicken, then she proceeded to get some of the cornbread dressing and baked beans.

"If you got an invitation to her retirement party a month or so ago, I guess they didn't expect her to go this quickly, or they thought she'd beat the cancer," Carey said.

"I just don't know..." Maurine responded.

"I thought she had three children? I only saw two at the service," Carey said.

"She does have three children. Unfortunately, her oldest daughter, Catherine, is in prison, and Beth was raising her three children. Now, I believe they'll be split between her son and daughter, Brandon and Lorraine."

"How old are Catherine's children?"

"I believe they range in age from four to ten," Maurine said, motioning toward a couple empty seats at a nearby table.

"Why is her daughter in prison?"

"From what I understand, Catherine was involved with a married man who was murdered a couple years ago. Supposedly, Catherine killed him in self-defense, but a jury convicted her of murder."

"Murder?" Carey frowned.

"Yes, murder. What really hurt her case was the fact that she drove around for days with his body in her car, then dumped it in a lake in Mississippi," Maurine said, stopping to pick up a couple buttered rolls.

"She drove from Texas to Mississippi to dispose of a body?" Carey questioned.

"Yes, she did," Maurine responded. "I know the court hearings and appeals took a toll on Beth over the last two years. Since the man had been a prominent businessman in the community, I heard the prosecuting attorneys crucified her daughter in court. She received life in prison. I believe her last child was the murdered man's. Taking care of those children meant the world to Beth. Now, I'm wondering if the stress from it all did her in."

"That's sad," Carey responded, getting a couple cornbread muffins. "Do you believe stress can play a major role in causing the onset of illness and disease — and its reoccurrence?"

"Chronic stress — living under never-ending stressful conditions — can affect your health. Worrying constantly about financial, marital, medical, legal, family, and workplace problems causes our bodies to produce adrenaline, a hormone that speeds up heart rates and produces rapid breathing," Maurine said.

"I've heard that," Carey responded. "Dr. Meyers says there's increasing evidence that stress is a contributing factor to medical conditions like high blood pressure and diabetes. The stress of Catherine's legal problems and the emotional suffering of her kids could have contributed to the return of Beth's cancer."

"And don't forget the financial impact. I know she had to take out a second mortgage on her home to pay for the team of attorneys," Maurine added.

"Wow!"

"Despite the unfortunate turn Catherine took, Beth was most proud of Brandon and Lorraine," Maurine said. "Their successes helped to overshadow her pain, suffering, and disappointment over Catherine's incarceration. They both pursued careers in the medical field. Brandon works as a counselor at the Sterling Diabetic Institute for Kids — a facility for kids with Type 1, insulin-dependent diabetes. Lorraine works as a chemical dependency counselor that focuses on adolescents."

"The other nurses always raved about Beth's work as a counselor. It was often said that she was the best at offering individual and group counseling services for cancer patients and their families. She was passionate and energetic about helping patients cope with the psychological and physical aspects of cancer."

"They're right. She was exceptional at helping them cope with the treatments — providing emotional support, education, and practical self-help techniques," Maurine confirmed. "Plus, she worked with the Healthcare Ministry at her church, giving services to their members and the surrounding community."

"I only hope someone was there to offer the same for her during the last stages of her life," Carey said. Reaching into the container of soft drinks, she stated, "I forgot to get a soda. Would you like one?"

"No, I'll take one of those ice teas," Maurine replied, extending her hand to accept an ice tea from Carey. "Thank you, Carey."

"You're welcome," Carey said.

"I only wish she would have thought more of our friendship to share the return of her cancer with me," Maurine whispered.

"Does the family need anything? I know that in lieu of flowers and money they're asking that donations be forwarded to the American Cancer Society. But, what about the three grandchildren she was caring for?"

"I know Beth planned for their futures," Maurine said, motioning them toward the available seats. "But I also know they'll need our continual prayers."

"I'll put her family on our prayer list at church."

"That's kind of you," Maurine said. "I'm sure the kids would appreciate that."

"I'll call Sister Robinson, our church secretary, tonight and give her the information."

"Carey, it's hard for me to wrap my mind around the fact that she's gone," Maurine stated.

"I know. You were really close to Beth and her family."

"While I was at the house visiting with the family the other night, her grandson, Bobby, asked about his grandmother. He asked why she wasn't at home and why were there so many people in her home. Brandon took him aside and told him that his grandmother had gone to Heaven to be with the Lord."

"I know it was probably hard for Brandon," Carey interrupted.

"He was remarkable. He explained that she died from a disease called cancer. Inquisitive as usual, Bobby asked what cancer was."

"Understanding cancer is complicated for adults, so how did Brandon explain it to a kid?" Carey interjected as she sat down with her plate and began unfolding her napkin.

"He explained to Bobby about the general makeup of the human body and how it's composed of trillions of cells. As simply as possible, he discussed how our body creates cells, replaces them when their life span ends, and regenerates new, healthy cells that keep us living."

"It's a lot more to it than that," Carey said, raising the can of soda to her mouth.

"He went on to say that sometimes, instead of returning back to a normal cell, the cell changes into an abnormal, sometimes harmful cell. Then it has the capability of multiplying quickly without dying, making a lot of other harmful cells. He explained how a tumor then develops, which is when abnormal cells group together in the form of a mass or a lump. He ended by saying that cancer is a disease that happens when the body makes cells that are not normal, and that the countless replicas take over the normal cells and spread to different parts of the body. It mimics the 'bad apple' syndrome, where one bad apple destroys the whole barrel."

"That was a lot for an eleven year old to comprehend. How can you make a kid understand how normal body cells grow and divide — then know to stop growing and die when they've fulfilled their purpose?" Carey inquired. "I sometimes have a hard time understanding how abnormal cells, that is, cancer cells just continue to grow and divide uncontrollably and don't die. Then there's the mystery of what causes them to become abnormal in the first place."

"Brandon did the best he could, under the circumstances. He explained to Bobby that his grandmother's cancer cells lumped together to form a tumor in her breast, and that it made her very sick. He said that the cancer cells broke away from the original tumor and traveled to another area of her body, the liver, where they kept growing and formed new tumors."

"I'm sure after all that Bobby had a lot of questions," Carey stated.

"He did, but mainly he asked why the doctors didn't heal his grandmother," Maurine responded. "Brandon assured him that they did everything imaginable, but the spreading of the cancer cells continued too rapidly, and the doctors couldn't stop their accelerated growth."

"I know that was a lot for a little boy," Carey said, holding back tears, picking at the brisket.

"Yeah, it was, but I think he got the gist of what his father was telling him," Maurine stated. "Bobby is very smart for eleven. He even asked about treatment for his grandmother. Brandon explained that the doctors did everything they could to heal her by using a combination of surgery, chemotherapy, and radiation to rid her body of the cancer."

"Beth was a beautiful person. I'm gonna miss her. She was spunky and tenacious. Everyone who knew her loved her. The comfort is that she's in a better place; no more suffering here on Earth. She loved the Lord with all her heart, and I know she's rejoicing with the angels in Heaven," Carey said.

"You're absolutely right! I know Beth would want us to remember her as one of God's Heaven-bound children," Maurine replied, sitting and staring at her plate.

"I've got to get back to the hospital," Carey said, admiring the pastry table from afar. "I need to put my food in a takeout container. They definitely had all of Beth's favorite desserts — Pecan Pie, Banana Cream Pie, Cream Cheese Pie, Mississippi Mud Cake, German Chocolate Cake, Rum Cake . . ."

"I know that's Georgia's Better-Than-Sex Cake at the edge of the table. All her pastries are made from scratch with real butter, eggs, and milk — whole milk, that is," Maurine added.

"I'm definitely gonna take a slice of that Pecan Pie and German Chocolate Cake to go. I'm working 12-hour shifts for the next four days," Carey said, looking at her watch. "It's been great talking with you, Maurine."

"It was good visiting with you, too. Maybe we can have lunch soon," Maurine replied. "We can talk healthy stuff. I need to start eating better. After listening to the remarks at Beth's funeral, it's evident that people will say wonderful things about you, but at the end of the service their own lives continue."

"Let's set a lunch date for next week," Carey said. "We can meet at Georgia's Country Kitchen."

"Although it's not exactly the 'healthy' I was thinking about, I look forward to it," Maurine confirmed. "We probably need to sign up for Trevor's healthy living class."

"I'll put it on my list of things to do next year," Carey responded, getting up from her seat.

CHAPTER 13

Considering the Errors of My Ways

The following week, as planned, Maurine and Carey met at Georgia's Country Kitchen for lunch. Georgia's Country Kitchen was one of Dallas' premier casual family-style dining restaurants. Family-owned and operated, they featured daily home-cooked country breakfast, lunch, and dinner meals. The restaurant was ten minutes from Methodist Memorial Hospital.

"What are you gonna eat today, Carey?" Maurine asked, reviewing the menu.

"I think I'm gonna try the barbecue chicken. They have a three-meat special for $8.99 with two sides, but I think I'm gonna get the one-meat entrée for $7.49," Carey said.

"Me, too — even though the better buy is with the three-meat special. I'm gonna get the brisket with macaroni and cheese and potato salad," Maurine said.

"I think I'll have the broccoli rice casserole and mustard greens," Carey said.

"Sounds good," Maurine replied.

Moments later, Maurine and Carey's server came and took their orders. After fifteen minutes of idle chitchat, their food arrived. Continuing their discussions, they enjoyed their delicious choices, along with soda and tea.

"Ever since last week, I've been thinking about our conversation at Beth's funeral, particularly what we said about cancer," Maurine said. "Thinking about Bobby and his question about what causes breast cancer made me take a look at my eating habits. His father mentioned the most common reason: family history. A woman whose mother, sister, aunt, or daughter has had breast cancer is more likely to get it herself. Also, as women get older, they're more at risk for breast cancer. Diet and lifestyle choices, along with smoking, eating high fat diets, drinking alcohol, and not getting enough exercise, are all factors, and the environment can contribute to it, as well."

"Aside from age, I definitely fall into the category of diet and lifestyle choices. I eat foods high in fats and don't exercise. I love to eat — as you can see by my plate — and that's probably gonna be my downfall," Carey said.

"Carey, you're dousing those greens with a lot of salt and hot sauce. That's a bad habit I have: adding salt before tasting my food. The greens are probably salty enough; Georgia only uses salt pork," Maurine commented.

"You're right; I should have tasted my food first," Carey said, continuing with the conversation. "I do think you have to exhibit some control over the kinds of foods you eat. That's the problem with most of us: We refuse to deny ourselves any of the foods that can be harmful down the road."

"You're absolutely right about that; we refuse to impose any restrictions. What we're really saying is, 'I'm gonna enjoy myself the best way I know how.' Unfortunately, that's usually through unhealthy eating," Maurine stated.

"Unfortunately," Carey agreed.

"Recognizing that there's a genetic connection to cancer, Beth's daughter, Lorraine, has gone to great lengths to overhaul her unhealthy habits. She avoids the traditional foods and exercises regularly," Maurine shared. "I read an article the other day that said diet and nutrition appear to be factors in a large percentage of women's cancers, men's cancers, and cardiovascular diseases. The author, who's a doctor, recommended that we reduce our intake of fat, red meat, smoked meats, and those preserved by nitrites, and eliminate white sugars from our diets. White flour products and soft drinks are harmful, too. He said soft drinks alone can cause many health problems because of the acidity, caffeine, and sugar."

"What do you mean 'acidity'?" Carey asked.

"Dark-colored sodas like the one you're drinking have phosphoric acid, which some experts believe may interfere with the body's ability to use calcium, leading to osteoporosis for women and the softening of the teeth and bones. Phosphoric acid also neutralizes the hydrochloric acid in your stomach, which can interfere with digestion, making it difficult for your body to utilize nutrients."

Carey picked up her cola and started to sip, admitting her addiction. "That's interesting, because I drink at least four cans of soda a day."

"I've cut my intake down to only one soda a day. After reading about the phosphoric acid and realizing how much sugar I was getting just from soda, I figured I'd better start reducing my intake. Did you know that one 12-ounce can contains anywhere from thirty-nine to fifty grams of sugar?" Maurine stated. "I'd started buying the 20-ounce bottles because of the better prices, and sometimes the 24-ounces if they were better deals. It's a proven fact that sugar increases insulin levels, which in turn facilitates the likelihood of developing diabetes and other related health concerns."

"That's interesting," Carey commented. "You know all that research can be biased, though, Maurine."

"Maybe so, but I still decided to keep my soda consumption low," Maurine replied.

"Sometimes I drink the diet sodas," Carey said. "Are those better, in your opinion?"

"Regular sodas have the high-fructose corn syrup, and most diet sodas have aspartame. Once again, according to researchers, there are numerous side effects associated with aspartame consumption. I've read that some side effects include brain tumors, birth defects, diabetes, emotional disorders, and seizures."

"Emotional disorders? That's really interesting. My cousin often complains about her boss at work. Apparently, the lady has erratic mood swings on a daily basis. According to my cousin, she drinks diet sodas all day, one behind the other, and I wonder if that could have something to do with her behavior. My cousin says that she's calm and accommodating in the mornings, but by the afternoon she's mean and disrespectful," Carey laughed. "I'm gonna tell my cousin that her behavior may be due to the diet sodas; maybe then they can get the lady to drink something else."

Maurine began to laugh. "Who knows? Nowadays, researchers, scientists, and health organizations say most of what we eat has harmful side effects. As far as the aspartame, its side effects haven't been validated by scientific studies. I just know I wanted to make some changes," Maurine stated. "If, for no other reason, I wanted to reduce my consumption after I was diagnosed with high blood pressure. According to my doctor, caffeine increases your heart rate and elevates your blood pressure, which can contribute to the development of heart disease. Like you, I was drinking about four sodas a day — I'm sure between the sodas and other unhealthy habits I was slowly killing myself."

"You're down to one soda a day? That's good," Carey responded, taking another sip. "I don't think I could do it."

"Sure you can! Even if I ate healthier, my doctor says caffeine blocks the absorption of some nutrients and can cause the excretion of not only calcium but also other essential minerals like magnesium, potassium, and iron in our urine. Instead of the vital minerals being stored in my body, the caffeine prompts them to make an untimely exit — one that can be harmful to my body's preservation efforts. When I took into consideration the potential impact of both phosphoric acid and caffeine, I knew I needed to make some changes. If we don't know anything else, we know how vital calcium is and that the loss of it leads to an increased risk of osteoporosis. And with the diet sodas, considering the possible impact of the aspartame, there's a triple whammy effect."

"Osteoporosis is really a debilitating disease. Working as an occupational therapist, I know you've seen a lot of it," Carey said.

"I have a patient with a broken hip bone that's forced her into a life of dependence since she's no longer able to walk on her own. I have other patients with spinal and vertebral fractures that have severe back pain, loss of height, and deformity. When you really think about it, all we need is a sufficient intake of calcium and bone-strengthening exercises," Maurine said, eating her macaroni and cheese.

"I recently heard a news report that suggested coffee has significant health benefits. Studies linked coffee consumption to lower occurrences of certain cancers and chronic diseases, lower risk for developing Type II diabetes, and added endurance during physical workouts. Researchers are saying that regular and decaffeinated coffee contain significant amounts of antioxidants, substances that have the potential to protect cells from the damage caused by free radicals."

Looking down at her plate, realizing that she had neglected to get some green vegetables, Maurine shared her thoughts on the subject. "It just goes back to whose research you believe. I tried to explain free radicals to a church member the other day when I told her about Beth's death."

"What did you tell her about free radicals?" Casey asked.

"I tried to keep it as simple as possible. You almost have to go back to our chemistry class and talk about atoms, nucleus, neutrons, protons, and electrons, not to mention the connection between molecules and free radicals. The main thing I wanted to stress was that our bodies have free radicals, but it's the ones outside our bodies, the ones that are inside insect killers, cigarette smoke, gasoline fumes, and air pollution that can cause us to experience health problems," Maurine stated.

"Absolutely."

"I don't think people understand how our bodies are breeding grounds for infection and disease. It's amazing how simple body functions like breathing the outside air or engaging in outdoor physical activities produce free radicals that attack healthy cells. Even though I don't exercise outside, I'm sure I'm at risk, as we all are, for infection and diseases."

Carey glared at her plate. "I know. When healthy cells are weakened or damaged, they're more susceptible to unfavorable health conditions. Even though I don't eat fruit, vegetables, and whole grains regularly, I inform my friends how foods that contain antioxidants, like Vitamin C, Vitamin E, and beta carotene can help protect healthy body cells and tissue from the damage caused by free radicals."

"I always use the analogy of what happens to an apple after it's cut into pieces and oxidation occurs," Maurine said.

"Oxidation? You're getting pretty technical, Maurine."

"Just hear me out, Carey. No one ever thinks about why an apple turns brown after being cut, but it's due to oxidation. If the apple is dipped in orange juice, though, it stays white. That same example of oxidation holds true in our bodies. Free radicals cause oxidation, or cell damage, and the antioxidants in our bodies work to counteract their effects. That's why it's so important to eat foods high in Vitamin C, like oranges, grapefruits, tangerines, sweet peppers, strawberries, broccoli, and potatoes," Maurine said.

"I know, and foods high in Vitamin E, like wheat germ, whole-grain products, seeds, nuts, and peanut butter. Also, foods high in beta carotene, like some dark-green leafy vegetables, carrots, sweet potatoes, broccoli, apricots, cantaloupe, mangoes, red and yellow peppers. Foods high in lycopene, like tomatoes, are good, too," Carey added.

"There have been a number of studies conducted that suggest that antioxidants may slow or possibly prevent the development of cancer."

Carey glanced at her watch. "We kind of got sidetracked; now back to my coffee. As I mentioned, there have been associations between coffee consumption and lowered rates of certain illnesses, like Parkinson's disease, Alzheimer's, Type 2 diabetes, colon cancer, and heart disease."

"We've traditionally thought about antioxidants being in the foods we've mentioned, and even in tea and cocoa, but never in coffee. Even if the studies *are* true about coffee, it still doesn't carry the nutritional benefits you get from vegetables and fruit," Maurine suggested.

Nodding her head in agreement, Carey admitted, "I can't see giving up my coffee any time soon. Your comments about the impact of caffeine are interesting. Even more powerful, it sounds like my risk for some medical problem is increased. I not only drink five to six cups of coffee, but I also drink about four to six cans of regular sodas a day."

"What?! Oh my goodness, that's a lot."

"Okay, this is my routine: on my way to work, I stop off and order a 16-ounce café mocha to drink with my morning blueberry apple-cinnamon muffin, sausage biscuit sandwich, or griddle cake sandwich. Around nine o'clock, I drink a 12-ounce soda, and sometimes two if I'm scheduled to see a lot of patients back to back."

"Two?!" Maurine shouted.

"Yeah, sometimes two," Carey admitted. "Around mid morning, I drink another cup of coffee. For lunch, I order a soda with my lunch, and I'll probably have at least one refill while seated, then take an extra for the remainder of my workday. Around three in the afternoon, either me or someone else in the office will make a fresh pot of coffee, so now I'm drinking another cup. Because my soda from lunch is probably flat, I'll buy another soda to drink during my drive home. When I get home for the evening, I usually make a half pot of coffee to drink, as well as have another soda with my evening snacks."

"That is entirely too much soda and coffee! And what in the world is a griddle cake sandwich?" Maurine asked.

"Girl, it's two sausage patties, egg, and cheese on pancakes. It's great!" Carey exclaimed, her face radiating in excitement.

"When do you ever drink water?" Maurine questioned. "If I were you, I'd start making some serious changes. I got an email from a friend that mentioned a good way to gauge how much water we should be drinking."

"How?" Carey asked.

"It said that a good rule of thumb is to take your body weight in pounds, divide that number in half, and that'll give you the number of ounces of water per day that you need to drink. So, if you weigh 170 pounds, you should drink at least 85 ounces of water per day," Maurine said. "It went on to say that if you exercise you should drink another 8-ounce glass of water for every fifteen to twenty minutes that you're active. If you drink coffee or alcohol, you should drink at least an equal amount of water. Plus, if you eat a healthy diet, you can get about twenty percent of your water from the foods you eat."

"That's a lot of water. I'm no way near that amount. I sometimes squeeze in three glasses. An article I read said to drink when you're thirsty. There appears to be a lot of controversy about the subject matter," Carey confessed, taking another sip of her soda. "I know you're probably right, though, but I have a hard time drinking water — and I know I can't drink the 64-ounces that's recommended. According to your email, I'm not even in the ballpark if I use my weight as the benchmark."

"If I were you, I'd just start cutting back little by little on the soda and coffee each week. Don't try to stop all at once. Make a commitment to reduce your daily intake by one soda and one cup of coffee. If you start gradually weaning yourself, within six weeks or so you could be down to one soda and one cup of coffee a day. Just remember that water is crucial to our daily well-being," Maurine said. "Our bodies are about 60 to 70% water. Blood is mostly water, and our muscles, lungs, and brain all contain a lot of it. We need water to help regulate our body temperature, and without it, the nutrients we get through food can't travel to all our organs; just another example of how we could be placing ourselves in harm's way. Water also transports oxygen to our cells, flushes out toxins, and protects our joints and organs."

"I know you're right..."

"Plus, if you're gonna start increasing your water intake, it's important to make sure you monitor and reduce your sodium intake. I know you're aware that sodium causes your body to retain water, and extra water in your arteries means your heart has to work harder at pushing fluids throughout your body."

"You've talked about the benefits of drinking more water, but, like you've said, too much water in your system can be dangerous. Drinking too much water can increase your total blood volume, and when that happens on a regular basis — that is, the blood volume being contained within your blood circulatory system — extreme stress is placed on your heart and blood vessels. Then, extreme stress is placed on the kidneys to flush the excess water out of your blood circulatory system," Carey commented. "On a different note, I read an article about diet and nutrition in Dr. Wilber's office the other day. It also stated that research shows that consumption of the right foods and supplements may not only prevent cancer but also boost the immune system and energy levels, safeguarding the body against cancer and increasing its ability to heal itself. The article went on to say that daily consumption of foods rich in essential vitamins and minerals strengthens the immune system, slows tumor growth, protects against further spread of the disease, and reduces the overwhelmingly negative side effects of radiation and chemotherapy."

"It's amazing how cancer cells can attack so many different parts of the body — the colon, rectum, stomach, lung, mouth, pharynx, esophagus, breast, bladder, pancreas, uterus, and larynx. What's really terrible is that we know this stuff — that is, we know what to do, but don't," Maurine said.

"Eating right, plus staying physically active and maintaining a healthy weight, can cut our cancer risk significantly; that should motivate all of us to do the right thing. Sometimes I feel like I'm gambling with my health, rolling the dice of unhealthy habits, hoping they'll land on the winning numbers: good blood pressure levels, good cholesterol levels, good blood sugar levels, good sodium levels — and above all, disease free," Carey said.

"Absolutely!" Maurine replied.

"One thing I do know: I'm not comfortable with the chemicals they're using. I'm afraid they're getting into our bodies. I'm thinking about going organic, but I need to do some more research," Carey added.

"Organic fruits and vegetables are so much more expensive, and I don't know if organic is any better than non-organic. True enough, organic farming restricts the use of chemicals, so vegetables and fruit that have been certified organic contain lower levels of pesticides, herbicides, fertilizer, and fungicides. However, the organic farmers have to be doing something to their soil. As you said, more research is needed. The only thing we know for sure is that a diet high in fruit and vegetables protects against diseases like cancer. We've got to get off the excuse train and get aboard the acceptance train and start doing the right thing."

"I'm definitely gonna try and do better," Carey said.

"Then there's the question of cooked versus uncooked," Maurine continued. "Although there's not a clear distinction between cooked and uncooked, there appears to be more favor toward uncooked. You know that everyone does a study — a study here, a study there, a study everywhere. But, some studies suggest that cooking destroys the nutrients in fruit and vegetables known to aid in cancer prevention. According to those conducting the studies, since the nutrients needed to prevent cancer are destroyed or corrupted by cooking and conceivably not properly assimilated or absorbed in the body's cells afterwards, it's their contention that uncooked fruits and vegetables are the best choices for cancer prevention."

"Funny that you mentioned cooked and uncooked," Carey said. "At the county fair last weekend, there was a company demonstrating their premier stainless steel, waterless cookware. The representative talked about how minerals and vitamins are lost through using too much water and cooking with high heat — high pressure boiling and microwaving. He actually boiled some leafy vegetables and showed us how the water turned green, saying that the green water represented the nutrients. I've always noticed the green water from my broccoli, greens, and spinach, but never made the connection that I was throwing away my nutrients. You know we can leave some collard or mustard greens on the stove until they're so tender that they're falling apart. Apparently, their cookware is designed to heat evenly across the bottom and along the sides to cook food naturally without water, thereby retaining the nutrients. The demonstrator stated that vegetables shouldn't be cooked for an extended period of time."

"I've always heard that steaming or stir frying vegetables conserves the maximum amount of nutrients," Maurine said. "I can tell that Georgia's mustard greens were cooked awhile. I'm sure the broccoli in your broccoli and rice casserole was cooked awhile. Did you buy the cookware?"

"No! First of all, I don't cook that often. Well, I do cook breakfast, but I wasn't about to spend $1,500 for the set," Carey said, eating a spoonful of her broccoli and rice casserole.

"Fifteen hundred dollars! That cookware better cook *for* me," Maurine exclaimed.

"It was a very informative demonstration, though," Carey admitted. "We actually tasted a medley of vegetables he cooked while we were listening: sliced carrots, broccoli, mini ears of corn, red bell pepper, and cabbage. It tasted great; he seasoned the vegetables with products like Mrs. Dash, garlic, and onion. He said to avoid frying, grilling, and microwaving because studies have shown that those styles of cooking create chemical compounds associated with disease."

"Sounds like it was very informative."

"It really was," Carey confirmed. "What vegetables and fruit have you heard are best for cancer prevention?"

"Basically, the foods high in antioxidants that we discussed. What I want to do is figure out some good low-fat, low-sodium dishes for incorporating the suggested carrots, squash, sweet potatoes, and dark green vegetables, like broccoli and spinach. I have to be creative with some dishes to get my husband to eat them. I might try preparing a vegetable medley using the seasonings you mentioned. The flavored vinegars like balsamic and sherry wine are good enhancers if we're doing a vegetable medley stir-fry," Maurine shared.

"Working as a radiographer, my focus is on operating the X-ray equipment that produces images of the tissues, organs, bones, and vessels of the body. Once people find out I work in a hospital, they never fail to ask me about the benefits of good nutritional habits. How do you generally describe the benefits of eating more fruit and vegetables and their ability to reduce cancer risks?" Carey asked rhetorically, placing a napkin over her plate. "I just keep it simple by saying fruit and vegetables may strengthen the immune system, which is the body's defense against diseases like cancer."

"Sounds simple enough," Maurine said.

Carey was about to drink the last of her beverage before she lowered her glass and said, "My brother was diagnosed with lung cancer a few months ago."

"Is he a smoker?" Maurine asked, sipping her drink with a grimace.

"Yeah, he is," Carey said remorsefully. "The doctors have started him on an aggressive treatment plan — we're hopeful."

"My friend's mother was diagnosed with lung cancer a couple months ago, and she wasn't a smoker. Dr. Milber says that lung cancer is one of the most common cancers."

"For years, I've tried to get my brother to stop smoking, and he's made attempts to try to do so: using the nicotine replacement products like gum, patches, nasal sprays, and even the quit smoking counseling programs, but..." Carey said, hesitating to continue. "I've given him tons of literature to increase his awareness that cigarette smoke has a lot of cancer causing substances that produce mutations. Unlike breast cancer, where you have the breast self-exam and mammography, there's no early diagnostic test for lung cancer — Seems like it just sneaks up on you."

"My friend's mother doesn't smoke, but her husband does," Maurine said. "Statistics show that 10-15% of lung cancer victims are non-smokers who inherit the disease through secondhand smoke, as well as radon gases, genetics, and pollution," Maurine added.

"It's really serious. The life expectancy—" Carey stopped in mid sentence before continuing. "My brother is simultaneously going through his treatments while getting his personal business in order. He has two children, ages eight and twelve. It's a shame that people don't consider the full ramifications of their lifestyle habits — More than likely, he'll leave a family behind to live with the consequences of what is now considered a preventable death."

"More importantly, not only is he harming himself, he's putting his wife and kids at risk for the disease," Maurine said.

"You're right. He's not one who goes outside to smoke his cigarettes. His mindset is that he pays the bills, so he's gonna smoke in his house," Carey said, rubbing her brow. "I know none of us know the day, time, or hour of our earthly departure, but it just seems as if more emphasis should be placed on living a life pleasing to God. When you think about it, our unhealthy lifestyles stem from selfish acts. We're only concerned with pleasing ourselves, rather than considering the impact of our actions on those closest to us — We dismiss the burdens and hardships that they'll impose on others." The thought of losing her brother and living with the remnants of his decision saddened Carey.

"I wouldn't lose all hope. With God, all things are possible. People are being healed and delivered everyday," Maurine said. "In some ways, we're no different than those we're talking about. The neglect that we've imposed on our bodies is opening the floodgates to an array of diseases. And who's left holding the bag? Our families, our children, and friends who love us — that's who. They're the ones burdened with caring for us, watching us suffer, and having to make medical decisions on our behalf."

"Smoking is in a league all by itself. To me, a smoker is comparable to a suicide bomber, in that they go in knowing the consequences of their actions. They go in knowing that the ultimate result is a horrible death," Carey said, frustrated.

CHAPTER 14

A Hard Look at Family Traditions

*A*n unpopular conversation for most people who are at an age when they start to question and confront a lifetime of decisions, Maurine and Carey discussed a wide range of issues, touching on such topics as politics, religion, the economy, and retirement. They narrowed in on how they had allowed family traditions to dismantle and overtake their years of medical education and training. They recognized that, if left unaddressed, their existing health conditions would fester and cause bigger problems. In transforming their unhealthy habits, they would have to take more responsibility for their actions by establishing preventive benchmarks, helping them be proactive rather than reactive.

"Where is our waitress? Is she gonna check on us at some point? I need some more tea," Maurine said, irritated.

"Here she comes," Casey said, motioning for their waitress while trying to calm Maurine. "I think most people understand that the inevitable will happen, and they're okay with it. One thing I'm gonna do is up the ante and start concentrating harder on doing the right things. First, I'm gonna start by limiting my intake of meat; I eat entirely too much. Beef links, bacon, and pork sausage for breakfast. Ham on the weekend. I'm not talking about the recommended portion sizes. I'm eating three to four slices of bacon or two sausage links plus eggs, hash browns, and toast," Carey said.

The waitress attended to the ladies, refilling their drinks. Maurine continued to nibble on her food selections during their conversation.

"What about your griddle cakes?" Maurine asked.

"Oh, yeah, my griddle cakes, too. And I love my pork chops, rib eye, chop steak, meatloaf, roast beef, beef stroganoff, spare ribs, sirloin roast, tenderloin, the occasional pig's feet and chitlins — You name it, I eat it. In some form or fashion, I'm eating either beef, pork, or chicken two to three times a day. I know my portion sizes have too much saturated fat, cholesterol, and probably trans fat, since a lot of it is processed food."

"You're definitely a prime candidate for the health threats related to high blood pressure, like a heart attack, stroke, or kidney failure," Maurine said.

"Thanks for the reminder, but you're right. Forty years of that kind of eating has surely impacted the amount of plaque building up in my arteries," Carey replied. "Stop staring! No, I'm *not* forty. I just mean that this has been my pattern of eating going back to when I was a kid. I don't know about yours, but my parents were big eaters of meat, eggs, and cheese."

"You sound like my husband about his beef and pork. Have you tried the turkey bacon and sausage?" Maurine asked.

"It's just not the same. I know it's supposed to be healthier. I guess it has less saturated fat, but I can't get into the turkey bacon and sausage."

"All that meat poses a much bigger risk — and that's the hormones injected into cows and possibly chickens. As I understand it, hormones are needed to help the cows grow faster, produce larger and leaner animals, increase milk production, and lower the producer's cost, which is also supposed to lower our cost. But, what does that really mean in the final analysis of it all? A large majority of producers feed hormones, antibiotics, growth promoters, or other artificial drugs to the animals," Maurine stated. "And now, all the talk about cloning is even more frightening for me."

"I remember back in the day when cows roamed free and ate grass in the pasture, and chickens did the same, eating grain. The animals were leaner because they weren't overfed and they walked around freely getting exercise. But these days animals are raised in factory farms and treated like commodities. They're kept in tight, enclosed spaces, unable to move more than a few inches, and they don't have access to fresh air and exercise — especially the chickens," Carey stated.

"As a child, I remember cows feeding off the land," Maurine said.

"We need to start questioning the type of feed the cows are eating. I want to know whether the feed contains hormones, antibiotics, growth promoters, color enhancers, or other artificial drugs. We also need to know if chickens, turkeys, or pigs are fed beef or a beef byproduct," Carey stated.

"Why is that important?" Maurine asked.

"The beef could contain hormones, which is one way they could be getting into the poultry supply," Carey replied. "And, like you, I definitely want to know if they're cloned. There's been mention of cloning in the news recently."

"Another question to ask is if the hormones in the cows make them grow faster, then what is it doing to us?" Maurine said. "It's amazing how quickly our kids are developing. Girls are developing breasts and starting their menstrual cycles much earlier than we did years ago."

"Forget the kids, what about me? I seem to be growing hair in all the wrong places, not to mention being an E cup size. No one in my family has *ever* had breasts this large." Carey looked down at her breasts. "Even though I'm small down below, I'm too large up top, and now I'm starting to have back problems."

"Carey, you're probably right. Who knows the long-term effects of those chemicals from your high-meat diet? Plus, it doesn't sound like any of us are getting many of the nutrients we need to keep our cells healthy and protect us from disease and illness."

Carey nodded her head in agreement. "I recently read that our liver produces about 1,000 milligrams of cholesterol a day, which is all the cholesterol your body needs. Another 200 to 500 milligrams can come from the food we eat. After looking more closely what I eat for breakfast, I'm right at 255 milligrams of cholesterol, and that's only if I eat one egg and two ounces of meat."

"Talking about all this is scary," Maurine said, picking at her brisket. "Since my husband retired, he does all the cooking, and he makes hefty meals for breakfast and dinner. I can always count on an egg most mornings, with either ham slices, pecan smoked jalapeno sausage, or pork sausage served with toast or biscuits. Sometimes, he'll whip up his famous fruity pancakes."

"I love frying those premium pork sausages. Just so you know: they're 180 calories, 30 milligrams of cholesterol, and 350 milligrams of sodium for a two-ounce serving. Do you know how small a two-ounce serving is? I'm sure your husband eats more than that," Carey stated. "One major concern of mine is the nitrites that meats contain."

"Now, you've got me: what's nitrite?" Maurine asked.

"I'll have to email you the information I found. But, they're preservatives — chemicals added to meats. They're in meats like sausage, hot dogs, cold cuts, bacon, meats in canned soups, and salt-cured fish. The information I read said they can convert into cancer-causing chemicals in our bodies. So, those of us who eat a lot of processed and red meat are at a high risk for cancer."

"I know you've said it, but we've gotta start making some lifestyle changes before it's too late," Maurine said. "That's why it's so important to eat fruit and vegetables to protect us from health threats. I'm gonna start this week by getting some zucchini, squash, and broccoli, stir-fry them in a low-sodium sauce, and throw them on top of some sautéed chicken strips. And I mean fresh chicken, without the hormones and chemicals. I just hope my husband feels the same about making better food choices — Looks like I need to take over his cooking role for a while. The drawback, though, is that I'll have to get back in the habit of coming home from work and cooking."

"That stir fry sounds delicious," Carey said. "I'm gonna start being more creative with eating healthier, and I'm definitely gonna stop eating so much processed meat. I guess we were raised to eat meat with every meal — sausage for breakfast, ham on a sandwich or on a chef salad for lunch, and spaghetti and meatballs, pork chops, steak, or a hamburger for dinner."

"Let's blame it all on our parents; they laid the foundation for our lifestyles now," Maurine replied.

"Funny, I don't know if it's right to play the blame game; we're adults," Carey said. "And you know we can't forget about exercise. All those studies we keep hearing about show that exercise is good for the heart and body. Considering my eating habits, though, exercise probably wouldn't make much of a difference. It's a good thing that, other than my E size breasts, I'm relatively small."

"Small people get sick, too," Maurine responded.

"You are so right. With our unhealthy lifestyles, I don't know if being small is something to brag about. Sure, obesity can lead to an array of health problems, but what we're doing does, too. It's funny how people always view small as healthy; thin people generally get 'tagged' with having a good metabolism or good genetics," Carey said.

"That's funny, I've always gotten comments like, 'You must have a tapeworm,' " Maurine replied. "There's a perception flaw that skinny people live longer, healthier lives, but they have their own set of potential health issues, too, like anemia, osteoporosis, fertility problems, heart irregularities, and hormone production problems."

"They're at greater risk of early death, may have problems with pregnancy, and have a higher risk of having a low birth-weight baby and premature delivery," Carey added.

"Being in the health field, I know that it's probably 70% genetics that keep us from becoming overweight. Although, some people are thin due to illness, while others are thin because of those fad diets or habits that help them stay really thin because that's what America idolizes," Maurine stated.

"One thing I know for sure, I'm gonna take your advice and start trying to reduce my excessive soda intake; it could be a contributing factor to my high blood pressure and elevated blood cholesterol levels. One thing I know: the caffeine causes me to have the jitters and sleepless nights."

"Well, just so you'll know what to expect: when I started weaning myself, I ran into some serious challenges. For the first three to five days, I had severe headaches. I was irritable, nervous, restless, and feeling sleepy all the time. If you can make it through the first few days, you'll be okay. My goal is to get to the point where I'm totally caffeine-free," Maurine stated.

Carey nodded a few times with a deep stare before asking, "How many years do you have with the hospital?"

"Twenty-nine and a half," Maurine answered with enthusiasm.

"Great. You're knocking on the door to retirement. I've got twenty-five," Carey said. "With everybody dying around me, I'm starting to wonder if I'll live another five years."

"During Beth's funeral services, I was thinking about how, as Christians, our spiritual lives are of utmost importance. Following our spiritual lives, we generally place extreme value on our family lives, work lives, financial lives, and social lives. Unfortunately, we fail to realize that an unhealthy life can impact all facets of our lives forever," Maurine said.

"Are you saying Beth's priorities were mixed up?" Casey asked.

"No, I'm not. Don't get me wrong; I'm not saying Beth's cancer was a result of unhealthy habits. I'm just saying I don't think we do enough to safeguard our temples against the attacks of diseases and illnesses," Maurine stated. "Speaking firsthand as someone with high blood pressure, and a husband with high cholesterol, I know we've gotta change the status quo. The challenge for me will be getting him to cross over to healthier choices."

"Personally, I've focused my efforts on making sure I'm financially secure when I retire: boosting my 401K contributions, saving money, and making the right investments since I'm single and won't have any other sources of income."

"I'm sure your divorce from Tom after twenty-two years threw a monkey wrench in your retirement plans," Maurine commented.

"It did. Although I've moved on, I sometimes resent his walking out on our marriage — You know he left me for a younger woman," Carey shared. "Somehow, he believed a younger woman would be more fulfilling. I think a lot of it had to do with his inability to keep an erection during sex, as well as not being able to perform adequately. Somewhere in his mind, I was the cause — His interest and attraction for me had dissipated."

"I've done some research on erectile dysfunction," Maurine shared.

"So have I. After reading tons of articles, I believe his high blood pressure was a contributing factor. With age and disease, such as high blood pressure, the blood vessels are affected, disturbing circulation of penile vessels, thus reducing blood flow and the erection. Other diseases, like diabetes and smoking, can also cause ED, as well as some medications."

"Now, that snapshot of the future should make *any* man want to be healthier," Maurine said. "My husband's sexual engine *stays* revved up. If I tell him that his high blood pressure and high cholesterol could result not only in a heart attack or stroke, but also impotence, he just might change his unhealthy ways."

"You're right. I think if men understood how an unhealthy lifestyle could impede their ability to maintain an erection, they just might do better. Eventually, my ex-husband sought an alternative to help him out: MEDICATION — then, after getting a boost in his energy, he sprinted toward a younger partner," Carey said.

"Medication is scary. You never know about the effects, especially when they are mixed with other prescription medications," Maurine revealed.

"At this point, I wish him the best. One thing about someone new: you take a risk that they'll be loyal, faithful, and committed. You won't ever know until you get really sick. Will the person you sacrificed everything for stay in your corner?" Carey stated.

"You're absolutely right about that," Maurine replied. "That same situation happened to a relative of mine: her husband left her for a younger woman, but when he got ill and bedridden, she left him hanging. Now, my cousin, his ex-wife, goes over to his house and cares for him."

"Does she still love him after everything he put her through?" Carey asked.

"I think because they shared thirty-five years of marriage and five kids together, she cares for him out of loyalty to her children."

"She's a better woman than I could *ever* fathom being. My ex-husband and I planned a fruitful retirement together, but now I have to play catch-up since I'm alone now. I do need to concentrate on my health, though. I can't rely on my son; he'll just tuck me away somewhere in a nursing home to die. After all you do for your children, you'd expect them to return the favor, but not these days."

"You just never know," Maurine said.

"My main focus has been on making sure I have enough money to do what I want to do when I'm retired. Even so, I'm gonna have to scale down my lifestyle tremendously to maintain my house, car payment, insurance policies, and taxes," Carey said. "Lately, I've even been paying more attention to those social security statements that come around my birthday, telling me how much I'm supposed to receive in benefits at various ages. I'm especially paying attention to my health insurance, including costs for prescriptions, doctor visits, and hospital costs. Seems like the body goes haywire after retirement; statistics show that we're living longer, but they're not saying with what kind of quality of life. We see patients everyday, their pain and suffering, and the reality is that I'll be in the same predicament if I don't change some bad habits."

"Retirement? What does it all matter if I can't enjoy myself due to health and physical constrictions?" Maurine admitted.

"You're right. We look forward to planning the retirement party and the beginning of a new era, but what's the point if everything hurts and we end up bedridden, unable to care for ourselves? What if we have to walk with a cane or a walker or we're confined to a wheelchair? What if we go blind?"

"It wouldn't be my ideal scenario, but if it happens my life wouldn't end because I needed a walker, cane, or wheelchair or go blind," Maurine replied.

"I didn't mean that it would." Carey said, trying to clean up her statement. "So many people in my building have died or become stricken with disease since the beginning of the year. It's so important for people to understand that their spiritual lives, including the values and relationships they hold so dear, are closely connected to the conditions of their bodies. If the body begins to break down, the endurance and energy required to work, serve, and be a blessing to others, as well as the ability to manage daily obligations — work, school, outside activities with kids, meetings, and participation in ministry — are severely compromised. On the brink of a fixed income, I can't afford to suffer a catastrophic health problem like a heart attack or stroke."

"I know that's right. The financial burden that I hear patients talk about is frightening. Some have gone bankrupt over their health crises," Maurine stated.

"I'm fifty now; I'm starting to think that it's too late," Carey said.

"It's never too late to start focusing on better health. Sure, the clock is ticking, but it's not too late. I think we're better off if we concentrate on our nutritional contributions rather than the financial ones. I'd rather have peace of mind about my health than my finances. Don't get me wrong: finances are important, but if I can't enjoy an active life with my husband, children, and grandchildren, then what good is money?" Maurine stated. "A major health problem would probably strip me and my husband of our finances and burden us for the remainder of our lives. The best safeguard is taking preventive measures."

"You're absolutely right. Implementing lifestyle changes that help to prevent, manage, or eliminate health concerns is paramount. For right now, I'm sorry, Maurine — but it's hard for me to envision healthier eating with this delicious soul food staring at me," Carey stated, removing the napkin. She started eating her barbecue chicken and mustard greens.

"I know that's right," Maurine replied. "I'll start my ambitious pursuits to eat more whole grains, fruit, vegetables, and low-fat dairy products *next week*."

"Me, too," Carey said.

"We've talked so long, I've got to get back to the hospital. I'm gonna get the rest of my food to go and order some of Georgia's German Chocolate Cake to take back to the office," Maurine said, motioning for the waitress. "I think our waitress forgot about us. She didn't check on us one time. The food here is good, but the service is horrible."

"I don't want any more of my food, but I'm gonna get some peach cobbler to go," Carey said.

"Lunch was great. Next time, we'll do healthy for real," Maurine said. "When I get home later this evening, I plan to give some serious thought to our conversation, and I think I'm gonna contact Trevor."

"Let me know if you decide to participate in his healthy living class. If you do, I might forgo my year delay and join you."

CHAPTER 15

Bringing Healthier Habits Closer to Home

*D*riving home, Maurine thought about her years in the medical field, particularly her work as an occupational therapist. She had treated people who had suffered strokes, head injuries, spinal cord injuries, and other major illnesses, and as part of her job she guided them toward the practical aspects of how to function with a disability: eating, dressing, hygiene, cooking, driving, and returning to work. She helped them become self-sufficient by learning or re-learning how to carry out regular daily living skills.

Working with those who had been diagnosed with osteoporosis, she helped them prevent fractures that could lead to loss of mobility and other medical complications.

She thought, *I could be headed down that same path if I don't start taking in more calcium, rich foods, and exercising. Without those changes, I might need therapy one day to reduce the consequences of disease-like fractures of the vertebra, hip, wrist, pelvis, and rib.*

Then there were those who suffered from incontinence.

Gripping the steering wheel, she continued to think, *I couldn't handle the loss of bowel or bladder control and having to wear an adult diaper.*

Through education and exercises, she worked hard to help her patients change their lifestyles in order to cope with the embarrassment stemming from such unpleasantness as unplanned urine leaking through their clothing. Looking back, she began to see the potential effects of an unhealthy lifestyle catching up with her.

Maurine began to reflect on the life she and her husband, Jack, had built together: they had lived in Westchase Village, a quiet community in Rockwall, Texas, for over thirty years. They had raised three sons, Dale, Dornell, and Douglas. Jack, a factory worker, had retired eight years ago on medical disability after breaking a bone in his neck during a fall. Now, he spent his time working as a volunteer at their church, cooking for Maurine, handling the bills, and taking naps.

To escape the hustle and bustle of city life, Maurine and Jack often retreated to their country home near Longview on the weekends. Fewer cars, clean air, and friendly people motivated them to make country living their final destination after Maurine retired. Although its location lacked some of the usual in-town conveniences, they treasured their beautiful home, the peace and quiet, the privacy in the woods, and living on seventy-five acres. Best of all, Jack enjoyed the hometown gatherings: family reunions, holiday festivities, graveyard rallies, and church homecoming services. Aunt Mabeline lived nearby, and she routinely prepared his favorites: Berry Cobbler, Berry Dumplings, Pineapple Upside Down Cake, Peach Cobbler, Mississippi Mud Cake, and Dirty Rice.

Maurine breathed a sigh of relief as she approached her driveway. *Six months to retirement.* The countdown had started. Spiritually, emotionally, and financially, she was prepared. Joining Jack with volunteering at their church would fill the void of going to work everyday. The best part is that she'd be on her own time schedule. She'd finally implement those lifestyle changes she had delayed for so long. No more excuses for neglecting the things she wanted to do, like taking computer classes to update herself on the latest technology.

Entering the living room, Maurine yelled out to Jack, "Hi, Jack. I'm home!"

"Hi, honey. I've got dinner on the stove," Jack said, walking in from the kitchen.

"Oh, honey, I'm sorry I didn't call you, but I ate a big lunch with Carey earlier," Maurine said as she sat on the sofa and started looking through their bills.

"I made beef stroganoff with the leftovers. Surely, you're gonna eat some. How is Carey doing? I haven't heard you talk about her in a while, at least not since her and her husband divorced." Jack said, handing Maurine a can of ice tea.

"Thanks, baby," Maurine said. "I'll eat some later on. I had some brisket for lunch. Carey has moved on and is planning for her retirement. We mainly talked about our health. It's funny, most of our life has revolved around the boys, work, finances, acquisitions, and whatever social life we managed to conjure up. But, we've never embraced the most important aspect of lives: our health."

"I don't know about you, but I was working and trying to make sure our family had the basic essentials and some extras," Jack responded, taking a seat on the sofa next to Maurine. "Like paying those bills you're looking at and making sure we had a roof over our heads and food in our bellies."

"That's not what I'm talking about. Now that I look back, I don't know if we had the right perspective on what was truly important," Maurine explained. "With all the hustle and bustle of life's obligations, situations, and events that have transpired through the years, have we really enjoyed being a family?"

"Okay, Maurine, I don't know where you're going with all this, but I've had a happy life with you and the boys," Jack replied.

"Sometimes I wonder if we spent the right kind of time with each other and the boys. They've grown up to be self-sufficient adults, but I don't know if we taught them about what's really important in life. They are so consumed with making it big, making more money, and getting expensive toys," Maurine said.

"They should be thinking about making more money. Bigger and better things aren't gonna fall in their laps," Jack responded.

"There's so much more to life than things. Maybe we didn't have an opportunity to instill the right values in them when they were kids with me working long hours at the hospital and you at the factory so much," Maurine stated. "With all the hustle and bustle, when was there ever time for us to sit back and really enjoy and appreciate our family? I know the boys are okay, but we never seemed to have an opportunity just to hang out. We never played together. Now, I'm afraid that when they have families it'll be more of the same, simply because they don't know anything different."

"We were no different than any other family," Jack replied. "We were about making it, chasing the American dream."

"You're right. We raised a generation the same way our parents did: all for the sake of the American dream. Like most, we weren't involved mentally, just actively. I know that has some sort of impact on kids growing up to be loving, caring, and passionate adults," Maurine said. "I hate that we didn't make time as a family for fun activities like walking, bicycling, skating, hiking, river rafting — fun outdoor, nature-exposing activities."

"Where did you hear about river rafting?" Jack asked.

"I read about it in a travel magazine. It sounds like fun. I hate I missed out on stuff like that, especially with my boys," Maurine stated. "Carey and I talked awhile about living healthier, eating healthier, and exercising."

"Sounds like you don't need to hang out with Carey again," Jack laughed.

Maurine continued, ignoring his comment. "I think if we had taken a different approach toward building our family, we might have established a solid trend for our boys to follow. As I look back over my life, working in the medical field has connected me with real people with real problems, who, through their circumstances, recognize the importance of implementing a healthier lifestyle. For many, that recognition doesn't occur until they're faced with a life-threatening situation. I hate that we didn't teach the boys more about proper health and nutrition; more than likely, they'll end up with the family tradition of high blood pressure, high cholesterol, and who knows what else as a result."

"I think we've done just fine. Everyone nowadays has some sort of health problem — high blood pressure, high cholesterol, diabetes, arthritis — and you know we'll all probably get some form of cancer," Jack stated.

"With the right attitude, I believe the inevitable doesn't have to happen. We've inherited the cycle of unhealthy practices from our parents, and now we've handed them down to our children," Maurine stated. "Had I put the knowledge that I've acquired over the years to good use, our outlook might be optimistic rather than pessimistic. Had I taken the time to educate the boys on sound eating habits rather than letting them gorge on candy, chips, cookies, and ice cream… "

"As long as they're not overweight or obese, they'll be okay. That's all you ever hear about anyway. You don't hear anything about skinny people being unhealthy," Jack stated.

"And that's a fallacy on the health industry's part," Maurine said as she got up and started to straighten some of Jack's magazines on the table. "Skinny people need to know that their health is at stake, too. I just don't want my boys to end up with chronic diseases like you and I have. Being young, they think they're invincible. But, the time will come when they can't dodge the bullet of disease and illness."

"How do you know they don't already eat healthy?" Jack asked. "And how long is this conversation gonna last? A rerun of *CSI New York* is getting ready to come on. Can you hand me the remote while you're up?"

Abruptly, and with irritation, Maurine handed Jack the remote. "Instead of watching your TV show, we could take a walk around the neighborhood."

"Not gonna happen," Jack responded, switching the TV on.

Maurine continued with their discussion, "I see what's in their refrigerators and pantries: they basically eat wherever it's cheap. Douglas is the worst because he's always looking for a bargain. Three pieces of fried chicken with a biscuit for $1.99, with maybe a side for $2.99, a burger, super-sized fries, and drink for $3.99, a pizza buffet for $3.49 — none of which is beneficial enough to protect their bodies."

"Okay, the chicken is protein, and the side is probably red beans and rice or coleslaw. The red beans are high in iron — Bet you thought I didn't know that!" Jack exclaimed. "The coleslaw is made with cabbage. There's lettuce and tomatoes on a burger, and a pizza is filled with the basic cheese, onions, tomatoes, mushrooms, and some sort of meat for protein."

"Okay, Mister. Yes, the chicken is protein, but when it's loaded with batter and deep fried in unhealthy oils, the chicken becomes a potentially artery-clogging food. The red beans are highly seasoned with salt, ham, and who knows what else, which translates to a high-sodium food, causing the heart to work harder. The mayonnaise in the coleslaw is more than likely high in fat, and that in itself negates any nutritional benefits of the cabbage. As far as the lettuce and tomatoes on a burger, the amount you're given is minimal. With the amount of cheese, pepperoni, sausage, and ham laying on a deep-dish crust, the pizza is also loaded with products high in fat, cholesterol, and sodium containing very little of any essential vitamins and minerals."

"Sounds like you're listening to everyone else's opinions of 'do's' and 'don'ts.' I think you're overreacting," Jack replied. "All I know is that I'm okay with what I eat. Don't expect me to make any drastic changes. As far as I can tell, I'm as fit as a fiddle."

"You know what? If we keep eating the way we've been eating, it's like playing a game of Russian Roulette. We don't know which unhealthy habit will trigger a health crisis — one that we may not be able to bounce back from," Maurine said, sitting on the sofa. "We have only two options: change some unhealthy habits, or keep on doing as we've always done and risk a stream of medical problems that'll hamper the life we've dreamed about after retirement — Which do you prefer?"

"You make it sound as if our future is at stake," Jack replied.

"Do you really understand high blood pressure and what it really means?" Maurine asked.

"My doctor tells me about the consequences of my high blood pressure every visit and how important my medication is. I know if left untreated, the excess pressure of blood on the arteries eventually scars and narrows them. Also, plaque can accumulate, which forces the heart to work much harder to push the red blood cells throughout the body. This makes getting sufficient levels of nutrients and oxygen to organs and tissues difficult, which compromises the proper function of the kidneys, brain, and heart," Jack replied. "But, the good news is, since our blood pressure is being treated with medication, we don't have to worry about those things happening to us."

"Medication shouldn't be our excuse for continuing unhealthy practices," Maurine stated. "Your doctor should be telling you how to implement better habits so you can get off the medication."

"Well, that's our best option..."

"If you really understood what was going on inside our bodies, you'd respond differently," Maurine suggested. "High blood pressure causes the heart and arteries to work harder because the heart has to pump harder and the arteries have to carry blood moving under greater pressure. If this process goes on for a long time, the ability of the heart and arteries to function properly is weakened. As a result, other vital organs, like the kidneys, eyes, and brain, may be influenced. Having high blood pressure puts us more at risk for strokes, heart attacks, kidney failure, loss of vision, and atherosclerosis, the hardening of the arteries."

"Maurine, once again, that's what the medication is for," Jack said, growing agitated.

"I don't want to get comfortable relying on medication to make me okay. If we start implementing better habits, we could probably rid ourselves of the medication. You know we can't dismiss the fact that medications have side-effects, and some are not so favorable."

"Leave it to you to put a black mark on the picture and ruin the outlook," Jack replied. "With all that said, what really causes high blood pressure?"

"Scientists and researchers really don't know the real cause for high blood pressure, but there are two types: primary and secondary. The primary type generally stems from genetics, obesity, stress, lack of exercise, diet — including salt intake — cigarette smoking, sex, race, age, and even personality. The secondary type can be connected to kidney disease, endocrine disorders, the use of oral contraceptives, and excessive use of alcohol. Some believe stress can be a contributing factor, but there's no evidence of that," Maurine said.

"Great! I'm not obese, and I don't have any stress — except for right now. Age, I'm good. Personality, I'm great. I don't smoke. Sex is good. Exercise — I get that with sex," Jack said, starting to laugh. "I don't have kidney disease or that endocrine disorder. I don't use oral contraceptives, and I don't drink."

"It's much bigger than what I've said, but that's it in a nutshell. The only thing we really don't have control over is our genetics, but we can't use genetics as a convenient cop-out. Carey and I came to the conclusion that the main culprits in our lives are salt and sodium."

"There goes that name again: Carey," Jack interrupted.

"Talking with her was a real eye-opener."

"Like I said, the medication helps treat my condition," Jack stated.

"Even though we're on medication, its effectiveness can be hindered if we keep eating foods high in salt. Most people don't understand the connection between salt and sodium; sodium does occur naturally in most foods, but the most common form of sodium is regular salt and commercial seasonings," Maurine said.

Maurine explained to Jack the amount of sodium hidden in the processed meats they ate, like bacon, sausage, and ham.

"We need to watch out for additives like sodium nitrite, sodium benzoate, trisodium phosphate — any word with sodium attached to it," Maurine told him. "I'm also talking about your Cajun, taco, and mesquite seasonings, and the variety of marinades, tenderizers, soy sauce, and onion and garlic salts you use to season your meats."

"Wait a minute! You're treading on my main meal enhancers!" Jack shouted. "And what do you expect me to season my meats with? Marinades are the key."

"I've found a great recipe for a barbecue marinade and a southwestern marinade," Maurine said, trying to convince Jack.

"What's in them?"

"The barbecue marinade includes a chopped onion, brown sugar, canola oil, cider vinegar, catsup, horseradish, and black pepper."

"Well la-di-da, Mrs. Madam. How do you make it?"

"It's simple: in a saucepan, cook the onion and brown sugar in oil over medium heat until the onion is tender. After about three minutes, add the remaining ingredients and keep cooking for three to four minutes. Then you follow the process as you normally do: remove from the heat and cool before adding it to your meat. The southwestern marinade isn't much different, except you use homemade salsa, chopped cilantro, fresh lime juice, canola oil, garlic clove, and ground cumin."

"Like I'm gonna make fresh salsa."

"It's easy. All you basically need is a couple cans of no-salt-added crushed tomatoes, a can of no-salt-added tomato sauce, cloves of garlic — diced, green chilies, cayenne pepper, cumin, ground rosemary, medium green pepper — diced, onion — diced, fresh cilantro leaves — diced, two tomatoes — diced, and jalapeno pepper — diced. SIMPLE! The main thing is cutting down the sodium we get in the over-the-counter brands."

"I can tell. All that 'no-salt-added' stuff is gonna taste a mess."

Maurine went on, "Aside from the meat, we need to stop using boxed and canned goods, such as rice, pasta, potatoes, soups, and stuffing. I figured out why I feel so bloated after I eat. It's the salt! Salt acts like a sponge in our bodies, retaining water. It causes an increase in blood volume, making the heart work harder at pumping the red blood cells throughout our bodies. That's one reason why our blood pressure is so high."

"I feel like that when we eat out," Jack replied, rubbing his belly.

Looking at Jack rub his belly, Maurine said, "If we don't stop eating those products, we'll never be rid of the medication, and our medical problems may get worse. Because your mother had high blood pressure, as well as my father, we're obviously genetically predisposed. More than likely, it's the same case for our sons. We need to start eating foods low in fat and high in calcium, magnesium, potassium, along with low-fat dairy, fruit, and vegetables to lower our blood pressure. The more we do on our own, the better our chances are for getting off the medication totally. Also, we have to start exercising. Exercise is essential to keeping the heart and blood vessels strong and healthy."

"I'm definitely not gonna start drinking that low-fat or non-fat milk. Whole milk is the only milk for me. Non-fat tastes terrible," Jack said, staring at Maurine. "And what kind of exercising? I get exercise on the weekends when we head to the country. Mowing the pasture and chopping wood is enough exercise for me."

"That is exercise, but we should be doing more."

"I'm getting mine. It sounds like you need to get started," Jack replied.

"According to health experts, we should be exercising at least thirty minutes most days."

"When I mow that pasture, it takes me about three and a half hours. That's my thirty minutes a day," Jack stated. "When I work around the church setting up chairs and tables, I'm getting exercise — and then there's SEX!"

Maurine ignored Jack's extra comment and continued, "That's true. It's a good start, but you need more exercise than that," Maurine said. "Being involved in a structured program is good for people with high blood pressure and high cholesterol, and it also helps reduce the signs and symptoms of other diseases and chronic conditions, like arthritis, diabetes, osteoporosis, and back pain. We're not getting any younger. Our sons will eventually get married and give us some grandkids, and I want to be able to lift, bounce, and play with them without restriction. Quite frankly, if we don't get serious about our health, that won't happen. All I'm asking is that you at least try some of the things we've talked about."

Jack said, "I know... What's the real connection between high blood pressure and kidney disease?"

"High blood pressure already makes your heart work harder and puts added stress on your blood vessels. As a result, the blood vessels throughout your body — including those in your kidneys — can be damaged. Your kidneys filter waste and extra fluid from your blood, so when the blood vessels in your kidneys are damaged, your kidneys are unable to do their job effectively."

"It's great having someone in the family with a wealth of health knowledge."

"It's only great if you follow their recommendations."

"Right! *CSI* is getting ready to come on, so hold any other recommendations, please. By the way, Douglas is bringing his new girlfriend over this weekend. He wanted me to prepare you: she's forty-two."

"Forty-two! What is that woman doing with my baby?" Maurine shouted.

"Watch your blood pressure," Jack laughed. "Your 'baby' is twenty-six. Sounds like he's really serious about this one — and — are you ready for this — she has two children."

"Two children? I'm gonna call him."

"Leave him alone. Trust his decision; he's a mature young man and able to exercise good judgment about his love life."

"Forty-two, and with two children? He *can't* have good judgment. She's had life experiences that he can't even begin to fathom," Maurine said. "She has more in common with me and you than Douglas. Anyway, I'll be back."

"Maurine, please don't call Douglas."

"Actually, I'm gonna call my sister. I need to let her know what time we're coming to Longview this weekend."

"Just make sure you're calling Linda," Jack responded.

CHAPTER 16

The Aftermath of Retirement

S ix months later, after thirty years in the workforce, Maurine was finally able to experience the joys of retirement. At the age of fifty-two, having treasured her family and job most of her adult life, it was now time to shift her focus, and her first step was to connect with Trevor MacElroy.

"Hi, Trevor. Thank you for calling me back; I didn't expect to hear from you so soon, especially over the weekend. Nevertheless, I've heard some awesome things about you. I'm hoping you can give me some ideas to help me and my husband start living healthier."

"Thank you for contacting me. Tell me a little about you and your family."

Maurine shared information about herself, her husband, sons, and parents.

"Well, I recently retired as an occupational therapist. My years of working in the medical industry have exposed me to all the things necessary to live healthier, but I've neglected to embrace the basics. I've always been good at telling others what to do, but . . ." Maurine paused.

"I understand; I hear the same from so many others. My goal is to encourage as many people as possible to make healthier lifestyle changes. If I can convey how critical it is to make better decisions about your lifestyle choices and habits, hopefully we can reduce your concerns about any impending healthcare crises, which, for the most part, are tied to lifestyle habits. My primary goal is to gain traction by helping people move beyond their comfort zone, educating them on how to stretch their thinking by engaging in candid reflections of their poor choices, and inspiring them to put forth the effort to achieve the results they're searching for."

"From what I've heard, you're gaining traction," Maurine replied.

"Being a healthcare professional, I know you know that I'm not the most experienced person you're gonna come into contact with, but what you'll hopefully say is that I have a strong message; a message of education; a message that fosters change; a message that combines reality with evidence; a message that stirs individuals to step back and say, 'Maybe I do need to make better choices because if I don't I'll probably have some real problems.' "

"I'm looking for that message and inspiration for me and my husband. I know that my traditions have overtaken the education and awareness I've been privy to," Maurine admitted.

"People are gonna have to reconcile two realities: one is the reality of eating foods high in calories, fat, and sodium, a tradition that's been passed on from generation to generation. Culturally, eating fried pork chops, fried chicken, meatloaf, and the other favorites have always been important to us. The other one is that, in the long run, these foods may prove to be harmful to our overall health."

Maurine and Trevor talked about strategies for doing things differently. He stated that an understanding of the impact and results of developing, implementing, and maintaining healthier lifestyle habits would help lessen risk and foster a state of healthy preparedness.

"My friend, Beth, was in one of your classes at Methodist Memorial Hospital."

"I remember Beth; I was saddened by her death."

"It was a shock," Maurine reiterated. "So how can you help me get on track?"

"First, let's set up a meeting. At that time, we'll discuss in greater detail your current health and fitness lifestyle and habits. I'm looking at my calendar: what about Monday?"

"That'll be fine. I'll see you then."

A week later, Maurine awoke, excited about her first week of retirement and her visit with Trevor.

"Jack, I made it!" Maurine exclaimed, lying in bed and watching the sun pierce through the curtains.

"You sure did, honey," Jack replied. "I'm so happy for you. I hate that you didn't want us to throw you a retirement party, though."

"You know, I didn't want a lot of fuss; I just wanted to leave quietly. Beth's death a few months ago hit me hard," Maurine admitted, rolling over to hug Jack. "Life is filled with such uncertainty, I didn't know if I would live to see this day. You work all your life, looking forward to the day when you don't have to, but so many don't make it. And if you do make it, you might be too sick to enjoy it."

"Honey, you made it," Jack said, kissing her. "And we're at a good point in our lives. Sure, we have to take medicine for high blood pressure and high cholesterol, but that's minor. We can eat what we want, when we want, and where we want."

Getting out of bed, Jack went into the bathroom to brush his teeth. "I'm gonna make your special retirement breakfast this morning. What do you want? Pecan smoked jalapeno sausage, blueberry pancakes, hash browns, and eggs, or maybe some of those pork sausage patties, French toast, and hash browns? Or, do you want me to take you out to Fred's Diner for his famous fried catfish, grits, and eggs?"

"I'm not that hungry this morning. I'm gonna eat some yogurt, a slice of toast, and some fruit," Maurine said as she began to make the bed. "I hope you haven't forgotten that I'm meeting with Trevor, the fitness consultant, this afternoon."

"Please don't come back with all that health and fitness mumbo jumbo," Jack said, sticking his head out from the bathroom door. "I'm gonna cook my breakfast. Don't forget about the homecoming at the fairgrounds this weekend. Aunt Mabeline is making me some berry dumplings and cobbler."

"Jack, I'm gonna pray for you," Maurine said, staring back at him.

"You do that."

As several weeks passed, Jack and Maurine settled into a routine of alternating between city life and country life. In the midst of it all, menopause made its entrance into their lives. Maurine began having hot flashes, night sweats, headaches, fatigue, and mood swings. A mixture of cold chills, vaginal dryness, irregular periods, sleep problems, and hair loss were all brought on by the hormonal changes, which signaled the start of a new era for Maurine.

As she faced menopause, she began to equate her hormonal changes with getting old. She particularly remembered her patients with osteoporosis, and knowing the disease caused bones to become less dense and prone to breakage, she was committed to following the fitness program Trevor had designed for her. She was amazed at how she was building strength and flexibility. To add variety to her fitness program, Maurine signed up for swimming lessons at the local recreational center. As a little girl, she had always wanted to learn how to swim, but she was afraid to go under the water. Trevor encouraged her to take swimming lessons, assuring her that the instructors would start her out very slowly.

"Jack, I believe I'm in menopause," Maurine said, reaching to turn on the lamp on the side of the bed.

"Is that why you're always irritated and difficult to get along with?" Jack asked, lying in bed. "And why you keep making excuses for not wanting to have sex?"

"Probably," Maurine answered.

"What about the pain from the vaginal dryness when we're trying to have sex? Can you do anything about that? You've been dealing with that for well over a year now. Then there's the waking up with night sweats and your daily hot flashes. Have you talked with your doctor or sought any relief?"

"It's all a part of the menopausal process. When estrogen declines significantly, the membranes of the vagina thin, lose elasticity, and decrease the production of lubricating fluids. I've been looking into some lubricants and creams that help ease vaginal dryness. As far as the hot flashes, my doctor recommended a natural progesterone cream to rub on my body."

"Sounds good to me. Seems like good old fashion Vaseline should help with lubrication," Jack said, beginning to laugh. "So what exactly is menopause?"

"I have a book in the study. I'll go get it. It'll be easier for me to explain it to you with it," Maurine said, leaving the room.

"Hurry back. I can't wait for the explanation," Jack said sarcastically.

Returning with the book in her hand, Maurine sat on their bed and thumbed through the pages she had flagged. "Okay! Explanation, Mr. Jack! 'Menopause is that period in time where a woman's body doesn't make the same amount of hormones anymore. Without hormones, the ovaries are not able to release eggs. It's generally defined as the time in a woman's life when her periods stop forever.' "

"Yeah, yeah. It's 'the change' you women go through," Jack interrupted.

Maurine continued reading the information, ignoring Jack's comment, " 'During menopause, a woman's hormone production drops below the level required to continue her periods. Menopause represents the end of nearly forty years of periods. A woman's ovaries have produced an egg cell every month for roughly four decades. At menopause, they have finally run out of eggs. It can occur anytime, but the average age is about fifty-one. A woman is considered menopausal one year after she's had her last period.' "

"Sounds great! Then we don't ever have to worry about you getting pregnant again," Jack added with excitement.

"Let me finish reading, Jack," Maurine commanded. "And it's especially great for me. There's no longer a need for contraceptives or sanitary napkins. I'm not gonna bore you with all the other stuff in the book."

"You're right; I've heard enough," Jack agreed.

"Here's something interesting I flagged. There's a relative new term being tossed around: perimenopause. It can start when women are in their thirties and forties. As with menopause, some will experience the same effects."

"I know Fred said his wife gained a lot of weight after she went through 'the change'."

"As we get older, the risk of weight gain is greater because our activity level decreases significantly. The fact that I'm retired magnifies the situation. That's why I plan on staying physically active," Maurine said, getting up to go into the bathroom.

"I hear so much about estrogen and hormone replacement on TV. How does it tie in with menopause?" Jack asked.

"Estrogen is generally referred to as a female hormone because it's vital in shaping the female body and preparing it for childbearing," Maurine said loudly from the bathroom.

Maurine went on to explain how vital estrogen is for the development of breasts and hips, and how the vagina, uterus, and other female organs depend on the presence of estrogen in the body to mature.

"Estrogen works together with progesterone, another female hormone made by the ovaries. It controls a woman's monthly period and prepares the uterus for pregnancy. While contributing to so many other bodily functions, it stimulates skeletal growth and helps maintain healthy bones. It protects the heart and veins by increasing good cholesterol and lowering bad cholesterol. It also affects a woman's sexual desire, and it maintains the function of a woman's vagina and surrounding tissues, uterus, urinary bladder, and urethra, the organ through which urine is passed from the bladder."

"That's a lot," Jack responded, reaching for the TV remote on his night table. "I really have heard enough. How can you be sure that you're at menopause?"

"There's a test I can take called FSH Blood Level Measurement. But, I haven't had a period in twelve months, and I'm at that age, so I'm pretty sure I know what's going on," Maurine replied while walking back into their bedroom. "I wish my mom were alive so I could ask her when she went through menopause. That's also genetic."

"How old was your mom when she died?" Jack asked.

"Sixty-five," Maurine responded, looking through a drawer for her swimsuit cover-up. "Maybe menopause won't be so bad because, after all, there'll be no more bloating; no more placing a towel on the bed; no more having two different types of underwear; no more replacing bed linens every six months; no more replacing spotted mattresses; no more traveling down that aisle of the grocery or drug store; and no more counting days or wondering if it's that time again."

"Wow, that's a lot!" Jack shouted. "What are you looking for?"

"I'm trying to find my new cover-up," Maurine responded, continuing her search. "I wish I would have done more research about menopause sooner. I probably could have curtailed the effects of the hot flashes that I've been in denial about for the past year. I read that eating spicy foods can trigger hot flashes. I guess putting hot sauce on my foods wasn't a good thing. Or, eating those pecan smoked jalapeno sausage you like to cook, and the ham and sausage jambalaya at Cajun Joe's. Caffeine is also a trigger. I probably would have stopped drinking sodas and coffee a lot sooner. Then there's alcohol, but since I don't drink I don't have to worry about that. Then there's the theory that soy products help curtail the effects of menopause."

"Is that why you've started drinking that soy milk?"

"Yes, it is, and even those soy nuts you think taste horrible," Maurine responded. "Great, I found it."

"What you have on looks like a big terry cloth T-shirt; too short to be wearing out of this house. Hopefully, you're gonna wear something else to your class, like warm-ups," Jack said petulantly.

Maurine stood in the mirror admiring her black St. John's cover-up. Ignoring Jack's comment, she continued, "To prevent the onset of osteoporosis, I need to start ingesting more calcium products. My soy milk does contain about 35% calcium."

"That's a pretty good percentage."

"I haven't bothered you lately about it, but I keep hoping that we can exercise together. In addition to my walking and swimming, Trevor has started me on a resistance training program using an exercise ball."

"That big blue ball in the guest bedroom?"

"Yes. He's shown me exercises to strengthen my legs, arms, and shoulders."

"Weight lifting? Not you!" Jack shouted.

"I feel so much better now that I'm exercising, and I want the same for you. See my muscles?" Maurine approached Jack, trying to force him to touch her bicep muscle.

"I'm glad you're benefiting from it all, but—"

Maurine cut him off, "Exercising together helps couples have fun at the same time. Playing together is a critical aspect of a healthy relationship," Maurine stated. She sat at the end of the bed.

"Sounds like some of that 'Dr. Phil' psychological mumbo jumbo. Don't we have a healthy relationship?" Jack asked. He slowly emerged from their bed. "We've been married for the past thirty years."

"Where are you going?" Maurine asked.

"I'm going in the kitchen to get something to eat. Are you coming?" Jack asked, looking around for his slippers.

Maurine followed Jack around in their bedroom, wearing her swimsuit cover-up to continue their conversation, "Looking back, we probably put too much emphasis on the wrong things. For years, our lives were centered on work, finances, and the boys. Since we can't go back, we can at least move forward enjoying our remaining days to the fullest. It's time we introduced some new activities into our marriage. We can have our pick of the exercises — rowing, canoeing, mountain biking, hiking, or tennis," Maurine said. "Maybe you'll consider the swimming lessons. We're learning to do the butterfly, something I thought I'd never be able to do."

"I can tell you now that I'm not interested in rowing, canoeing, or hiking. Maybe tennis, but not mountain biking," Jack responded. "And definitely not swimming. Let's finish this conversation downstairs while I get something on the stove to eat."

"Okay," Maurine said, trailing him to the kitchen. "I'll check into a tennis class, but for now we can walk together. Also, we need to talk about changing our eating habits."

"Maurine, I hope you're not gonna start bombarding me with a bunch of changes," Jack said, opening the refrigerator door. "Don't let this menopause stuff get in the way of happy times. I'm ready to start traveling more, and when I travel I want to eat as I please. I said I'll exercise, but don't push it."

"It's not my menopause that's gonna get in the way. I guarantee you we won't be traveling at all if we don't stop eating all that pork and beef," Maurine stated. "I want you to consider visiting with Trevor."

"I don't need someone telling me to eat cottage cheese and peaches, or tuna and crackers, or fish and a garden salad. I'm definitely not gonna eat those rice cakes you've been eating or that granola mix," Jack commanded, getting out a package of sausage patties and a can of biscuits.

"Jack, it's not about totally giving up your favorites; it's about reducing your overall intake of them," Maurine replied.

"You can't keep eating beef or pork at every meal, every day. Heart disease runs in your family; your father and brother died from complications of it, and you will, too, if you don't change your ways. I don't want to see you suffer a heart attack like your father or a stroke like your brother."

"A heart attack?!" Jack shouted.

"Yes, a heart attack, Jack. When Carey and I talked a few months ago, she shared with me what she found out about the meats that she eats. Ever since our conversation, I've been looking at the contents of some of the meats we eat, and it's not pretty — look!" Maurine said, opening the refrigerator door behind Jack.

"You said her name again — and look at what?" Jack responded.

"Three slices of this hard salami you love so much is 100 calories and contains 510 milligrams of sodium and 25 milligrams of cholesterol," Maurine said, reading the nutritional value.

"Okay. I'll only eat two slices," Jack responded.

"And look here: two ounces of your premium pork sausage is 180 calories and contains 350 milligrams of sodium and 30 milligrams of cholesterol," Maurine said, as she handed Jack the package. "You eat a lot more than two ounces."

"Yeah, yeah, yeah," Jack said, looking at her as she continued to roam through the refrigerator.

"A four-ounce serving of those smoked turkey necks is 520 calories and contains 1540 milligrams of sodium and 100 milligrams of cholesterol. Four ounces of the smoked turkey leg is 180 calories and contains 1540 milligrams of sodium and 100 milligrams of cholesterol," Maurine kept reciting. "With the size of a turkey leg, I know you're eating a lot more than a four-ounce serving. You don't stop until you're at the bone of the leg — and keep in mind your daily allotment of sodium is 2300."

"Okay, okay, okay, you've made your point — so now what? I can't change lifelong habits overnight. I guess I shouldn't have the smoked turkey leg at the county fair this year or the funnel cake, or the sausage on a stick, or the fried ice cream, or the fried pickle, huh?" Jack asked, forming his sausage patties. "What about the fried peanut butter and jelly sandwich?"

"Fried peanut butter and jelly sandwich? Whew! I'm not saying we have to make drastic changes overnight, but I do think we should make a concerted effort to scale back on the foods we know are potentially harmful over the long haul," Maurine said.

"Woman, we don't eat fried peanut butter and jelly sandwiches every day. This is a once-a-year occasion," Jack said.

"We already have health concerns, and they'll only increase if we don't change our ways. The ingredients on the bologna you like mentions stuff like mechanically separated chicken, sodium phosphates, sodium diacetate, sodium erythorbate, sodium nitrate," Maurine said, handing the package to Jack. "There are more chemicals in this stuff than I care to comprehend."

"I don't need to see it," Jack responded. "Just tell me."

Maurine placed the package back into the refrigerator and went into the family room to get a printout of information she'd researched earlier on the Internet. She returned with the information. "From what I've researched, sodium erythorbate is an additive that slows down flavor and color change in food when exposed to air; sodium nitrate stabilizes the red color in cured meat and adds flavor. Without it, meats would look gray," Maurine said.

"If it was all that bad, they couldn't sell it," Jack responded.

"Maybe, maybe not," Maurine said. "For me, it's all worth considering. I don't think the manufacturers and researchers realize how much of these substances we eat all day, every day, with our huge amounts and variety of meats. For those with sensible eating habits, there's probably small health risks, but I just don't know if that holds true for us with hefty food allowances. I bet if you look on the back of your sausage packaging you'll see the very things I'm talking about."

Opening the refrigerator, he grabbed the package and looked for himself. "It does — Now what?" Jack admitted.

"We need to start making some changes," Maurine responded.

"So I guess you're willing to give up your favorite blueberry loaf cake and those banana nut mini muffins you love for breakfast? What about those honey buns?"

"You're absolutely right, now that I know the consequences of doing so. Most important, I'm not getting any essential vitamins or minerals."

"What are we supposed to do when we go to the movies?" Jack asked. "You know how I love popcorn and nachos."

"Your box of hot buttered popcorn is roughly 1650 calories and 93 grams of fat, and that doesn't include the extra butter you order; I'd hate to imagine the amount of sodium in that. Your 32-ounce soda is about 450 calories," Maurine said. "I think we should take our own snacks."

"And what would that consist of?" Jack wondered, his eyebrows raised. "Rice cakes and granola bars?"

"I don't know yet — Maybe air-popped popcorn from home." Maurine paused. "Oh, yeah, one more important point: Carey mentioned to me how high blood pressure can lead to erectile dysfunction."

"Maurine, if you mention that lady's name one more time . . . You didn't start all this madness until you spoke with her — and I hope you're not saying what I think you're saying," Jack replied, making sure his meat was cooking thoroughly.

"Yes, Jack, impotence: your inability to keep it up," Maurine said. "You're worried about my menopause, but you need to be worried about the impact and consequences of your continued unhealthy lifestyle. At some point, it'll catch up with you in a way you definitely don't want it to."

"Okay, I'll bite: How does high blood pressure hinder me from performing my manly duties?" Jack asked, while getting a paper towel to soak up the excess oil from the patties.

Maurine went on to explain the number of causes she had read about that led to sexual failures in men.

"I'm sixty, and my little men are rolling out just fine. In the event of stoppage, though, it's good to know that there are medicines out there for me," Jack answered. "There are ads all over the newspaper now; I saw one the other day for a risk-free trial of an all-natural formula that boosts male sexual performance."

"But, you don't know the global impact of combining those drugs with medicines for conditions like your high blood pressure. It can all be simply alleviated by implementing healthier habits," Maurine suggested. "The bottom line is that you're either gonna get on board the healthy ship or get left behind on shore to deal with the consequences of your actions."

"I think I'll take my chances."

"You're hopeless," Maurine said, moving hastily with a hurried purpose. "I need to get ready for my swim class."

"Just remember to put on your warm-ups!" Jack shouted as she rushed out the kitchen. He grabbed a baking pan to butter and cook his can of biscuits.

Maurine gave up trying to sway Jack's unwillingness to change and moved forward with implementing her own healthy initiative. She started by focusing on foods that contributed to her well-being. First order of business was breakfast; she eliminated her intake of high-fat, high-sodium, and high-cholesterol sausages and links, along with high-fat and high-sodium muffins, honey buns, biscuits, and pancakes. More fruits, vegetables, and whole grain products were the target. On Monday, a bowl of oatmeal, with an eight-ounce glass of soy milk and fresh fruit. Tuesday, a bowl of cold whole grain cereal added to a glass of soy milk, and fresh fruit. Wednesday, an omelet, filled with spinach, tomatoes, bell pepper, mushrooms, and onions, sautéed in olive oil. It included a sprinkle of low-fat mozzarella cheese, seasoned with Mrs. Dash and cilantro, and served with a slice of whole grain bread, a smear of honey, and fresh fruit. The next order of business would be to refine her options for lunch, dinner, and snacks.

CHAPTER 17

Unwillingness to Change – The Heart Attack

After another year of unhealthy lifestyle habits, Jack suffered a massive heart attack on the Fourth of July. The end of a day filled with a sea of Jack's favorites came in the agonizing discomfort of what he thought was indigestion. A team of paramedics arrived to perform CPR at their home in Rockwall; the years of unhealthy habits had finally caught up with Jack.

Five o'clock in the morning, Maurine sat still in the waiting room with their three sons. To add to the stress she was already feeling, Douglas' girlfriend appeared with her two children.

"Mom, what are they doing to stabilize Dad and make him well again?" Dale asked.

"How did this happen? Dad is healthy. He's always busy doing something physical," Douglas said.

"Was he feeling sick?" Dornell asked.

"I don't know, boys. It all happened so quickly. Your father went to bed early after complaining of indigestion; he took a couple pills. I just thought he ate too much at his cousin's

Fourth of July party. About one o'clock this morning, he got up and collapsed on the floor, holding his chest. He thought the indigestion had gotten worse and asked me to help him to the living room because he wanted to sit on the sofa. Because he was in so much pain, I called 911. When the paramedics arrived, he was barely alive. They said he was having a heart attack, and they gave him an aspirin and administered CPR. For a few minutes, they lost him, but through the grace of God, they were able to bring him back to us."

"What exactly is a heart attack?" Dale asked.

"A heart attack occurs when the supply of blood and oxygen to an area of heart muscle is blocked, usually by a clot in a coronary artery," replied Tiffany, Douglas' girlfriend, who was a nurse practitioner for a local hospital.

Interrupted by the physician, the family was informed that Jack had had a massive heart attack that resulted in significant damage to a major heart artery. The surgeon then explained the emergency surgery they had performed to open the blocked artery, but the sounds emerging from the surgeon's mouth were muffled as Maurine and the boys thought about Jack's survival chances.

"Angioplasty involves opening the blocked artery. A catheter — a narrow tube containing a fiber optic camera — was threaded directly to the blocked vessel. We then opened the blocked vessel using balloon angioplasty, in which a tiny deflated balloon is passed through the catheter to the vessel. The balloon was inflated to compress the plaque against the walls of the artery, flattening it out so that blood can once again flow through the blood vessel freely. In order to keep the artery open afterwards, a device called a coronary stent, which is an expandable metal mesh tube, was implanted at the site of the blockage. Once in place, the stent pushes against the wall of the artery to keep it open."

"Will my husband be okay?" Maurine asked, trying to process all the information.

"We won't know for a few days," the surgeon replied, "but we're watching him closely."

A couple weeks later, Jack was released to go home, but his departure was not without fear. Sitting in the living room, he thought to himself, *Can I ever recover from the shock of this near-death experience? What are my chances of having another heart attack?*

Jack struggled to gain a fresh perspective on readjusting his thinking toward adopting healthier lifestyle habits.

Doctors and insurance companies began to get the best of Maurine. Her biggest fear, a catastrophic illness, had become a reality. Their portion of the hospital bill was $20,000. For months, Maurine nursed her husband, supervising his every move, as well as bathing him, dressing him, and feeding him. His spirits were low, and he experienced seesaw moods, sudden bursts of tears, and irritation at family members. It was all part of his trying to cope with the traumatic ordeal. Maurine held on to her faith that they would emerge victoriously.

"What would you like to eat this morning?" Maurine asked, looking in the pantry. "The doctor says oatmeal is good for heart health."

"Oatmeal is okay today, but I don't want to eat it everyday. I wonder when I'll be able to drive," Jack muttered, sitting at the kitchen table.

"I don't know. The doctor said for you to take it slow. The church members are calling, wanting to see you. Are you ready for visitors?"

"I've lost so much weight. I don't want anyone to see me like this."

"Don't worry about that. You'll get your weight back. Everyone understands what you've been through, and they're praying for you."

"We'll see. Maybe next week. I'm gonna go take a shower while you get breakfast ready. Fry me a couple of those sausage links," Jack said, moving slowly from the table.

"Jack, you shouldn't be eating sausage links. They're high in fat, cholesterol and sodium. You sure you don't want the bowl of oatmeal?"

"Maurine, I said I want sausage links, and that's what I want," Jack said forcefully before leaving the room.

Moments later, while in the kitchen, Maurine heard a loud bang coming from the bathroom.

"What's happening?" Maurine shouted, running down the hallway.

As she opened the bathroom, Jack was holding onto the shower rod, trying to balance himself.

"What did you clean this tub with? It's slippery," Jack said angrily.

"I used the same solution as always. Did you lose your balance, Jack?"

"No, I didn't lose my balance."

The months that followed proved to be a challenge for their marriage. Jack's mental state was dark and solemn most days; he hated the fact that he was now forced to take a variety of medications to stay well.

"Some days I feel like I'm just gonna stop taking all this medication and take my chances with whatever happens to me."

"Jack, you can't think like that," Maurine said, standing in the kitchen, preparing lunch. "Before your heart attack, you were already taking medication for high cholesterol and high blood pressure."

"You're right, but now I've gone from two pills to ten pills. Just look at this bag: Simvastatin, Metoprolol Tartrate, Hydrochlorothiazide, Felodipine, Irbesartan, Lorazepam, Naproxem, Toprol XL, Norvac, Potassium Gluconate 99, and Temazepham," Jack called off, sitting at the kitchen table and pulling the medications out of his pill bag one by one.

Maurine sat down beside him and began to gather the printed drug information Jack received with his prescriptions. One by one, she read some of the information, "The Simvastatin is a cholesterol-lowering medicine that inhibits the production of cholesterol by the liver. Metoprolol Tartrate is a beta-blocker used to treat high blood pressure and angina pectoris, which is chest pain. Your doctor probably prescribed it because it's also used after a heart attack to improve survival."

As Maurine continued to describe the other medications, Jack remained silent.

"Toprol XL is a beta-blocker used to treat high blood pressure, angina pectoris, and congestive heart failure. Hydrochlorothiazide is a water pill used to treat excessive fluid accumulation and swelling of the body caused by heart failure, cirrhosis, chronic kidney failure, corticosteroid medications, and Nephrotic syndrome. Felodipine is another medication used to treat high blood pressure. It relaxes your blood vessels so your heart doesn't have to pump as hard. Irbesartan is a drug that blocks angiotensin II, a chemical that causes the arteries and veins to narrow. As a result, the arteries and veins become larger and blood pressure is reduced. When the blood pressure is reduced, the heart doesn't have to work as hard to pump blood. Norvac is another medication for patients who have high blood pressure, and it's often used to treat chest pain."

"I don't know why he prescribed the Lorazepam," Jack said, looking at all the medicine bottles. "According to the pharmaceutical handout, Lorazepam is used to relieve anxiety, nervousness, and tension associated with anxiety disorders. It's also used to treat certain types of seizure disorders and relieve insomnia."

"The aftermath of the heart attack has been traumatic for you, so I'm sure it's only to aid in relieving anxiety and nervousness. I know it can be habit-forming, though, so hopefully you won't need to take it for very long," Maurine paused then continued. "You know that potassium is an essential mineral needed to regulate water balance, levels of acidity, blood pressure, and neuromuscular function. It also plays a critical role in the transmission of electrical impulses in the heart."

"I know one thing: I don't need to take this Hydrochlorothiazide for too long. One of the side effects is that it can cause impotence," Jack said.

"We'll see. You should discuss it with your doctor. It's important to avoid a diet high in salt. Too much salt may cause your body to retain water, which would decrease the effects of Hydrochlorothiazide. We've talked about your diet and the sodium for months now."

Six months after his heart attack, Jack's doctors discovered that Jack's stent didn't work and that they needed to repair his heart valve. The balloon had to be removed because his artery was filled with blood, which led to the development of an aneurysm.

Sitting in his doctor's office, Jack asked, "Doctor, why doesn't the stent work?"

"I don't know, Jack. Sometimes they just don't work," Dr. Madden responded.

"How did the aneurysm develop?" Maurine asked.

"Because a section of Jack's heart wall was damaged after the heart attack, it caused scarring, and consequently the heart wall grew thinner and weaker. As a result, tests have revealed the formation of a ventricular aneurysm. As you stated, you're experiencing shortness of breath, chest pain, and, based on your test, an irregular heartbeat," Dr. Madden said while staring at Jack. "All this is making your heart work harder to pump blood to the rest of your body. It's best that we do surgery to correct the problem. If left untreated, there's a risk that the aneurysm will burst, causing you to bleed to death."

"What about the irregular heartbeat?" Jack asked, looking for reassurance from the doctor.

"Sometimes scarring of the heart muscle after an attack causes a short in the heart's wiring, resulting in irregular beats. To correct this problem, we'll implant a defibrillator. Implanted defibrillators shock the heart back into a normal rhythm when it starts beating irregularly."

Jack was scheduled for surgery to repair the heart valve. Four days after the surgery, a defibrillator was implanted.

With his brothers trailing behind him at the hospital, Douglas asked, "Hi, Mom. How's Dad doing?"

From afar, Maurine saw Tiffany coming down the hall with her children.

Staring at the procession of two children with dolls and video games trailing behind their mother, Maurine tried to conceal her irritation that Tiffany was at the hospital during such a difficult time for their family when she responded, "The doctors are optimistic that your dad will be fine as long as he takes care of himself. I sure hope his doctors can come up with compelling arguments on how critical it will be for him to change his ways. For years, he's treated his health like a situation that can be swept under the carpet like dirt, not to be dealt with until the bulge underneath becomes too noticeable. Unfortunately, his bulge of unhealthy habits grew out of control, and now he's gonna need all the strength I can give him to remove it."

CHAPTER 18

The Road to Recovery

After a year, Jack resumed most of his normal activities. He was farming and driving. His capacity for physical endurance was diminished, but he was in tune with his body and knew when to slow down. Although the medication kept him tired, he was managing a fulfilling life, aside from the fact that his ability to enjoy sexual intercourse was hampered due to his erectile problems. The tables had turned, and Maurine was doing all the cooking. Months of analyzing the foods they had spent the majority of their lives eating sparked ongoing debates between Maurine and Jack.

Sitting in front of the TV watching a home and garden show, Maurine sounded off, "A healthier lifestyle is not a switch you can turn on and off. You have to be in it for the long haul. You've been doing well since your last surgery, but I see you slipping back into some old familiar ways."

Tossing the remote back and forth while pondering a channel change, Jack replied, "I guess I got that unexpected wake-up call."

"Yes, you did, and now it's gonna be up to you to turn the tide on the habits that caused your heart attack. All that you've been through should inspire you to do things differently."

"It's hard to imagine giving up the food I love so much."

"Don't think of it as giving them up; think of it as cutting back on those things that can place you back in a life-threatening predicament. Frankly, I'm tired of fighting with you about what you need to eat," Maurine responded, walking into the kitchen to get a glass of water.

From the family room, Jack shouted, "What do you expect me to do? All I know is what I've done all my life!"

"I'm telling you," Maurine said, "the buck stops here. No more ham, pan pork sausage, bacon, and hot links. It's gonna be fish and chicken — and more fish than chicken." Returning from the kitchen, she continued, "I'm gonna try a different recipe each week so we don't get bored. I know you're tired of oatmeal and cold cereal."

"I know that's right," Jack said as he got up to go in the kitchen. "What about one final round of bacon, eggs, and pancakes?"

"Nope, not on my watch. Today, it's yogurt, whole grain toast, and fresh fruit for you, Mister."

"Sounds yummy, but I'd rather eat that Meat Lover's Omelet at Fred's. It has bacon, pork sausage, shredded beef, ham, onions, green peppers, cheddar cheese, and that great tasting hot salsa."

"I don't think so, Mister."

Jack sat at the kitchen table. "Not looking forward to this meal."

"I'm starting to consider the nutritional impact of the foods we're eating. Good nutrition is what's gonna be the key to your continued recovery."

"Okay," he responded, taking a glass of orange juice. "I guess this fresh-squeezed orange juice is okay."

"Jack, I'm not doing any of this to punish you. I know how hard making these changes is for you, but I don't want to relive that moment when I thought you would die. I know we're all gonna leave this Earth, but I want us to be here together for as long as possible with our boys. Trevor has me on a wonderful program, and I know he can do the same for you."

"I thought you were gonna check on tennis lessons for me?" Jack asked.

"I will, as soon as you clear it with your doctor."

"By the way, I'm glad you're starting to accept Tiffany."

"Looks like I have no choice for now. I'm just hoping our son will come to his senses and find someone closer to his own age."

"Maurine, he's talking about buying her a ring."

"Jack, let's not have this discussion now."

"I'm just trying to prepare you."

"There's nothing to prepare me for."

Continued debates over Jack's quality and quantity of life persisted, which led him to start changing some of his unhealthy ways.

During another follow-up visit, Dr. Madden asked Jack, "Have you started exercising?"

"Not yet, Doctor Madden. My wife keeps worrying me. I did tell her that I was willing to try tennis. She told me I needed to talk to you about it, though," Jack replied.

"You've been through rehab. Plus, the results of the stress test we recently conducted were good. Tennis requires a lot of energy, so I would prefer you start off with walking to build up your strength and endurance."

"I do mow my pasture. That's about seventy acres," Jack stated. "That's exercise, right?"

"I'm sure you're on a riding mower," Dr. Madden replied.

"Yes, I am," Jack responded.

"The best kind of exercise for your heart is regular aerobic exercise. Aerobic exercise, such as swimming, bicycling, or walking at a brisk pace, helps build up endurance. I'd rather you try one of those activities first, then we'll see about the tennis. The bottom line is that research has shown that people who exercise regularly after a heart attack live longer than people who don't."

"Okay, doctor, I'll start. My wife's been nagging me about it for the longest time. It's just... I've never exercised formally. I've always been busy moving around, working all my life. It never seemed that important."

"I understand. For generations, people have centered their lives on family, work, and pleasure — everything except the well-being of their bodies. I'm glad you're willing to make some changes; I just need for you to do more on a routine basis."

"Also, doctor, I've had some problems with an erection — Can you give me something? Better yet, what's causing it to happen to me?"

Dr. Madden explained that medicines, such as those related to blood pressure, fluid pills, chest pain, irregular heartbeat, and antidepressants, could affect a person's sex drive and function. "Some men experience an inability to achieve or maintain an erection, or they may have premature ejaculations — or none at all."

"My problem is that I'm having trouble *getting* an erection. My wife said that I'd face this problem one day if I didn't change my ways."

"Fortunately, for you and millions of others, there are options: vacuum pumps, penile injections, and medications."

"Since my heart attack, I don't think I'm interested in the medications. What's the pump all about?"

"Once you and your wife decide to engage in sexual relations, the device has some options for you to consider: a plastic cylinder that you place your penis into—"

Jack stopped Dr. Madden short, "I'm not placing my penis into *anything*."

"There are also implanted devices known as prostheses."

"I don't think so — not for me, anyway."

"Never forget the impact of diet and exercise. A healthy circulatory system provides blood flow to the penis that's needed for an erection. Conditions like high cholesterol can destroy the walls of your veins. It can harden, narrow, or block the arteries leading to your penis, causing erectile problems. Smokers are particularly at risk," Dr. Madden shared.

"I'm not a smoker," Jack said.

"Good," Dr. Madden replied, "because medical experts believe that smoking is a large contributing factor to erectile problems."

"Okay, doctor, tell me more about the pump," Jack said, sounding discouraged.

Energized by his expectations of longevity, Jack and Maurine fully embraced their rights to break their generational curses. While Maurine continued her swimming classes, Jack enjoyed long walks along the perimeter of their land. Tired of his own litany of excuses, Jack succumbed to Maurine's wishes to incorporate a healthier lifestyle. The occasional deviations to indulge in fried chicken from The Fried Chicken Hut, T-bone steaks from Fred's Diner, donuts, bowls of ice cream, and sausage and biscuit sandwiches were the exceptions rather than the norm. They both enjoyed an active sex life. Jack admitted to needing some assistance and decided to use a pump that his doctor had recommended. Maurine minimized the effects of menopause with better eating habits and exercise.

The consequences of an unhealthy lifestyle became a reality for Jack and Maurine. A permanent reminder was the scar that stretched from Jack's chest to his stomach — the effects of a generational lifestyle. Increased knowledge of heart disease and age-related diseases and illnesses propelled them to a state of implementing habits that would add years to their lives. They finally recognized the impact of misplaced priorities: keeping work, finances, family, and friends at the forefront had jeopardized the start of healthier lifestyles for them.

"Thank you, Maurine, for not giving up on me. I love you, and I thank God for you. You've brought out the best in me, and I appreciate you for it every day," Jack said.

"You're welcome, honey," Maurine replied. "You know, this aging process really isn't all that bad. The road would have been less traumatic if we'd just taken some preventive measures."

"I feel like I was thrust into living healthier with blinders on," Jack said. "Nevertheless, I'm not gonna worry about the past; I'm gonna move forward and continue what I've now started."

"I only hope that the generations following behind us will recognize the impact of poor choices and begin their process for understanding and implementing a healthier lifestyle. Unfortunately, for me, I didn't accept the consequences of my actions until Beth's death. I'm glad to see the boys are starting to make some changes. The knowledge they gained after your health scare has really made a difference. With all the relatives that have passed before us, we denied and dismissed the root causes for too long."

Hindsight is powerful! You might not understand or realize the consequences of your actions at the time, but hopefully you'll survive your health scare or crisis with a newfound vigilance to live a longer, healthier, and better life.

HEALTH AND FITNESS
REFERENCES

NUTRITION

Eating Breakfast – American Dietetic Association – www.eatright.org

Tips for eating Mexican food – American Heart Association – http://www.americanheart.org/presenter.jhtml?identifier=1100

Sodium in Processed Foods – The Center for Science in the Public Interest – http://www.cspinet.org/new/200511081.html

Nutrition Fact Label – U. S. Food and Drug Administration – Center for Food Safety and Applied Nutrition – http://www.cfsan.fda.gov/~dms/foodlab.html

Trans Fat – American Heart Association – http://www.americanheart.org/presenter.jhtml?identifier=4776

Portion Distortion – National Heart, Lung, and Blood Institute – http://hp2010.nhlbihin.net/portion/

Dietary Supplements – U. S. Food and Drug Administration – Center for Food Safety and Applied Nutrition – http://www.cfsan.fda.gov/~dms/ds-oview.html#what

Vitamins and Minerals – National Institute of Health – Office of Dietary Supplements – http://ods.od.nih.gov/Health_Information/Vitamin_and_Mineral_Supplement_Fact_Sheets.aspx

Iron Deficiency – National Institute of Health – Office of
Dietary Supplements –
http://ods.od.nih.gov/factsheets/iron.asp

Kids and Breakfast – KidsHealth –
http://www.kidshealth.org/kid/stay_healthy/food/breakfast.html

Diet and Cancer – American Cancer Society –
http://www.cancer.org/docroot/ped/content/ped_3_2x_
common_questions_about_diet_and_cancer.asp

Diet and Cancer – American Institute for Cancer Research –
http://www.aicr.org/site/News2?abbr=pr_&page=NewsArticl
e&id=10261

Nitrite and Cancer – U.S. National Library of Science
Medicine and the National Institutes of Health –
http://www.nlm.nih.gov/medlineplus/ency/article/002096.htm

WEIGHT LOSS

Counting Calories – American Cancer Society –
http://www.cancer.org/docroot/PED/content/PED_6_1x_
Calorie_Calculator.asp

Effective Weight Loss – U.S. Department of Health and
Human Services – Office on Women's Health –
http://womenshealth.gov/faq/weightloss.htm

Quick-Weight-Loss or Fad Diets – American Heart Association –
http://www.americanheart.org/presenter.jhtml?identifier=503

Fad Diets – American Academy of Family Physicians –
http://familydoctor.org/784.xml

Weight Control – American Academy of Family Physicians –
http://familydoctor.org/197.xml

Body Mass Index (BMI) – Department of Health and Human Services – National Institute of Health – http://www.nhlbisupport.com/bmi/bmicalc.htm

Body Mass Index (BMI) – Department of Health and Human Services – Center for Disease Control and Prevention – http://www.cdc.gov/nccdphp/dnpa/bmi/index.htm

ILLNESSES/DISEASES

High Blood Cholesterol – National Heart, Lung, and Blood Institute – http://www.nhlbi.nih.gov/health/dci/Diseases/Hbc/HBC_WhatIs.html

Healthy Cholesterol Levels – American Heart Association – http://www.americanheart.org/presenter.jhtml?identifier=183

Stroke – American Stroke Association – http://www.strokeassociation.org/presenter.jhtml?identifier=3030387

Osteoporosis – U. S. Department of Health and Human Services National Institutes of Health – National Institute on Aging – http://www.niapublications.org/agepages/osteo.asp

Anemia – National Heart, Lung, and Blood Institute – http://www.nhlbi.nih.gov/health/dci/Diseases/anemia/anemia_whoisatrisk.html

Urticaria – American Osteopathic College of Dermatology – http://www.aocd.org/skin/dermatologic_diseases/urticaria.html

Urticaria and Histamine – American Academy of Dermatology – http://www.aad.org/public/Publications/pamphlets/Urticaria-Hives.htm

Menopause – Mayo Clinic – http://www.mayoclinic.com/health/menopause/DS00119

Lupus – National Institute of Arthritis and Musculoskeletal and Skin Diseases – http://www.niams.nih.gov/hi/topics/lupus/shades/ Resources _ 277

Pre-Diabetes – American Diabetes Association – http://www.diabetes.org/pre-diabetes.jsp

Diabetes – American Diabetes Association – http://www.diabetes.org/about-diabetes.jsp

Diabetes and Kidney Disease – National Kidney Foundation – http://www.kidney.org/atoz/atozItem.cfm?id=37

Alternatives for Taking Insulin – National Institute of Diabetes and Digestive and Kidney Diseases – National Diabetes Information Clearinghouse – http://diabetes.niddk.nih.gov/dm/pubs/insulin/

Insulin Pumps – American Diabetes Association – http://www.diabetes.org/diabetes-forecast/may2004/pump.jsp

High Blood Pressure and Kidney Disease – National Kidney Foundation – http://www.kidney.org/atoz/pdf/hbpkidneys.pdf

Cancer – American Cancer Society – http://www.cancer. org/docroot/CRI/content/CRI_2_2_1x_What_Is_Cancer. asp?sitearea=

Breast Cancer – American Cancer Society – http://www.cancer.org/docroot/CRI/content/CRI_2_2_2X_ What_causes_breast_cancer_5.asp?sitearea=

Tobacco and Cancer – American Cancer Society – http://www.cancer.org/docroot/PED/content/PED_10_2x_ Tobacco-Related_Cancers_Fact_Sheet.asp?sitearea=PED

Sodium Intake – Mayo Clinic –
http://www.mayoclinic.com/health/sodium/NU00284

Salt and High Blood Pressure – American Stroke Association –
http://www.strokeassociation.org/presenter.jhtml?identifier=
3027283

High Blood Pressure – National Heart, Lung, and Blood Institute –
http://www.nhlbi.nih.gov/health/dci/Diseases/Hbp/HBP_
WhoIsAtRisk.html

Heart Surgery Overview – Texas Heart Institute –
http://www.texasheartinstitute.org/HIC/Topics/Proced/

DISORDERS

Emotional Eating – Mayo Clinic –
http://www.mayoclinic.com/health/weight-loss/MH00025

Sleep disorders – National Sleep Foundation –
www.sleepfoundation.org

OVERWEIGHT/OBESITY

Overweight Kids – Department of Health and Human Services –
Centers for Disease Control and Prevention –
http://www.cdc.gov/nccdphp/dnpa/obesity/index.htm

Costs Related to Obesity – American Obesity Association –
http://www.obesity.org/treatment/cost.shtml

Economic Impact of Obesity – Department of Health and
Human Services – Centers for Disease Control and Prevention –
http://www.cdc.gov/nccdphp/dnpa/obesity/economic_
consequences.htm

Obesity – National Center for Health Statistics –
http://www.cdc.gov/nchs/pressroom/06facts/obesity03_04.htm

GENERAL

Antihistamines – American Academy of Family Physicians – http://familydoctor.org/857.xml

Erectile Dysfunction – American Academy of Family Physicians – http://familydoctor.org/109.xml

Vagina Dryness – Mayo Clinic – http://www.mayoclinic.com/health/vaginal-dryness/DS00550

Radon Gas and Cancer – American Cancer Society – http://www.cancer.org/docroot/NWS/content/NWS_1_1x_Radon_Gas_Confirmed_as_Second_Largest_Lung_Cancer_Risk.asp

ABOUT THE AUTHOR

Recognizing the pitfalls of misplaced priorities, Bridgette Collins launched MAC Fitness (Making-A-Commitment to Fitness) in 2002 to educate, coach, and motivate individuals who struggle with implementing healthier lifestyle habits. She is skilled at creatively crafting solutions to help her clients overcome the physical, financial, and emotional consequences of physical inactivity and poor nutritional habits.

Bridgette has worked as a certified personal trainer, both privately and for Bally's Total Fitness, and she holds a personal trainer certification through Aerobics and Fitness Association of America. By combining her fitness training and passion for healthy living with nearly twenty years of human resources and program development experience, Bridgette delivers practical health and fitness solutions.

Understanding that the quest to incorporate a healthier lifestyle is often hampered by daily demands and obligations, she equips her clients with a collection of lifestyle tools which help to close the gap between understanding and doing what is right to reduce the risk of disease and illness.

As a motivational speaker and facilitator, Bridgette travels throughout the country to deliver a message that empowers audiences to make positive lifestyle choices. She writes a health column for various print and online magazines and has also served as a fitness coach for an Internet radio station and an online lifestyle management program.

Bridgette has been an avid runner for more than ten years, participating in a host of 5K and 10K races. She has completed four marathons and two half-marathons. In an effort to share the benefits of a consistent running program, she has coached several group training programs to provide beginner walkers and runners with weekly instruction for improving their fitness level.

A native of Houston, Bridgette resides in Grand Prairie, Texas, where she is an active member at Golden Gate Missionary Baptist Church. She enjoys running, watching football, traveling, and going to movies and stage plays. She has a degree in business administration.

Bridgette would love to receive your feedback on Destined to Live Healthier. To contact her, please write or email:

Bridgette L. Collins
P.O. Box 542671
Grand Prairie, Texas 75054-2671
bridgette@bridgettecollins.com

For more healthy living tips and information
on Bridgette's other book, visit:

www.DestinedToLiveHealthier.com